HARPER'S BIZARRE

MIKE THORNE

outskirts
press

Harper's Bizarre
All Rights Reserved.
Copyright © 2023 Mike Thorne
v4.0

This is a work of fiction. Names, characters, businesses, places, events, locales, and incidents are either the products of the author's imagination or used in a fictitious manner. Any resemblance to actual persons, living or dead, or actual events is purely coincidental.

The opinions expressed in this manuscript are solely the opinions of the author and do not represent the opinions or thoughts of the publisher. The author has represented and warranted full ownership and/or legal right to publish all the materials in this book.

This book may not be reproduced, transmitted, or stored in whole or in part by any means, including graphic, electronic, or mechanical without the express written consent of the publisher except in the case of brief quotations embodied in critical articles and reviews.

Outskirts Press, Inc.
http://www.outskirtspress.com

ISBN: 978-1-9772-5902-8

Cover Photo © 2023 www.gettyimages.com. All rights reserved - used with permission.

Outskirts Press and the "OP" logo are trademarks belonging to Outskirts Press, Inc.

PRINTED IN THE UNITED STATES OF AMERICA

Dedication

*To Wanda, the love of my life, for her steadfast
encouragement and assistance.*

PROLOGUE

Serious crime is a rarity in Harper, a small Southern college town. But in a relatively short time frame, several interconnected events undermine the town's sense of security, and unfounded rumors abound.

Some unexpected deaths prove so disturbing that the police chief, Grady Noland, questions remaining in Harper, a town he loves. He also fears his health is being affected.

Set in the mid1980s, DNA testing and other model forensic techniques are not yet in the underfunded and understaffed Harper Police Department's arsenal. In addition, the period predates commonplace personal computers, cell phones, other electronic devices, and social media.

Harper's Bizarre is a fictional account inspired by a couple of actual events in a small town.

CHAPTER 1

At 44, health and safety were serious matters to Peter Dewberry. He watched his diet, always wore his seatbelt, and was sold on the benefits of regular exercise.

Walking and occasionally jogging were Peter's favorite exercises, and his favorite shoes were a pair of nearly new Nikes. Only one flaw marred the Nikes: A spot of paint had gotten on them the second time he wore them. Nancy had asked him to help her paint a bookcase they'd built, and Peter, impatient to go for his walk, decided he could surely paint half a bookcase without getting paint on himself. If they had been old shoes, there was no way the paint drop would have fallen the way it did–straight for the toe.

Peter immediately soaked a paper towel in turpentine and scrubbed, mentally cursing his carelessness. The turpentine only made the spot worse, lightened it but spread it out, making it bigger and more noticeable. Peter still liked the shoes, but not as much as he had in the store.

Except for the spot on the toe, the Nikes were white with a sporty red stripe along the sides. Peter had chosen them because the colors matched the colors of the college where he taught and because they were on sale.

From the laundry room, he retrieved a leash. At the sound of its clinking, Skipper bounded off the couch where he'd been curled up next to Nancy. The dog circled Peter expectantly, making little whining sounds.

"Settle down, Skipper," Peter said, trying to get the hook of the leash onto the metal loop on the dog's collar. Skipper's tongue slathered his hands, and he wiped them on the back of his jeans. He stood and allowed the dog to tug him into the family room where his wife waited to give him the ritual peck on the cheek.

"Love you," she said, already turning back to the novel she was reading.

"See you in about an hour, Hon," and he was gone.

On the outskirts of downtown Harper, Jefferson Street rises gently before meeting Main. Beyond Main, Jefferson falls gradually over its course through a lower-class neighborhood. The houses along lower Jefferson are small but mostly neat, with lawns freshly mown and cars parked in carports, not on the street.

On the south side of the Jefferson-Main intersection stands a branch of the Farmers & Merchants Bank. At the rear of the bank, an electronic message board looms over an empty parking lot. "SHOP DOWNTOWN HARPER" is followed by, "KEEP HARPER MONEY AT HOME." Next is the time and temperature: "11:33 ... 87°."

"How can it still be 87 degrees this late?" Peter asked his dog. The aging animal looked at his master, tilting his head as though trying to discern the meaning. The pair stood under a streetlamp on the corner, their shadows stretching toward lower Jefferson.

"Wanna look for Danny's bike, Skipper?"

At the sound of his name, Skipper's tail increased its tempo, and his mouth gaped in a doggy smile. Assent noted, Peter crossed the street, Skipper at his heel. He whistled tunelessly, mild anxiety competing with anger at the thought of the bike's theft. Danny had ridden the new 10-speed to school on Thursday morning, and then had walked home that afternoon, carrying the clipped chain. This morning one of Danny's friends said he thought he'd seen the bike on lower Jefferson.

Skipper trotted beside Peter, sometimes edging ahead, sometimes falling behind, occasionally stopping to anoint a telephone pole or a fire hydrant. Peter made no effort to get the dog to heel.

Peter hesitated on the corner of Roosevelt and Jefferson. Overhead, the streetlight hummed, an angry sound like trapped wasps. Beyond Roosevelt, working streetlights were far apart, with most of the street in darkness. Passing cars were sparse at this time of night in Harper, even though it was the first night of the weekend. Skipper looked up at him, then sat when they didn't immediately move forward.

"Hell," Peter said to the dog. "There's nobody out anyway. Let's have a look, old boy." He stepped off the curb briskly, decision made. Skipper stretched quickly before trotting to his side.

A Baptist church loomed on their right, scaffolding gilding its side. Pete remembered the summer he and Nancy toured Europe. They began to think that every cathedral's exterior was either being cleaned or repaired. It was hard to get a good picture with all the scaffolding.

Houses began after the church, each a rectangular bulk swaddled in darkness.

"Can you see anything, boy?" Peter asked the dog in a softer voice than he had used earlier. "I sure can't." He walked a little faster. "We'll go to the end of the block and then turn back, Skipper."

Near the block's end, the corner streetlight sent tendrils of light between houses. Three houses from the corner, Peter caught the gleam of handlebars in a side yard. He slowed, certain it wasn't Danny's bike but hating to admit the anxiety-filled walk down Jefferson had been for nothing. Check it out, he told himself. What have you got to lose?

"C'mon, Skip," he said, as though the dog had a choice. Talking to the animal somehow made him feel better.

Ten feet away, he knew it wasn't Danny's bike. "It's a girl's bike," he whispered, turning back toward the sidewalk. The whole idea of trying to find Danny's bike had been foolish, he now realized, particularly in the dark. Tomorrow, he and Danny would cruise the streets in this neighborhood, and then, if they couldn't find the bike, he would file a claim Monday on his homeowner's policy. Even with his deductible, the bike had cost so much that they would get something back.

He crossed the street at the corner, feeling better now that he had a plan. Maybe he would jog home—let his speed get his pulse rate up for the cardiovascular benefits. He smiled in the darkness, picturing how excited Skipper would be when he started running.

Peter saw the bike under a carport, next to a very large and nearly antique Ford Fairlane. He stopped on the sidewalk. Skipper tugged at the leash, and Peter unconsciously jerked him back.

Go home, something told him, remember the location and go home. Come back tomorrow in the daylight and check it out. But another voice, sounding equally rational, argued that the bike might be gone in the morning. And what a surprise Danny would have to find the bike waiting for him in his own backyard. Peter decided to check it out.

It *was* Danny's bike. Peter was pretty sure of that from the street, and he was certain by the time he got to the rear of the Ford. Danny had mounted a decal of the high school mascot, a lion, on the rear reflector. Peter rubbed his fingertips over the embossed animal, assuring himself with contact. He had really found it! But it was locked, chain through the front wheel and around one of the carport's wrought-iron supports. Peter briefly toyed with the idea of detaching the front tire and taking the rest of the bike home, but he would have to carry it and he didn't think he could manage both a bicycle and a dog.

A low-pitched whirring sound startled him until he recognized it as the sound of an air conditioning unit starting up. "Let's go home, Skip," Peter whispered, and the dog growled in response.

"Hush, Skip," Peter whispered, concerned more with keeping the dog quiet than with what might have triggered the growl. Then another whisper, "Whatcha looking at, Skipper," following the dog's gaze.

CHAPTER 2

A large drainage ditch separated the backyards on Jefferson from those on Grant, and the neighborhood children played in the ditch when it was dry. Over the years, unexpected thunderstorms had dropped so much water on the yards and ditch that a few kids had been swept to their deaths, and if there were the least hint of rain, mothers warned their youngsters not to play in the ditch. In the '50s, mothers up and down the street thought the ditch, and its standing puddles, harbored polio germs.

Barely over, the summer had been hot—not unusual for Harper—and it hadn't rained in nearly 3 weeks. Forgetting the spring floods, Harper residents had begun to think it would never rain again. Utility bills at the end of the month would reflect the excess water used to keep lawns and gardens alive. Any run-off from watering instantly disappeared into the cracks crisscrossing the steep sides of the ditch. Tonight, the ditch held two brothers who companionably sweated, smoked a joint, and talked desultorily.

"I hate that sumbitch," the younger brother said softly, punctuating his words by pressing the button on his knife. Kerchunk, the blade sprang into place.

His brother grunted and took a drag on their butt. He swallowed the sweet smoke and held it, savoring his mild buzz.

"One of these days," the first one said, taking the cigarette from his brother.

"Shit, he's our old man, for chrissake," the older one said, smoke dribbling from his nose and mouth.

To look at them, it was hard to believe that the two had the same father. The younger one was whipcord lean, small, ferret-faced, whereas the other, who looked at least 4 years older, was huge, solid, muscular, built like the star lineman he had been. There was no rivalry between the two. The younger boy knew his brother was so superior to him there was little chance he could best him at anything. So he didn't try. He was content to bask in his brother's reflected glory, which was rapidly diminishing since he had dropped out of school.

"Prick," the younger boy said, venomously. His hatred was justi-fied—like almost everyone who knew the brothers, their father dis-criminated against his younger son. He started to say something else but was silenced by a finger to his lips.

"You hear that?" the older boy whispered.

Overhead, the end of a dog's bark hung in the air, followed by a man's quiet voice. The voice was too far away for them to make out the words.

"Sounds like it's at our house," the younger brother said, his eyes glittering. He sheathed the blade of his knife and slipped it into a pocket. He took a quick drag from what was left of their joint and stubbed it out in the dirt at his back. He and his brother eased up the side of the ditch until their heads were above the rim. They saw the dark figure of a man and his dog beside their carport, which was about 50 feet away.

"Looks like he's foolin' with my bike," he whispered, forgetting that he had stolen it from school just a few days earlier.

"Les give the fucker a scare," he mouthed, pulling himself out of the ditch. "I'll go round the house and come at him from the front. You slip up on him from behind." Without waiting for a response, he trotted in the direction he'd indicated. The grass and weeds muf-fled his footsteps.

CHAPTER 3

"Whatcha doin' in there, Jack?"

Peter whirled to stare at the figure between him and the sidewalk. The guy was short and slender, and he looked relaxed, arms folded across his chest. His nonchalant stance signaled that this was his territory, that Peter was an intruder.

How could he have slipped up so quietly, Peter wondered, pulse pounding, mouth dry as cotton. At his side, Skipper continued to growl. Without looking, Peter knew the dog's teeth were bared, and the hair along his back and shoulders was stiffly erect.

"This is my son's bike," he said. His voice quivered like it did on the first day of class each semester. At his words, the figure grinned, teeth gleaming in a dark face. Peter saw it was just a boy, probably not much older than Danny. He wore thick glasses.

"Whatcha gonna do about it?" the boy asked, uncrossing his arms and reaching casually into his pants pocket. In one smooth movement, he extracted an enormous knife, pressed a button, and a large blade appeared. Peter hadn't seen a switchblade in years. Despite the temperature, he shivered.

"Nothing," he said. "You can have it. Insurance'll pay for it anyway," he said to the grin. The boy's stare was unnerving; the eyes seemed empty, nothing behind them.

"We're leaving now," Peter said. "The bike's yours."

"I know that," the kid said. He switched the big knife to his other hand.

Peter licked his lips, thinking irrationally about applying his chapstick. "So, what do we do now?" he said. "You gonna let me by, or what? I said you could keep the bike."

"You said it, but I don't believe it, Jack. I ain't stupid, you know. Soon as you leave here, you'll be callin' the cops to tell 'em where your kid's bike is and who's got it and then what'll happen?"

The boy's words didn't frighten Peter as much as the tone of his voice. There was no feeling in it, no rhythm, no cadence. For the first time since a college misadventure, Peter feared for his life. At this point, he really would have given the bike to the boy, signed it over to him, anything to gain the safety of the sidewalk. Once there, he would jog home, no two ways about it. Jog, hell, he would run as far as his wind would take him.

"C'mon, Skip," he said, starting forward. The boy didn't move or change expression. The grin seemed painted on.

Skipper howled.

"Wha...," Peter began, then finished with "hunhhh," as he was grabbed from behind. Arms like tree limbs bound him implacably. He smelled grease and sweat and his own fear. He dropped Skipper's leash. Liquid warmth coated his legs.

"The fucker pissed hisself," a deep voice said, chuckling. Peter kicked and missed, his right foot traveling between his captor's spread legs. Skipper barked shrilly. Peter swiveled his head, straining to see behind him. Nothing. When he looked back, the boy was almost upon him, still grinning. Peter couldn't see the knife. He drew breath to yell, then exhaled with a hiss as six inches of steel slipped between ribs to pierce his left ventricle. Peter never felt a thing.

CHAPTER 4

"What'd you do?" the older brother said when he felt the man go limp. He released the body, which settled at his feet, legs twitching reflexively in a parody of running.

"Stuck the fucker," his brother said. "Sumbitch reminded me of the old man." He giggled. Skipper barked uncontrollably, creating an incredible din in the space between the houses.

"Shut that goddam dog up."

"Here, doggy." the boy crouched, holding the knife behind his back, trying to suppress his giggles. Skipper snarled, backing away, canine brain trying and failing to understand what had happened to his master. There were suddenly too many strange signals. Skipper turned and ran, his leash clattering on the sidewalk behind him.

The brothers stood over Peter's body, watching the legs pumping. They moved slower now, more rhythmically.

"Think he's still alive?" the younger one said, followed by "I'll fix 'im." He hefted a brick he'd picked up from the yard. He knelt and struck. Once. Twice. Then again and again until the man's head was flattened, gray matter oozing into the grassy stubble of the yard. The twitching had stopped.

He stood, panting, still grinning, holding the soiled brick. "What we gonna do with 'im?"

"Sheeit. You killed 'im. You figure it out." The older brother slipped out a cigarette and lit it with a disposable Bic. The brief flash illuminated ordinary features: a low forehead over eyes the color of dark chocolate, broad nose, thick, unsmiling lips. Their father looked much the same.

"They's a trash bin behin' the church. We could stuff 'im in that. Burn 'im, maybe."

The older brother shrugged. It sounded like as good a plan as any. He wasn't worried about anybody recognizing the man's face after what his brother had done with the brick. Burning would take care of the rest of the body. They could use the garden hose to wash away the gore in the yard.

"Grab his arms," he said, lifting the man's feet and slipping them under his armpits. His brother wiped his knife on the man's shirt sleeve before thrusting it back into his pocket. Still grinning, the boy hefted his end. The top of Peter's head bumped along the ground as the brothers struggled to the church with their load.

"Fucker didn't look this heavy," the boy said, between gasps.

"Jes shuddup," his brother answered. "Sooner we git this fucker outta sight, better I'll like it."

On a Saturday night, the trash dumpster was less than half full. It would be picked up and emptied on Monday. Fortunately for the brothers, the dumpster was hidden from the street by the new educational wing under construction. They lay the body beside it while considering their next move.

"Git inside the thing and see if there's somethin' that'll burn."

"Why do I hafta git inside?" the boy asked, grin gone at the thought of how his brother always ordered him around. "Won't the fucker's clothes burn?"

"Naw, his pants is wet, and the shirt's all bloody. Anyways, you stuck 'im." The unfinished thought was that it was the boy's responsibility. He knelt and began to undo Peter's shoes. "Them shoes is too good to burn," he mumbled.

Muttering under his breath, the boy climbed into the metal box. "Ain't nothin' here but trash sacks and paint cans," he hollered to his brother.

"Can't you keep ya voice down?" the brother hissed back. "Anythin' in the cans?"

"Naw, they empty. All but thissun." Sitting on the top edge of the container, the boy dropped a half full can on the body. His brother picked it up, and his lighter flared.

"Shiit, this is jus' what we need. Turpentine. Les git 'im in and soak 'im with this. He'll go up like a rocket."

The brothers worked quickly now that they had a plan. Empty paint cans and black plastic bags were Peter's funeral bier. The body reeked of turpentine when the boy finished.

"Git down from there, bro'. Les' fire it up and git the hell outta here."

"Aw, jus' one more sniff, man," the boy said, hopping off reluctantly. "That's some good shit." He leaned back over the edge and inhaled deeply.

"You go through his pockets?"

"Shit, no. Never thought of it."

"Too late now," he said, dropping a lighted piece of paper over the side.

Whump! Instantly, the bin was filled with flame. Heat licked the brothers' faces as they stared, awed. A roar filled the still night. Smoke curled up and over the sleeping houses.

"Goddam, somebody'll notice that, fo' sure." He sniffed. "Smell jus' like bobikew."

"Yeah," the boy said, grin threatening to split his face. His teeth gleamed in the firelight. "What we gonna do 'bout it?"

"Shut the lid, I guess. Mebbe it's already burned enough."

The lid hung down the back of the bin. The boy grabbed one corner and screamed. "Shit, that's hotter'n a pistol." The dropped lid clattered back against the bin.

"Here, use this as a glove," the older brother said, handing his brother one of Peter's shoes. He put the other one on his own hand and lifted his side of the lid, holding his breath to keep from inhaling the pungent smoke. Heat scorched his sweating face. Together they raised the lid until they could drop it closed.

11

"Let's git outta here," he said, but his brother needed no urging. They trotted home, the boy carrying the shoes. Back in their house after cleaning up as much of the blood as possible, the older brother whispered, "There ain't nothin' to make 'em think we done it." His brother grinned in the dark.

CHAPTER 5

They were about to pull onto the interstate when Sandy said from the back seat, "Did you notice how hot it was at Uncle Doug's?" The temperature was the first thing Brad had noticed about his uncle's room, but he never agreed with his sister about anything, so he kept his mouth shut. His father flipped on the right turn signal and slipped between a Toyota and a massive tractor trailer.

"Ninety degrees outside, and he had on an electric heater," his mother marveled.

The highway ahead shimmered in the heat, and the air conditioner's hum blocked the road noises.

"Doug's dying, Mary," his grandmother, Ellie Reynolds, had said on Friday evening, before they had even unpacked the car, referring to Douglas Oldham, her younger brother. Their duty visit was scheduled after church Sunday morning.

"We'll only stay a few minutes, Hal," his mother had assured his father. "We can say we need to leave early to have lunch and get on the road."

They had stayed 27 minutes, to be exact (Brad had timed the visit), but it felt like the longest 27 minutes of his life. It probably seemed like hours to his father.

Brad, his parents, his sister, and his grandmother had crowded into a room with his aunt and uncle—actually, they were his great-aunt and great-uncle—but Brad always called them Aunt Reba and Uncle Doug. With two couches at right angles to each other, a large recliner, a wheelchair, and a console television set, the room would have been cramped with three people.

Doug, the dying uncle, lay back in the recliner, his bare feet hanging off the recliner's foot. He looked much as Brad remembered him from previous visits: liver-spotted, bald, puffy-faced with reddish-white eyebrows, little round mouth pursed like he was sucking a persimmon. His eyelids were half closed, but all the people on Brad's mother's side of the family had this trait. An electric heater glowed beside Uncle Doug's chair, sending waves of heat to battle the over-taxed window air conditioner rumbling at the far end of the room.

After greeting his uncle, Brad took a seat next to his sister. He tried not to touch her. Their grandmother sat on the same couch, while his mother, father, and Aunt Reba shared the couch next to Uncle Doug's recliner. Aunt Reba didn't have her teeth in, and she continually puffed her wrinkled lips in and out, looking at times like a dried apple doll.

"Are you in any pain?" Brad's mother asked, and everyone leaned forward expectantly, anxious to know what Uncle Doug was experiencing.

"What's that?" Uncle Doug said.

"He can't hear you," Aunt Reba mumbled, screwing her mouth into indescribable shapes. "He won't wear his hearing aid." Like you won't wear your false teeth, Brad thought.

"I said, 'Are you in any pain?'" Mary Childers shouted. Brad's father drew away slightly, although he continued to hold his wife's hand. Brad knew his father well enough to recognize that his distant smile meant, "I wish I were anywhere but here."

"Naw," Uncle Doug said. "It's a cancer and that don't cause any pain."

Expressions of amazement greeted this statement, but the uncle was as oblivious as he was deaf. "The doctor says it's got my liver and stomach," he said, tracing the afflicted areas with his hand over his pajamas. "Started in my pankcreas or whatchamacallit."

"Gone to his brain, most like," Aunt Reba muttered. "They want him to go into a nursing home, Ellie," she said to Brad's grandmother, "but he's too stubborn."

"What's wrong with the nursing home, Doug?" his father asked.

"I helped 'em put two old women down the street into a nursing home," his uncle said, "and they died all hunched over. Got shoved into the casket like that."

"He don't know what he's talking about," Aunt Reba said under her breath to Sandy. Louder, she said, "That wouldn't happen to you, Doug. You need to go to the home 'cause I can't take care of you by myself." Brad watched in fascination as his aunt's mouth kept moving after she finished speaking. She reminded him of characters on a television show with unsynchronized sound.

"I'm okay right chere, old woman," his uncle said, his face reddening. "I got my bathroom over there in the corner, and I got my chair, and I can walk a little when I have to."

"He musta got up 10 times last night, Ellie," Aunt Reba said, "an' it's a mess in the bathroom when he gets through."

"I built this room," his uncle said. "Cost me $36,000." Brad thought he probably meant it cost $3,600; he wasn't sure the whole house was worth $36,000. "I own this home, and they're not getting me out of it to go to no nursing home."

"How much would it cost him in the nursing home, Reba?" his grandmother asked.

"Nine hunderd a month," Aunt Reba said, "but the doctor said he only has a couple of weeks left."

"I got a pacemaker last month," Uncle Doug announced. Aunt Reba shook her head and sucked her gums.

"Didn't you have a pacemaker put in, Hal?" His father said he hadn't, but Brad didn't think his uncle heard him. Brad was pretty sure his uncle wasn't responding to anything in the immediate environment.

"Anyway," Uncle Doug continued, "I got this pacemaker, so I can't get mad. Since you got one, you can come to the nursing home with me, Hal. We can have the beds next to each other. Wave to each other." He waved to Brad, perhaps mistaking him for his father.

"Is he like this all the time?" his grandmother asked.

"Pretty much," Aunt Reba said.

"What grade do you teach, Mary?" Uncle Doug said.

"I don't teach anymore, Uncle Doug," his mother said, but her reply was lost in his uncle's next observation.

"That's the best load you ever shot, Hal," he said, fixing Brad with a rheumy stare. His father laughed, and Brad thought it was funny too, although he wasn't exactly sure what his uncle meant. His mother blushed, and his aunt just shook her head and worked her mouth.

"We're having turkey tonight, Ellie," Aunt Reba said, perhaps trying to distract her husband from any other sensitive subjects. "It's one of Doug's favorite dishes."

"What's that, Reba?"

"I said, 'We're having turkey tonight,'" Aunt Reba hollered, leaning forward to look at her husband. Brad thought it was the first time she had looked at him since they'd been there.

"I'm not eatin' no turkey-a-la-goo-goo," Uncle Doug hollered back.

CHAPTER 6

"You think Reba's right, Hal?" his mother said from the back seat. "That the cancer has affected Doug's brain?"

"How could you tell, Mary? He's always been that way if you ask me."

"Kinda crazy, huh, Dad?" Sandy said.

"Right," said her father. "You remember the time Doug got to picking at Sandy, Mary? Saying she was large when he meant fat? It was so ridiculous, because she was just a tiny thing at the time."

It fit now, though, Brad thought, and when they were alone, he would find some way to remind Sandy of it. Around him the family's talk wove desultorily, finally dying away when they had exhausted the topic of the craziness of his mother's family. Things were no better on his father's side, but they never went to visit his relatives.

They were off the interstate now, on the home stretch. His father had swapped places with Brad at Bud's Truck Stop; they always stopped at Bud's so that his mother and his sister could go to the bathroom. His mother got into the back seat after the pit stop when Brad took over driving duties. Brad hadn't pee'd when they stopped, and he had been regretting it for the last few miles.

Brad first saw the truck at the top of the ridge, still a good quarter mile away. It was a big rig, probably speeding, its grill resplendent with the Stars and Bars. Staring at the truck, Brad sensed a disquieting thought creeping into consciousness. He tried to look away—and failed. The truck grew as the two vehicles neared on the two-lane road.

Brad kept a steady pressure on the accelerator, not slowing like his mother tended to do when approaching traffic. They were very close now, the car and the truck, and Brad could imagine the expression on the other driver's face. It would be blank, the man lulled by the nearly empty road.

In the instant of their passing, the obsession that controlled his mind would take control of his muscles as well. Only a small twist of the wheel, that's all it would take. "Jesus H. Christ," the truck driver would scream, stomping the brake and swerving his rig to the right.

Too late.

How long would it take, Brad wondered. Would he feel anything? He didn't think so. He could see his body trying to continue forward but being stopped by the compaction of the car. In a fraction of a second, he would be crushed nearly flat, bones breaking, blood and guts squirting, going from something alive and human to dying protoplasm. He remembered his biology teacher saying that sensory systems were too slow to respond to the almost instantaneous changes his body would experience. His father, sharing the front seat, would go as quickly as he would, crushed into an unrecognizable pancake of protein and congealing jelly.

Maybe, just maybe, his mother and sister, dozing in the back seat, would awaken to a moment of terror and agony as they fused with the hunk of metal and plastic and glass that had been their car. He didn't care about his sister, but he hoped his mother wouldn't feel anything.

"Whatcha thinking about, Brad?" his father asked. The truck roared past.

"School," he said, images gone but not forgotten. Was he losing his mind?

"How do your classes look this year, Son? Better than last year?"

"Yeah, I guess." Anything would be better, he thought. How could he have failed three courses? He, Arnold Bradley Childers, IQ of 137. Most kids didn't even know their IQs, but trust his father to take advantage of anything free. When the guy from the college came looking for kids to test, he and his sister were volunteered. Well, he hadn't minded the test; it had been kind of fun, actually. What he resented was the way his father threw his high IQ up to him whenever he made a bad grade.

"Want me to try to get something on the radio?"

Brad shrugged. His father rotated the tuning knob very slowly, trying to find a country music station without too much static. But it was Sunday evening, and his search was futile. He stilled the radio with a plastic click.

Brad shifted his left arm, trying to find a comfortable position for his elbow. He had been driving for nearly an hour, and he was getting tired, although he would never have admitted it. Also, there was no way he could admit how badly he needed to piss.

"What kind of team is your school going to have this year, Brad?"

He could feel his father's eyes boring into his right cheek, and he had an almost uncontrollable urge to tell him to fuck off, to leave him alone. He knew what he would see if he turned to face his father—the old man sitting there with his "I'm concerned about you, Son" look on his swarthily handsome features, features that Brad saw palely reflected in his own mirror.

"Don't know, Dad."

"Mmmm. Seems like I've read they're supposed to be as good this year as they were last year."

And that had been pretty good, Brad knew. In fact, the Harper Lions had been so good they won all their games and the state championship in their class. He knew it bugged his father that he had so little interest in football, but Brad didn't care. Or maybe he did care and feigned lack of interest just to spite his father. Sometimes, when his hormones were at low ebb, he wondered what had happened to his relationship with his father. After all, the old man was usually pretty reasonable.

"Going to any of the games?"

"Probably not." Brad spotted lights along the roofline of the car in his rearview mirror and eased back on the accelerator.

"I sure hope you're going to do better this year than last. Your mother and I can't afford to send you to college to make the kind of grades you've made the last couple of years."

Brad kept his eyes glued to the road ahead, thinking about how badly he needed to take a piss and how much he wanted a cigarette, in that order.

"Lord, just let me hold it until we get home," he prayed silently. And let Jesse have some smokes at school tomorrow. Somehow it didn't seem right to include that thought as part of his prayer.

The highway patrolman swept by.

CHAPTER 7

Saturday afternoon in Harper. Down the street a dog barked incessantly, his yip growing shriller as whatever triggered it came closer. Humid air smelled of barbeque, newly mown grass, and lawn mower exhaust. An occasional breeze rustled pine needles. Many fell, and Mickey "Bone" Ludlow's yard was thickly carpeted. He hated raking pine straw even more than he hated mowing grass.

Ludlow planted a size 13 shoe on the side of his mower, pushed the throttle to Start with the heel of his right hand, and yanked the rope. The motor spun but didn't catch. He pulled again.

"Goddam," he said, sweat trickling down his face and back. A smile twitched his thin lips, ending short of blue eyes nearly hidden by puffy lids. He saw himself upending the gas can over the mower, then throwing his lighter on it. "Give that fuckin' machine something to think about," he muttered. He yanked the cord again. And again. The smell of raw gas tickled his nose, and he knew he had flooded it.

"Shit," he said, aiming a kick at the engine housing. Bone ripped the throttle back to Off and stalked away, back to the house. He entered the kitchen through the back door, blinking in the relative darkness. To his left hummed an aging Frigidaire. He took a Bud from the refrigerator, standing with the door open to let the cold air chill his naked chest. A roll of flab hung over the top of his faded jeans.

The chilled air felt good, and the sight of leftover chicken beckoned. Bone groped under the plastic wrap for a drumstick.

"I was saving that for supper," Vicki said behind him, and Bone jumped, startled. He dropped the drumstick back into the bowl, slammed the refrigerator door so hard that it popped back open, and he had to close it again, firmly this time. He turned, glowering at his wife.

"Go ahead and eat it, Bone," she said, "now that you've touched it." Although she spoke softly, there was a hard edge to her words.

Bone said nothing, just stared. He popped the top on his Bud, feeling the spray mist the back of his hand. A sharp odor of hops entered his broad nose, triggering salivation. He took a sip without taking his eyes from his wife. She dropped her eyes from his, pulled out a chair from the table, and sat.

"Through with the grass?"

"No, I ain't through with the grass," he said, settling his bulk into the chair catty corner to hers. He slipped a mashed pack of Camels from his pocket, fumbled out his lighter, and lit up. Smoke filled the air between them.

"Mower wouldn't start."

Vicki said nothing, just sat looking at the table, finger tracing a nonexistent pattern. Bone read disapproval in her nonlook, her finger tracing, the set of her narrow jaw. He thought of popping her a quick one, somewhere it wouldn't show, and then felt guilty about this thought; it wasn't her fault the mower wouldn't start. He took another pull from his beer and wiped his mouth with the back of the hand holding the can.

"You been talkin' to your momma again?" he asked. Her involuntary glance, pupils dilating, gave him the answer. Her and her momma, always talking about what a worthless husband he was. Anger flared, fueled by frustration with the mower, with life, with his job, with the disapproval of his wife and mother-in-law. He drained the Bud and crumpled the can.

"Get me another one," he said, testing his control.

"Get it yourself," she said, resentment flashing in green eyes.

She said it quickly, before she had time to think, to weigh the consequences.

And just as quickly he struck, openhanded, palm lashing across her freckled cheek.

Whap!

Vicki's cheek paled, reddened, then stiffened as the first tear spilled over, tracing a familiar path. Just for a moment Bone saw hurt, humiliation, hatred in his wife's eyes, and then she was gone. He heard the bedroom door slam.

He looked at his right hand, felt its tingle from the slap. Why had he hit her? Maybe he could still make it up, go down the hall to their bedroom, apologize, have make-up sex. "Fat chance of that, Ludlow," he told himself. "She's really pissed this time."

"Vicki," he yelled down the hall, not really expecting an answer. He decided to have another beer. Then maybe he would go apologize.

CHAPTER 8

Flattened beer cans littered the table. Bent butts filled the ashtray. The darkened room reeked of stale smoke and dried sweat. Bone levered himself from the chair and lurched toward the bathroom, taking short, wide steps to maintain his balance. As he neared, he could see that the door was shut; Vicki must be inside.

He tried the knob. Locked.

"Vicki," he yelled. "Open up and let me in. I gotta take a piss."

"Go away, Bone," came the muffled reply. "You can go in the yard for all I care."

"Aw, c'mon, Hon," he said. "I didn't mean to slap ya. Probly didn't hurt anyway."

"That's not the point," she said, and her voice sounded so close Bone was sure she was just on the other side of the door. "You promised the last time. . . ."

Bone crossed his legs and thrust his hand down his pants, squeezing himself to keep from urinating. "Open up, Vicki," he yelled. "I really gotta go." Not for the first time, Bone had the thought that they really needed to add another bathroom.

"No," she said, and he heard her moving away. Still tight from all the beer, Bone unzipped his jeans, scrabbled in his jockey shorts for his cock, found it, ripped it out and aimed it for the bottom of the door. His relief was profound.

"Bone! You better not be doing what it sounds like you're doing." Vicki jerked open the door, and Bone, startled, lost control. His warm urine struck Vicki's shin, traveled right to soak her other leg, then kept going to water the side of the tub.

"That does it," Vicki said, as Bone's stream dwindled and died. "I'm leaving." She turned away from Bone to rinse her legs under the faucet in the tub. Bone's stupid grin sagged as he realized what she had said.

Sobered, Bone stood looking in at his wife as she rinsed her legs. She did first one, then the other, taking care to avoid getting her shorts wet.

"I'm sorry, Hon," Bone said, feeling life creep into his still exposed penis, life stirred by the sight of his wife's damp legs. Her legs looked good, not all fat and crepey like the cashiers' legs at the store. And Vicki's behind was firm and small; Bone mentally compared it with the bottoms on so many of the store's customers, and his fear grew that his wife might really leave. Vicki cut off the water and stood on the bathmat drying her legs, not looking at her husband.

"I'll clean up the mess, Vicki," he said, "soon as we get through."

Vicki turned then, impaled Bone with a look of daggers. "Soon as we get through with what?"

"You know what," he said hoarsely. He grinned.

"Just get out of my way, Bone," Vicki said, turning off the water. She started forward as Bone backed away from the door. "There's no way we're gonna have sex after what you did this afternoon. Are you going to let me by?"

"Sure," he said, defeated. He stepped back, and Vicki walked past him into the bedroom. "You're not really leaving, are you?"

"I don't know, Bone," she said, looking more sad than angry. "I just might." Vicki left the room.

"I'm gonna clean up the piss," Bone said, struggling to get his penis back into his pants as he hurried to follow his wife. "And then I'll mow the grass, Vicki," he said to her back. "And I won't ever hit you again, Hon," he promised, as he had done so many times before.

CHAPTER 9

Sandy heard the toilet flush in the hall bathroom and wrinkled her nose in disgust. Brad spent hours in there. What could he be doing all that time, she wondered, and then decided she didn't want to know.

She lay across her bed, gazing unfocused at the Raggedy Ann wallpaper on the far wall. Fourteen on her last birthday, Sandy was too old for the print, but she found its familiarity reassuring.

Her room was cluttered but comfortable. A blue chest-of-drawers (when she was little, she thought it was Chester Drawers) dominated the wall opposite her bed. Her mother had spent hours painting the chest after her father put it together from a kit. He still laughed about the chest, talking about how it came in a thousand pieces and took him days to build. He embellished the story but not all that much. One drawer was open halfway; underwear peeked over the rim. It was plain cotton underwear, not fancy or frilly.

Homemade bookshelves covered the room's outer wall, and Sandy's doll and stuffed animal collection covered them. There was no pattern to the collection; Raggedy Ann slumped against a teddy bear; a one-armed, glass-eyed doll that said "Mama" hugged a faded Snoopy.

Overhead a ceiling fan turned slowly, casting flickering shadows over the solitary goldfish swimming in circles in the bowl on Sandy's nightstand. Poor Harry. Looking for Herman, no doubt. Sandy had found Herman floating on his back only the week before. She still missed him.

The fan's gentle breeze stirred the pages of an opened diary. Sandy resumed writing.

> ... got back this afternoon from Atlanta where we had gone to visit Granny Reynolds. She's really getting old.
>
> And mean. I guess I'd never noticed how she picks at Dad. But then he doesn't help. Sits around muttering under his breath and giving Granny dirty looks.
>
> We went to visit Uncle Doug and Aunt Reba 'cause Uncle Doug's dying. He really acted weird, which we agreed coming back wasn't too unusual. He didn't act like someone who's dying, or at least like I imagine a dying person would act.
>
> Coming back Brad drove some after we left the interstate.
>
> Mom and I dozed in the back seat. I never quite trust him—he's so moody all the time lately. Dad tries to be nice to him sometimes, but I think Brad just shuts him out. Like last weekend. Dad asked Brad if he wanted to go out to the gun club. Do some target shooting. Brad said no, he was busy, then spent the weekend in his room with his radio blaring. When I asked him to turn it off, he shot me the bird. I thought of telling on him, but what's the use.
>
> Brad's not bad looking when he smiles, which isn't very often. Looks kinda like Dad except Brad's taller and thinner and paler. Some of my friends even think he's cute, but I would never tell *him*. Speaking of cute, Diary, I saw the cutest boy in the mall in Atlanta.

Sandy chewed on the end of her pen, remembering the tow-headed boy in a muscle shirt and jeans. What a hunk. Not that he would ever look at her. She turned to her back and kneaded her hips with stubby fingers. Too much fat. Thick, that's what she was, thick like her father.

Why couldn't she have taken after her mother? She was so petite, although she had big boobs. Sort of like Dolly Parton. No, she had inherited her father's body. Maybe she would start exercising, turn all her flab into muscle. That was it. She would start jogging. Just as soon as she could get her mother to buy her some running shoes.

CHAPTER 10

Grady Noland stretched, opened his right eye halfway, and did a mental check of his body. Stiff, sore in places, badly needing to take a leak, but otherwise all in working order. Tendrils of sunlight streamed into the room where Marge hadn't quite pulled the shades down far enough the night before. With his half-opened eye, Grady watched dust motes drifting in the light. Before it could disturb his wife's sleep, he turned off the alarm. Grady scratched himself until his wife mumbled "Quit fidgeting," and then he rolled out of bed and into the bathroom.

Ten minutes later he was on the street in front of his house. He loved the stillness of the nearly deserted streets. Beside his mailbox, Grady began jumping jacks to get his heart rate up to tempo. One anna two anna three anna. . . . When he got to 20, he stopped, set his stopwatch, and loped off.

Funny how he looked forward to the jumping jacks now, when he had hated them so in boot camp. But that was long ago, before Vietnam. He had smoked then, and exercise had hurt his chest. Plus, he *had* to exercise in the military. That was the difference, he supposed. Having to do something versus wanting to do it.

At 6'2" and 185 pounds, Grady wasn't built for marathon running. Still, he ran easily, long legs effortlessly devouring the blocks. He was starting to sweat already, less than 6 minutes into his run. How could anyone run at noon, he wondered, thinking about the joggers from the college he often saw passing the police station. Guys older than he was, running in 95-degree weather. Had to be nuts.

Like many a reformed smoker, he snorted disgustedly at the odor of cigarette smoke from a house on his left. Then it was behind him, and he could breathe freely again. He ran on, breathing evenly through his mouth. He felt good, powerful, immortal. A couple of streets away Grady saw a big man leave his carport, padding on bare feet to retrieve his paper. He hoped he wouldn't have to speak. No such luck. The man spotted Grady, stuffed the newspaper under his arm, and waited.

"Hiya, Grady," the man called as the chief drew even with him. Grady waved, forcing a smile. There were things about Bone Ludlow that bothered him. Perhaps it was his too-friendly manner in the grocery store, always greeting Grady like the chief was his long-lost buddy. Sure, they had gone to high school together, but that was 20 years ago. They weren't in the same circle then, and they had little more than nodded since. A few pleasantries and some talk about the local football teams was about the extent of their relationship.

Then, too, there were the rumors. Marge said she'd heard Ludlow beat his wife. Grady wouldn't put it past the man. He quickened his pace, anxious to be away from Ludlow's block.

Grady turned another corner and smiled. He was now heading into a slight breeze. God, it felt good. As he ran, he thought about Jon Evans and the murders over a year ago in Harper. Amazing how all that had turned out. At the time Grady had gone to visit Jon in the mental institution, the former professor had indicated that he was satisfied with his situation. He had status and time to work on his novel based on the events that had gotten him incarcerated and institutionalized.

In fact, he had finished the book, sent Grady an autographed copy, and the notoriety of the case had gotten him a New York agent. The agent quickly sold A False Suggestion to a major publisher.

The success of the book, which revealed that Jon had not really committed the crimes attributed to him, was phenomenal. His agent had asked Jon to consider seeking his release from the institution so that he could go on book tours.

Jon had reached out to Grady, who had immediately offered to help him in any way he could. One major factor in proving his innocence was the murder in Canada that occurred when Jon's therapist, Henry Andrews, was in Montreal. Grady had contacted Lieutenant Paul Davide, and he had agreed to come to Harper to give his evidence implicating Andrews.

Still deep in thought, Grady turned another corner. The street he was now on would take him back to his neighborhood. Coming toward him was a person in a car delivering newspapers, and Grady briefly jogged in place when he and the newspaper deliverer arrived at the same driveway at the same time. He returned the woman's wave before continuing his run.

Grady had met Lt. Davide at the small, regional airport near Harper. After they greeted one another, Davide introduced his traveling companion, an attractive brunette who appeared to be in her early 40s. It turned out that she was Bethany Andrews, Henry Andrews' widow.

"I really want to thank you for putting us together, Grady," Davide had told him. In subsequent conversations, Grady had learned that Bethany was much more than just his traveling companion.

Davide's part of the story of Henry Andrews proved to be helpful at Jon's hearing, and with the evidence that Grady had amassed, the former English professor had gained release from the facility quickly.

The hiss of bike tires on asphalt startled Grady, and he looked over his shoulder to see a black-clad figure rapidly approaching.

"Morning," the man said, and then he was by. The breeze of his passing flung Grady's answer back at him. He checked his watch. 29:38. Only a few more seconds, and he could slow down.

"Git," he hissed, startling a cat feasting on table scraps from a torn garbage sack. The cat darted under a parked car.

Grady slowed to a brisk walk. He waved to a woman passing in a car. She returned his greeting, and he thought about how friendly people were in Harper. His stomach rumbled, and he realized how hungry he was. What would Marge have fixed this morning? Oatmeal? No, they had that a couple of days ago. Maybe some kind of homemade muffins. He would wash them down with skim milk, while Marge clucked approvingly, and their son complained. Grady Jr. didn't understand why they wouldn't let him eat junk cereal anymore. Well, at least the kid was young enough to be somewhat controllable. Grady could imagine what it would be like to try to get a teenager to eat a "good" diet.

He turned into his driveway and bent to retrieve the paper. Slim this morning, he thought, folding it out. He ambled to the carport door, scanning the front page. Usual stuff. College needed more money. Predictions of afternoon thundershowers. Some feature on a local author. Grady slipped inside the house.

"Hi, Dear," Marge said, turning her cheek for his kiss. Grady, looking over her shoulder, saw an egg-white omelet in the skillet.

"Grits, too?"

"Yep," she said, "and hashbrowns."

Grady sat at the table to exchange his running shoes for slippers. He smiled at his wife's back. Their new diet had really done wonders for her figure, and looking at her standing there, muscular calves showing below her nightgown, hand with spatula resting on hip, curves suggested beneath thin cloth, Grady felt something stirring. Something they didn't have time for this morning. Reluctantly, he wrenched his gaze away from his wife and back to the paper.

"That woman called again," Marge said, "the one from last night."

"Husband come home?" Grady asked, hopefully.

Marge came to the table with knives and forks, arranging them carefully at their places. She put a spoon at Grady Jr.'s place. "No," she said. "She wanted you to call as soon as you got in. Number's by the phone."

Grady sighed, stood, and punched the number on the wall phone. Half a ring and it was answered.

"Hello?" In that one word, Grady heard the woman's hope and fear.

"Mrs. Dewberry?"

"Yes." Disappointment.

"This is Grady Noland. Your husband still missing?"

A half sob, checked. "I can't imagine what could have happened, Chief," the woman said. "What should I do?"

"I'll stop by on my way to the office," Grady said. "Should be there before 8:00. What's the address again?" Nancy Dewberry told him, and he replaced the receiver.

He sat back at the table, frowning over his steaming meal.

"Go ahead and eat, Grady, before it gets cold."

Mechanically, he took a bite of the egg. "I've got a bad feeling about this, Marge," he said. "Man takes his dog for a walk near midnight, and the dog comes back without him." He sprinkled a little salt on the grits, and then followed that with a touch of margarine.

"Maybe he decided to run away from home. Met his girlfriend or something."

"Hmm," he said, disbelieving. He speared a few cubes of his hashbrowns and used them to scoop some grits. Reflexively, he shoveled the bite into his mouth. Chewed.

"These are pretty good, Marge," he said, pushing away his disquiet for the moment.

CHAPTER 11

Hannah Green lived with her oldest daughter Ida and her eight grandchildren in a five-room house on King Street. King intersects Washington less than a quarter mile from Roosevelt.

At 5:13 Monday morning, Hannah slipped quietly out the back door of her daughter's house, wrapped her gnarled hands around the handle of a rusty A & P shopping cart and headed for the street. A dusty haze around the rising sun signaled the beginning of another scorcher. Despite the pending heat, Hannah wore a thin brown sweater over her dress. She muttered as she walked, her quavering voice the only company she'd needed the past 25 years.

"Gonna be hot, Hannah," she said, shuffling along. Her left foot, layered in newspaper, slipped loosely inside a size 9 black wingtip. On her right foot she wore a tennis shoe one of her grandsons had discarded. Half a day's search through her daughter's trash had not uncovered its mate. Ida had offered to take her to the Salvation Army to find a pair of shoes that fit, but Hannah had refused. Her shoes felt right; new used shoes would have to mold to her feet, and Hannah didn't like change. Inside her shoes, Hannah wore black socks that flopped about her ankles.

Hannah spotted her first can, an upright Old Milwaukee. "Goddam," she said, stopping her cart. "Got somethin' in it, too." She brought the can to her nose and sniffed. "Beer, aw right," she muttered. If it had rained the night before, beer cans sometimes had water in them, and occasionally she found one filled with piss. Hannah drained the can and licked the last drops from her upper lip. "Good shit." Hannah threw the can into her cart. She rattled on.

At the corner of King and Roosevelt, Hannah hesitated. "I went right yestaday," she muttered, wheeling left.

She trudged across the street. The right front wheel of her cart kicked a rock, then circled crazily until Hannah ran it into the curb. She hiked her skirts a little higher on hips no wider than the front of her cart, walked to the cart's front, and lifted it to the sidewalk. A dog on a rope at the corner house pulled at his tether and barked loudly as the little woman clattered by. Hannah looked warily at the animal and shuffled faster.

Hannah spotted another can in the gutter and beside it lay most of a cigarette, its tan filter lipstick marked. "My lucky day," she said, squatting to retrieve both. The empty Bud banged against the Old Milwaukee can, and Hannah pulled a kitchen match from her sweater pocket to light the cigarette.

"Ah," she said, savoring the nearly fresh tobacco smell. She moved on, filter clamped between toothless gums.

Quiet on a Monday morning. Not much traffic yet. Hannah shuffled past a house where two brothers lived. One slept fitfully, dreaming of a stranger about to steal his bicycle. The other lay awake, wondering how their little trick had gone so wrong. Hannah found another cigarette in front of that house and slipped it into a Marlboro box in her left skirt pocket. "After lunch," she muttered.

The cart clattered busily, filling nicely with beer cans. "Monday mornin's nice," Hannah observed. "Lotta drinkin' on the weekend." Cigarette ash dusted the sleeves of her sweater. The church grew as she approached.

"Ida's church," she said, working the cigarette to the opposite side of her mouth. Hannah thought of Ida ready for church, wearing her red dress with the size 40 black belt. If Ida could leave her fat in the collection plate, the church would be rich, Hannah thought, chuckling at the image. It reminded her of an Oprah show when the star brought in a container of fat to show how much weight she had lost. Ida had watched the show with Hannah, but it just made her hungry.

Hannah stopped, arrested by the bacon smell drifting street-ward from the house behind the church parking lot. "Gawd, that's good," she said, and would have knocked on the door if she'd known the people. For all Ida's weight, she didn't cook breakfast. The kids ate Pop-Tarts and Fruit Loops, and Hannah had never liked either. Reluctantly, Hannah moved away from the smell, a vision slowly fading of greasy bacon strips, fried eggs with brown lacy-edged crispness, and a mound of creamy white grits with a pond of melted butter in the center. Or maybe under a pool of white cream gravy.

Beyond the good smell, there was another, faint smell, like something dead left out in the sun. "Probly in the trash bin," Hannah muttered. Cat or something. Lord only knew what the neighbor-hood kids had put in there. Hannah always checked the trash con-tainer behind the church. Once she had found a baby, its brown skin still slightly warm even though it was dead. Hannah had stum-bled away, blinded by tears. She didn't even tell Ida about the baby. Turned out to belong to a high school girl who lived on Washington. They had convicted her of manslaughter and sentenced her to 8 years, which Ida said seemed awfully harsh to her. Remembering the beauty of the baby's face, Hannah decided the sentence wasn't long enough.

She rounded the corner of the wing of the church under con-struction and stopped. "Gawd," Hannah said. "Burned the sucker." Maybe she wouldn't look today. Anyhow, she probably couldn't even get the thing open. She couldn't remember the container ever being closed before, even when she found the baby.

"Jus' pass her on by, Hannah," she said to herself. "Go on over by the new shoppin' center." The one the white folks love so, with all the fancy stores and expensive cars parked in front. This ear-ly, Hannah could cruise the front of the stores. Do a little window shopping. Then she would check out the liftainer behind the stores.

Might be some good stuff back there. Plastic coat hangers, empty boxes, maybe even a soiled or torn piece of clothing. Empty beer cans. Treasure. Hannah turned her cart and started back around the wing.

And stopped again.

"What they try to burn in there?" she wondered. Hannah took out her other cigarette, the one in the Marlboro box, and lit it. She sucked deeply, staring at the black smudge-swirled metal box. "Looks like a giant coffin or a coffin for a giant," she chuckled. "Way Ida goin', she be needin' somethin' like that when she pass."

"Jus' a peek, Hannah," she said. "Then get over by the shoppin' center." Leaving her cart, Hannah shuffled to the box. Her cigarette dangled from her mouth, gray smoke blocking most of the sickly sweet dead smell. "Jus' a peek," she said, standing on tiptoes, pushing the smoke-stained lid up enough to peer over, straining to see inside the container.

Hannah dropped the lid and backed away, hands pushing at the air as though to ward off the sight burned into her memory. She tripped over a brick, fell heavily on the asphalt, but kept moving, scrabbling toward her cart. Blindly. Her cigarette still dangled from her bottom lip, smoke from it fogging her vision and burning her eyes. Tears streamed down her wrinkled face, but not tears like those she wept for the little black baby.

"Dam' smoke," she said, swiping the butt from her lips. She blinked, rubbed her eyes, and bumped into the front of her basket. Hannah stood, reversed her cart, and moved both it and herself as fast as she could back to the sidewalk.

"You didn' see nothin', Hannah," she muttered, heading back to Ida's, her fine day destroyed.

CHAPTER 12

"Should I go, Mom?" Danny said, looking like a younger version of his father. It was all Nancy could do to keep from crying. But she mustn't. Not yet. Not until they knew for sure. Until then she had to keep up appearances. For Danny's sake.

Nancy nodded and held out her arms. Unhesitatingly, Danny gave her a full-body hug, not the A-frame variety he usually begrudged her. She smelled aftershave and almost said something about it, but she didn't want to discourage his shaving by calling attention to it.

"Bye, Mom," Danny said, and then he was out the door and heading for the bus stop.

"Bye, Dear," Nancy said, waving at her son's retreating figure. She walked back to the table and sat, feeling numb and distracted and alone with her thoughts. The image of Peter lying somewhere—injured or worse—kept trying to surface, and Nancy kept thrusting it back, with only partial success. She wouldn't let herself imagine the worst. If she didn't think it, maybe it wouldn't come true.

She picked up the paper and went through it rapidly for the third time, scanning each page for something about Peter. Nothing. She should have known. Someone official would've called if there were any news. Nancy blew on her tepid coffee and sipped without tasting it. Where was he? Why hadn't he come home? Was there any explanation for his disappearance that might have a happy ending?

Skipper barked tentatively, his "too-lazy-to-get-up" bark. Startled, Nancy looked at him. "Hush," she said, sharply. Then, "Sorry, boy," as she stroked him. No need to take it out on the dog, Nance, she told herself. It isn't his fault he returned and Peter didn't. She heard the car door shut and sat, staring dejectedly at the door, waiting for the bell. There was a knock instead, and Nancy forced herself up.

"Mrs. Dewberry? I'm Grady Noland," the man said, looking somehow rumpled even though it was only 8:00. He wore a navy sports coat, a carelessly knotted tie on the collar of his white-on-white shirt, khaki pants, and scuffed loafers. The chief opened his wallet to display some sort of badge, but Nancy hardly noticed.

"Come in," she said, standing aside. Skipper ambled over, whuffed, sniffed the intruder, liked what he smelled. Tail wagging, the dog raised his head and pushed against the man's hand.

"Don't mind the dog."

"It's okay. I like dogs," Noland said, idly stroking Skipper's head.

"Would you like some coffee?"

"No, thanks."

The man's gaze swept the room, and Nancy knew what he saw: a very ordinary and somewhat-messy kitchen, refrigerator plastered with message magnets, sink filled with dirty dishes, no pots or pans on the stove. She wanted to tell him she was a better housekeeper than it looked, but she didn't. She would have to start cooking again—Danny needed something warm.

Noland stopped petting, and Skipper wandered to the kitchen table, sinking with a sigh under one of the chairs. "Now, about your husband," the chief began, extracting a notepad and pen from his coat pocket.

"Why isn't there anything in the paper?" Nancy said, suddenly angry.

"Why isn't what in the paper?" Noland asked, looking directly at her for the first time. She noticed his eyes weren't perfectly symmetrical.

Nancy wondered if he would write her description in his notepad. She remembered what she had seen in the mirror this morning: a stranger with a face puffy and red from lack of sleep, wearing no makeup, dressed in baggy sweatpants with a t-shirt that read "Downtown Harper Business Association 5K."

"Anything about my husband not coming home."

"I really don't know, Mrs. Dewberry."

"But I called the police."

The chief looked surprised. "You did? Who did you talk to?"

"A woman answered the phone and connected me with Buster... Buster something or other."

"Detective Buster Mixon," the chief said, and Nancy saw him write the name in his notepad, underlining it. His look said he would deal with Mixon later. "Why don't we sit down so you can fill me in on what happened, Mrs. Dewberry?"

Nancy led the way to the table. "Call me Nancy," she said. The chief started to sit at Peter's place. "Not there," she said, too harshly. He pushed in the chair and sat in Danny's seat instead, moving the cereal bowl to clear a place for his notepad. Nancy sat across from him.

"What time did your husband leave?"

"A little after 11:00." They had finished watching something on HBO. She couldn't remember now what it was, probably because Peter had watched the program while she intermittently dozed. She could see him standing by her chair in the family room, Skipper nudging his heel. "Love you," she'd said, disoriented with drowsiness. Peter bent down, kissed her cheek, and then left. Now she wished she'd said, "Be careful."

"And the dog..."

"Skipper."

"...Skipper, returned when?"

"I guess it was after midnight. I was dozing in the chair when I heard him scratching at the carport door."

"What did you do then, Nancy?"

"Got Danny up and...."

"Who's Danny?"

"Our son. We took the car and drove around awhile looking for Peter."

"I see. Where did y'all look?"

"In the neighborhood and then down Washington to where it runs into the highway."

"Then what?"

"We came home, and that's when I called the police."

"About what time was that?"

"A little after 1:00."

"Where does your husband work?"

"At the college. He's in the sociology department."

"Uh huh. Any enemies?"

"No."

The chief stopped scribbling and looked at Nancy, smiling apologetically. "Now, I hope you won't be offended, but I need to ask you some personal questions." Nancy nodded, dreading.

"Anything unusual going on? Any reason you can think of he might have run away from home?"

She shook her head. "Have you ever thought of running away from your family, Chief?" she said, with just a hint of hostility.

"Not really," he said.

As he said this, she saw his eyes, and she knew he would believe her and do everything in his power to find Peter.

"What was he wearing?"

"A green t-shirt, blue jeans, a new pair of running shoes. Nike, I think."

"Where else do you think he might have gone other than where y'all looked?"

Nancy didn't want to think where Peter had gone because she was sure it was where he didn't belong, particularly not at midnight. "He was obsessed with looking for our son's bike. It was stolen last week, and Danny heard it was over on lower Washington." She picked up her coffee cup and sipped the cold liquid mechanically.

"Is your husband the cautious type, Nancy?"

"Not always," Nancy admitted, remembering their last trip to Gatlinburg. On the sidewalk that ran beside the stream, they spotted a coiled large black snake. While she screamed and pulled

Danny down the block, Peter prodded the snake with the tip of his umbrella. The snake struck and bit off the tip. "Sometimes I think of him as a little kid."

"I see," he said, trying to smile with more reassurance than he felt. Throughout the interview, Noland had had the urge to talk of Peter in the past tense, and he was sure Mrs. Dewberry feared the worst. "We'll get a picture in the paper tomorrow, post some flyers around town, and I'll put several men on the streets looking for him today. Have you checked the hospital?"

Nancy nodded. All Sunday she had hoped for a call from the hospital telling her Peter was there. "Mrs. Dewberry," she had imagined the caller would say, "your husband's been in an accident. Slight concussion, a little amnesia, nothing to worry about." But the phone hadn't rung and gradually hope had faded.

"Do you have a recent photograph?"

Nancy stood, turned away from the policeman, and left the room. She pulled an album from the bookshelf in the study and returned to the kitchen.

"Pick one," she said, handing the album to the chief. "I can't right now."

"Thanks, Nancy," Noland mumbled, standing. He had chosen a picture of Peter with his arm around his son. Danny straddled his new bicycle. Grady assumed the newspaper could crop out the son. Or maybe leave him in to show the bicycle Peter had gone looking for.

In his car a few moments later, Noland studied the picture. Pretty ordinary-looking guy, he thought. Nice, friendly, good family man. Again, he felt an emotional tug, and he remembered telling Marge about his bad feeling. Dewberry was dead, he was sure of it. He sighed, slipped the picture into his coat pocket, and started the motor.

CHAPTER 13

The truck stopped, and Winston opened the door and climbed down. "Yo," he called, and the truck crept forward, steel arms slowly rising, aiming for the slots on the sides of the garbage bin. With hand signals, Winston guided his partner slightly right, then forward until the arms were firmly seated.

"Take 'er up," he yelled, stepping back out of the way. The liftainer rode steadily skyward, then swung back over the cab to dump its load into the truck's belly.

Winston watched its descent before resuming his seat in the cab. Bob backed away from the bin, bluffed his way into the street, and, grinding gears on the downshift, pulled away from the shopping center. Rotten odors formed an almost palpable aura around the two men, but Winston didn't smell them; he had lost that ability shortly after he took the job. And that was over 10 years ago.

Winston Brown was 26, a school dropout with a steady job. More brawn than brain, he liked his work. "But I'd like it better if I ever got to drive," he told Sheritha, his wife. All she ever said was, "Get a shower."

At the corner of Roosevelt and Washington, Bob stopped and looked both ways. The big truck swung left and then pulled into the parking lot behind the church. Bob killed the motor and climbed down from the cab, stretching. Winston joined him.

"Got a smoke?" Bob said, patting an empty pocket.

Winston handed him one, then took one for himself. The two men lit their cigarettes companionably and took deep drags in the shade from the truck.

Bob examined his gift cigarette as smoke dribbled from his nostrils. "How come you smoke these filtered fuckers, Winston?"

Several thoughts rumbled through Winston's mind, thoughts like "Beggars can't be choosers," and "When you gonna start buyin' again," and "Why can't I drive the truck sometimes?" But he knew why he couldn't drive the truck. He'd gotten caught driving under the influence, and the company would never forget it.

"I only had a couple of beers with the guys," Winston had tried to explain, but he could see his words were falling on deaf ears. Hell, one of the guys was Bob, and Winston would have bet anything that good ole Bob hadn't called a cab to get home. But Bob hadn't gone down the street with the roadblock.

"I smoke Winstons 'cause my daddy smoked Winstons." And named his firstborn after his cigarette brand, according to Winston's mother. "Damned good thing Daddy didn't smoke no Marlboro or Old Gold or Herbert Tareyton," Winston once told Sheritha. "Do I look like a Herbert to you?"

"Get a shower," Sheritha had answered.

"I thought maybe you smoked Winstons 'cause your name is Winston," Bob said, and then he laughed his bad fat man laugh, beer belly jiggling under his sweat-stained t-shirt. He took another pull on his gift cigarette.

"You ever think of finishing high school, Winston?"

Winston shrugged. "Naw," he said. Winston had quit school in the eighth grade, while Bob had made it through. Winston had had his driver's license when most of the kids in his grade were just learning to whack off. For a while there, he was a big man, cruising around Harper in a '66 Plymouth Valiant, money from his weekly paycheck in his pocket, Lawanda White on the seat next to him, ready to drop her drawers when he turned down any deserted road.

Lawanda got knocked up, said it wasn't Winston's, then married somebody else. Thank God she married somebody else, Winston always said to himself when he thought of this chapter in his life. If he had married Lawanda, he wouldn't have met Sheritha, and Sheritha had definitely been the high point in his life. Sheritha and Winston Jr. and Angelica and the twins. Still, sometimes Winston felt he was trapped, forced to ride on the garbage truck while Bob Fatso Broadnax drove it.

The men finished their cigarettes, Bob lumbering toward the cab, while Winston stood in front of the truck, ready to guide it to a docking with the liftainer behind the church.

"That's it. Keep on comin'. To your right. Lef' a little." Winston gave the signal, and the blackened trash bin climbed slowly, its top swinging open to let its load drop. The flapping top hid the spilling contents from Winston. "That's neat," he breathed, impressed as always by the mechanical marvel. Bob put the arms in reverse, and the metal box eased down.

"We all set?" Bob asked.

"Yo," Winston said, closing his door. "You see how that can was all burned?" He was thinking maybe they should tell someone back at the Sanitation Department office.

"Naw," Bob said, looking in the side mirror. "I see what you mean though, Winston." He surveyed the traffic flow in the street.

"Think we should report it?"

"Naw. We're paid to empty 'em, not worry about how they look." Bob eased the big truck into the street, away from the church and its burned liftainer.

CHAPTER 14

Stopped at the light across from the church, Grady watched the garbage truck enter the street. The big man driving waved at his car, and Grady waved back. The light changed, and the chief eased forward, staying out of odor range. As he drove, he smiled grimly, remembering his encounter with Buster Mixon.

"Hiya, Grady," Mixon had said when the chief entered the station. Grady ground his teeth, wanting to say, "Chief Noland to you, Mixon," but at the same time not wanting to harm the station's camaraderie.

"Morning, Sheritha," he said to his secretary.

"Mornin', Chief," she said, smiling broadly. Detective Mixon, who had been leaning over a railing next to Sheritha's typewriter, straightened, face reddening from the rebuff.

"Any calls?"

"Nope," she said. "How was yore weekend?" Mixon started to edge away.

"Not bad. Mixon, I want to see you in my office."

They had gone into the chief's office, Mixon fawning as always.

"That's a great looking tie, Grady," he said. "Is it new?" Then, before the chief could respond, Mixon threw in "You still losing weight with the diet and running?"

"No, it's not a new tie and no, I'm not still losing weight. Did you get a call from Mrs. Nancy Dewberry late Saturday night, early Sunday morning?"

"Missing hubby? Yeah, I remember her calling," Mixon said. "Sounded kinda hysterical."

"Did you fill out a missing person's report, Mixon? Go interview Mrs. Dewberry?" Noland toyed with a pencil, not letting his anger show.

"No, but ..."

"But what, Detective? Don't you know the procedure for a missing person call?"

"I just figured ..."

"You figured a man would go walk his dog and decide to run away? Dressed in t-shirt and blue jeans and tennis shoes with no suitcase? Happy family man?" Noland was leaning forward now, eyes narrowed, voice no longer expressionless, although he was still speaking softly.

Mixon shrank back from the chief's desk without leaving his chair. "It sounded like a family fight to me, Chief," he said. "Man goes off awhile to cool down. Maybe checks into a motel or something."

"But what if you were wrong?" Noland said, easing back. "The man's still gone, and we've missed out on running his picture in the paper today."

Finally, Mixon apologized, and Noland sent him to canvas the Dewberrys' neighborhood, checking to see if anyone could remember seeing Peter and Skipper Saturday night. Why had he let Mayor Wainwright talk him into hiring Mixon, he wondered. The guy had been nothing but trouble since the day he joined the force. He was the type who either became a policeman or a criminal. Always cutting corners.

Noland turned right on King Street, heading for Ida Ivory's house. If anybody had seen anything in this neighborhood, it would be Hannah. A lifelong Harper resident, Grady had seen Hannah and her shopping cart many times.

Noland eased his Ford over to the curb and killed the motor. He spotted Hannah's shopping basket on one side of her daughter's house and smiled to see that she was home.

He strode past the white-painted tire planter in the middle of the tiny front yard, stepped over the purple tricycle lying on its side, one rear wheel mashed flat, and stopped at the door. He rapped twice and waited. Inside he heard a child's squall followed by a loud, "Shut up." Louder crying produced the unmistakable sound of a slap, and then Ida Ivory appeared at the door, balancing a quietly weeping toddler on one enormous hip.

"Is your mother here?"

"Whatcha want wif her?" Ida said. She absentmindedly wiped snot from the child's upper lip with a broad thumb, then cleaned her thumb on a fold of her skirt.

"I just want to ask her a few questions, Ida. About something she might have seen. She's not in any trouble." At least he didn't think she was.

"Mama," Ida yelled over her shoulder, without taking her eyes off the chief. At the yell, the child jumped, screwing up his eyes in preparation for crying, then thought better of it and resumed sniffling instead, popping his right thumb into his mouth. Brown eyes the size of quarters stared without blinking at the man outside the door.

"Can I come in?" Noland asked.

Ida ungraciously cracked the screen door but didn't move, letting her bulk prevent Noland's entry. Over her shoulder, the chief saw Hannah sidle into the room. "You wanna talk to the chief, Mama?" Ida asked, still regarding Noland with hostility and suspicion.

"I don' mind," Hannah said, scratching a kitchen match on a box from her skirt pocket to light a cigarette stub. The light from the match revealed another pair of dark eyes peering around the doorjamb at the rear of the living room.

"Just aks your questions and go, Chief," Ida said, finally unblocking the door. She lumbered away, the child, thumb still firmly in place, rotated in the crook of her arm to keep his eyes on the stranger in his house. Noland remembered the time he had mistakenly entered a local dive in Saigon. Twenty pairs of Vietnamese eyes had impaled him with the look he saw in the boy's unwavering gaze.

Noland perched gingerly on the sprung sofa with Hannah facing him from the depths of a chair that was vintage Salvation Army. A picture of Jesus, done in glow-in-the-dark colors, occupied the place of honor on the wall behind the old woman. There was a feeling of poverty in the house, touching everything from the console TV set with rabbit ears wrapped in aluminum foil to the broken toys littering the living room floor.

"How've you been, Hannah?" Noland asked, hoping the woman was in a talkative mood.

"Tolerable," she said, watching him closely.

"Pretty hot, isn't it?"

Hannah nodded and took another drag on her cigarette. "Gotta get up real early to beat the heat," she said.

"I'm looking for a man, Hannah," Noland said, "a white man who might have taken a walk down Roosevelt late Saturday night. You know anything about that?"

"Dumb," Hannah said.

"You're right," Noland said. "It was a dumb thing to do, and something might have happened to him. What do you think?" Hannah nodded, not giving anything away, just being agreeable.

"Have you seen a white man around here in the last few days, maybe hurt, maybe dead, wearing blue jeans and new tennis shoes?"

Hannah froze. "No shoes," she whispered, sweat glistening on her forehead.

"What was that?"

"I ain't seen nothin' like that," the old woman said. She levered herself out of the chair, slowly, arthritically. "I got things to do, Chief," she said, dismissing Noland, hobbling toward the back part of the house.

"If you see or hear anything, let me know, Hannah," Noland said, lamely addressing the old woman's retreating back. Her reaction convinced him that she had seen something that perhaps had something to do with the missing shoes. Unfortunately, Hannah's retreat to the back of the house told him that he would get nothing more from her today. He resolved to talk to her again at a more neutral site, perhaps try to catch her on one of her walks.

CHAPTER 15

Lids half shut, Brad Childers let his gaze settle on the tree outside the classroom window. It was an old tree, broken-limbed, covered here and there with moss, and today, because there had been a football game Friday night, festooned with remnants of at least one toilet paper roll. Brad sometimes imagined jumping into the tree from the window, shinnying down, and leaving the school campus. He could see the startled look on Mr. Packard's ruddy face and hear the oohs and aahs of his classmates when he leapt.

But maybe he would miss the main branch nearest the window. Maybe it was farther away than it looked from his seated perspective. Or perhaps he would reach it, but the moss would be so slippery his grip would fail. Three floors, thirty feet—would the fall kill him? Probably not. It would probably just leave him a cripple like that kid horsing around in the annex hall last year who fell down the elevator shaft. Brad didn't think he would like to ride around in a wheelchair all the time.

Brad wrenched his eyes from the tree to look instead at Mr. Packard at the front of the room. One of Harper High School's finest, Brad thought, with the corners of his mouth curling downward in disgust. Vance Packard was dozing, his chair tilted back on two legs with his head resting against the blackboard. Looking at the teacher's exposed throat, Brad stiffened his hand, picturing himself karate-chopping Packard, crushing the man's windpipe. Then jumping out the window.

Brad had Mr. Packard for both study hall, where he was now, and for chemistry, where he would be in 15 minutes. After chemistry, which he had failed the first time he took it, he would go to lunch. Packard, a zero in study hall, was laughable as a chemistry teacher. When he wasn't flirting with the girls on the front row, he was arm wrestling with some of the guys in the class. All except Brad.

"Wanna arm wrestle, Arnold?" Mr. Packard had said last Thursday, flexing. The man was always flexing his arms.

"I go by Brad or Bradley," he had said for at least the 10th time since school started, "and I don't want to arm wrestle."

Packard's expression implied names like sissy, queer, and fag, as though any "real" man would want to arm wrestle.

"I'll arm wrestle you, Mr. Packard," Mark Thompson said. "Thanks, Mark," Brad thought, grateful to him for distracting Packard's attention. Mark was the center on the football team, had 17-inch biceps, and could probably rip Packard's arm off his body. But he wouldn't, Brad knew, because he wanted to keep his "A" in the class.

Despite Mr. Packard, Brad liked chemistry better than his other courses. For one thing, Jesse Watkins, Brad's best and only friend, was in the class because of a scheduling mistake. Brad and Jesse sat next to each other and made fun of Packard and most of the rest of the class whenever they got the chance.

Then there was chemistry lab. For some reason, Brad was attracted to the rows of chemicals in the locked cabinet, all the powders and metals and benign-appearing liquids in the brown jars.

Poisons and acids were his favorites. HCl. Now that was a good one. Hydrochloric acid. What if he put a few drops on his pale forearm? Would it eat a hole all the way through? What would his burning flesh smell like? Could he get enough of it to fill the bathtub to "bathe" the old man in? And what would it do if he drank it? Once he and Jesse had done a reaction with HCl, and he had had to pour a small amount from a glass bottle with a glass stopper. The acid "steamed" on contact with the air, and Brad had an almost overwhelming urge to breathe the vapor. When he told Jesse later about this urge, Jesse had reassured him he wasn't going crazy by saying, "Me, too." Still later, it occurred to Brad that maybe he and Jesse were both a little off.

At the far left in the laboratory cabinet was a brown bottle that fascinated Brad. The bottle contained a waxy, silver-white metal identified as As, and the label's skull-and-crossbones had sent Brad on one of his few trips to the library. "Arsenic compounds," he had read in a book with brittle pages, "are used by poisoners more than any other class of poisons because of their odorless and almost tasteless qualities." This statement so intrigued Brad that he copied it down, printing laboriously on the back page of his nearly empty chemistry notebook. The old book's next sentence was almost equally appealing: "In several cases they have been introduced into the vagina, rectum, or urethra." Brad's mind was filled with images of his sister, spread-eagled on the dining room table, with himself spooning arsenic into some bodily cavity. With her screaming.

Disgusting! But exciting, too. Brad didn't think it would be hard to get some arsenic from the cabinet. He would wait until Mr. Packard's attention was diverted by arm wrestling or some girl whose boobs he could ogle, then whip over to the "A" end of the cabinet and swipe a few grams of the old As. A few grams would be more than enough to do in his old man and his sister. According to the library book, a lethal dose of most arsenic compounds was from a 10th to half a gram.

"Have you ever thought of how easy it would be to steal some arsenic?" he asked Jesse one day when they were smoking under the bleachers on the football practice field. It was hot under the bleachers and smelled of smoke and dirt and piss.

"What would you do with it?" Jesse said, and his eyes got a faraway, dreamy expression when Brad told him how little it took to kill someone.

The bell rang and Mr. Packard's head jerked forward, red-rimmed eyes spearing a frequent target. He stood as the study hall students exited and his chemistry class filed in.

"Childers," he said when all were seated, "get up here and put problem 15 on the board."

"Uh, I didn't do it."

"Didn't do it, huh. Did you do any of your homework?"

"Nossir," he admitted.

"Whatsa matter, Childers? Too busy playin' Pac-Man?" Titters from the class. Brad flushed, wishing he had already gotten the arsenic.

"Want a Coke, Mr. Packard?" he would ask, pretending to be trying to improve his grade. Maybe he would give Packard a whole gram.

CHAPTER 16

"Man, you shoulda seen your face when old Packard said that about how you been playin' Pac-Man," Jesse said, the cigarette's glow in the semidarkness under the bleachers giving his face a saturnine look. "Was he right?"

"About what?" Brad took a deep drag on the cigarette Jesse had given him and locked the smoke in his lungs, pretending he was smoking a joint.

"About you playin' Pac-Man."

Brad shrugged. "I don't even have Pac-Man. I just wish I had had some arsenic," he said.

"Yeah, that sounds like some good shit, Brad. Hell, we could do the whole school. Put it in some Kool-Aid or something like that."

Brad coughed on his smoke, reflexively putting his hands over his head like his mother had taught him to do when he got choked. Sometimes Jesse was downright scary. Brad periodically thought of killing his father, often dreamed of getting rid of his sister, and hated Mr. Packard with a passion, but he could never have imagined poisoning the whole school.

"You okay, buddy?" Jesse said, his voice expressing unusual concern.

"Yeah, smoke just went down the wrong way." Brad coughed a couple more times, stifled a cough and said, "What made you think of that? The Kool-Aid, I mean."

"You remember the guy down in Mexico, South America, wherever? The religious guy killed his whole group. He put poison in grape Kool-Aid, Brad, but it wasn't arsenic. It was somethin' else even better."

"Cyanide," Brad said. He had read about Jim Jones in the library, too.

"Right, cyanide," Jesse repeated, nodding and smiling to himself, his eyes going out of focus.

The two finished their cigarettes in companionable silence, Jesse with his dreamy expression and Brad wondering about—but afraid to ask—what his friend was thinking.

CHAPTER 17

Hal Childers' State Farm agency occupied a converted house on the south side of Harper, nestled between a struggling camera repair shop and a combination self-service gas station-mini mart. The mini mart had good sandwiches; Hal belched softly, his breath momentarily reminiscent of roast beef and gravy.

Hal leaned forward, studied the form he had been filling in, yawned. He knew the problem. It happened every day about this time. Lunch made him feel lethargic, and it was all he could do to stay awake between 1 and 1:30. He stood, stretched, and padded softly to the door connecting his office to the reception area. Feeling almost guilty, he watched his secretary.

Neat, intelligent, efficient, conscientious Vicki Ludlow was talking on the phone, supplying information, probably. Hal had no illusions about his business; he knew that Vicki performed much of the actual work of his agency. His task was mostly public relations, joining local organizations, pressing the flesh, selling a product.

And he was pretty darned good at it, if he did say so himself. He knew himself to be a good-ole-boy with education. The beauty of his position was that good-ole-boys stuck together. They supported each other. "You scratch my back, and I'll scratch yours" was the unwritten and unspoken rule.

So, Hal joined the Rotary Club and the Lions Club and the Chamber of Commerce and the Harper Gun Club, and he had been a Jaycee when he was younger. He was a long-time member of First United Methodist Church, where he sometimes pledged more than he could afford. He joined and went to the meetings and when work needed to be done, Hal volunteered. Without campaigning, he had held most of the elected positions in the various organizations he was in.

Watching Vicki, Hal was struck by her sexiness. She wasn't blatantly sexy, not like women who were sure of their erotic attraction and used it. Vicki's attractiveness was more subtle, a combination of fresh, wholesome, innocence that lately Hal found almost irresistible.

Face it, Childers, he told himself, turning away from the door. You're halfway in love with your secretary. He smiled ruefully. Waste of time to think about himself and Vicki Ludlow; for all he knew she was as happily married as he was.

It had been a busy afternoon, calls and clients coming in waves, threatening to swamp both Hal and Vicki at times. For no particular reason he could figure, some visitors were more memorable than others. For example, there was the professor and his son, the boy sullen and silent while the father urged Hal to warn the youth about the dangers of drinking and driving. They had come straight from the drivers' license office.

Then there was the man who looked sick. Millard Long. Millard coughed and wheezed and mopped his forehead and talked of getting some additional health insurance. When Hal told him preexisting conditions were excluded, Long made a hasty exit.

"Too much to do," he had said once to his secretary at the entrance to the walk-in storage closet separating the reception area from his private office. He had gone to get another batch of claim forms and had met Vicki coming out of the closet with a box of computer paper.

Vicki smiled, looking so frazzled that Hal had an almost over-whelming urge to rip the paper out of her arms and pull her back into the closet. Shut the door. Turn off the light. Clients and the rest of the world be damned.

Vicki stood over his shoulder now, front door locked for the last half hour, handing him one form or letter after another, waiting for his signatures so that she could mail the pieces on her way home. Hal was pleasantly aware of her warmth, her smell, her vitality where she almost pressed against his back. This was a familiar, end-of-the-day ritual.

Vicki leaned still closer, arm crossing his, skin so close to touch-ing that static electricity raised the hair on his forearm. He looked up into a nest of brown hair, inhaled its shampoo fragrance, willed Vicki to look at him. To see his desire.

"Look what you just wrote," Vicki said. She was looking at Hal, but it was with a slight trace of amusement, not the come-hither expression he had secretly hoped for.

He followed her finger to the signature he had just penned and saw that it read "H. Vicki," not H. Childers. "Good grief," he said, feeling flushed and foolish. "It must be getting late. Just print out another copy, and I'll sign it tomorrow, Vicki.

CHAPTER 18

"Where you get them shoes?" Larraine Jackson asked, cornering the boy in the kitchen, her bulk a barrier. "Uh, uh, from Cooter. He foun' 'em over by the park." Her grandson edged away from the refrigerator, clutching a pint of Jungle Juice.

"Was they lost?" Larraine distrusted her daughter's youngest kid and had little faith in her own ability to control the boy. Lord knew she had tried to raise the two boys, but her daughter was no help. Pregnant at 15, the girl told her mother the father was Randy something-or-other, a kid her age who lived a couple of streets over. She also said she didn't think the boy would be any help with a baby. Sulie moved out after Charles was born, leaving the baby with her mother.

Apparently Randy Watkins—Larraine had learned his last name—had worked his magic on Sulie again, because her worthless daughter came back pregnant a couple of years later, staying just long enough to produce the boy in front of Larraine.

After the second child was born, Larraine paid a visit to Randy Watkins, who turned out to be a responsible young man, albeit one who had a thing for Sulie and didn't like to wear protection. Randy moved in with Larraine and helped with the two boys as much as he could. The arrangement had worked well until the accident.

"What you mean?" the boy asked, looking at Larraine with eyes like twin lakes of fudge, beaten to the dull gloss stage. Light went in, but none came out. Larraine often wondered if the boy was dead inside.

"I mean, is they stolen?"

"Not by me," he said, feigning innocence.

"And what about that bike in the backyard? Cooter fine that too?"

"Hell if I know."

Larraine swung so quickly the boy had no warning. The slap caught him high on his left cheek. Without thinking, he reached for his knife.

"Jus' go right ahead if you is man enough." Larraine stared menacingly at her grandson, her bulk quivering. She was afraid of many things, but his knife wasn't one of them.

"Lemme by, Granma," he said finally, grinning.

Larraine felt like slapping the boy again, knocking his grin right off his face. "Not 'til you answer me one mo' question. Ida Ivory tole me a po-liceman be by to see Hannah this mornin', aksin' about a white man missin' since Saturday night. You know anythin' 'bout a missin' white man?"

Her grandson blinked, his grin slipped, and he nearly dropped the Jungle Juice. "Naw, me 'n Stump ain't seen no white man." Larraine didn't believe the boy, but she let him pass. Why had he mentioned Charles? Was his brother in on it, too?

The two brothers hunkered in the darkness in the ditch behind their grandmother's house, sharing a joint.

"What we gonna do, Stump?" He had told his brother about Larraine's questions.

"Get ridda the bike."

"How we gonna do that?"

"Not we. You. Ride it to school tomorrow an' leave it."

"What if somebody sees me on it?

Stump sucked on his joint, the glow illuminating his sullen features. "Hell, they ain' gonna notice you. Go a little late. They all be in the buildin' by then."

"Yeah, thass a good plan. You remember the way that fucker tried to run after I stabbed him?" He started giggling.

Stump stared at his brother. Sometimes the boy scared him. He wasn't sorry they had killed the white man, but he wasn't glad about it either. What went on behind the grin?

"Bes' to jus' put it outta your mind. Forget about it. Don' say nothin' about it to nobody."

"Mum's the word, Stump," Jesse said, trying to look serious. The grin surfaced, bubbled across his lips.

"You disgustin'," Stump said, flicking the butt into the blackness.

CHAPTER 19

Randy remembered exactly when it happened. It was 11:33 on Friday, the 14th of July. It was no hotter than you would expect for that time of year in the South; in fact, the summer had been almost mild. Still, the temperature was above 90, and the humidity had plastered his khaki shirt to his body like wallpaper.

Randy's crew was struggling with one of the mowers. The big machine had propelled itself halfway up the board ramp they used to load it onto the pickup, when the board on the right slipped. Now it teetered precariously, right rear wheel spinning as it fought for traction. Whitey, his face all eyes and his neck veins distended like steel elevator cables, held most of the mower's weight; a moment before he had been guiding it up the ramp. Behind him, waiting to load his mower, Sonny killed it instead.

"I'll get it," Randy yelled, leaping to grab the right front wheel and part of the metal housing. He wasn't a hands-off type of supervisor, and he knew the men respected his willingness to help whenever an extra hand was needed. With a grunt, he took most of the machine's weight and lifted it while Sonny moved the errant board back into place. Randy heard the crack when he lowered the mower to the board. Afterwards he would tell his friends that it sounded like a rifle shot, and for a moment he thought he had been shot. He fell like a dead man, unconscious before he hit the ground.

He came to a few minutes later, lying flat on his back on the newly mown grass. Its smell reminded him of picnics with Sulie out back of the high school. Whitey loomed overhead, his face a mask of concern. A bead of sweat dropped off his nose to strike his boss on the forehead.

"What happened?" Varley asked. Varley had been dozing in the cab of the truck, while the mowers were being put away.

"He just fell down," Sonny said. Sonny was a college kid working with the crew for the summer. Sometimes the college kids were lazy and spent most of their summers trying to avoid work, but Sonny had been one of the good ones. Randy was planning to try to get him on his crew the next summer.

But there hadn't been a next summer. When his crew got him to the hospital, Randy (Randall Ronald Watkins Jr. on the hospital chart) discovered he had ruptured a disc in his lower back. His injury was so severe that he was quickly transferred by ambulance to a large, regional facility.

"Ordinarily we would try conservative treatment for a ruptured disc, Randall," the neurosurgeon told him that evening. "Send you home and hope the problem would resolve itself. Most do in a few months with a combination of bed rest, heat, muscle relaxers, pain-killers—things like that."

"Sounds good to me, Doc," Randy said. "When can I get outta here?"

The doctor pulled a chair closer to Randy's bed, turned it around backwards and straddled it with his arms over the back. The doctor looked like he could be in his mid-20s, although Randy was sure he must be older than that. Randy noted with just a twinge of envy the Rolex watch, the immaculately clean hands (Randy's hands were never completely clean), the pale unblemished skin that came from a life inside hospital walls, not out in the sun doing manual labor. The doctor's supper breath took away Randy's appetite. Larraine had been in earlier but had gone to get the boys their suppers. She had promised to bring the two back with her.

"I said that ordinarily we would send you home to see if your back would mend on its own. Unfortunately, you've got other problems that rule out that action. How does your left leg feel, Randall?"

"It don't hurt, if that's what you mean. Just feels kinda numb." To check it out, Randy tried to wiggle his toes under the sheet covering the bottom half of his body. They didn't move.

"Can you feel it at all?" the doctor asked. Randy thought the doctor had an odd way of smiling at inappropriate times. Like now, the doctor was smiling broadly as Randy realized he couldn't feel much below his waist on the left side.

"Will the feelin' come back?" Randy asked, fear pumping sour acid into his empty stomach.

"It might," the doctor conceded. The CT scan shows you really did a number on one of your lumbar disks, and the ruptured part is putting pressure on your sciatic nerve—the sciatic nerve runs all the way down your leg—and that's why you have little feeling in the leg. If the feeling does return, there might be a lot of pain with it."

"So, what do you recommend, Doc?"

"We go in and take out the ruptured disc and that should fix you up."

In one respect, that first operation had been a success. After it, Randy's left leg wasn't numb, and he could move it easily enough. Unfortunately, when the anesthesia wore off the pain began.

"The sciatic nerve's just irritated," the young doctor had told him. "In a few weeks it'll go away."

Two operations later, Randy's pain was, if anything, worse. The pain was about a "10" when he hauled himself out of bed after a night of fitful sleep; he could sleep only if he took something to knock him out.

In addition to the constant pain, the guilt of not being able to work added to Randy's evil moods. The family survived on Randy's disability payments, welfare checks, and food stamps. Although Charles made some money working at his uncle's garage, he didn't contribute enough to the family's finances to offset what it cost for him to live at home. Randy thought often of asking his son to move out.

Sometimes after a hot shower, the pain level went down maybe to a "4" or "5," but that was about as good as it got.

"I walk like a goddamned crab," he thought one day, catching sight of himself in the bedroom mirror, clutching things, handing himself off from one piece of furniture to another. He almost smiled then because he looked like a baby learning to walk, staggering on bandy legs a few feet at a time, ready to catch himself if his legs should buckle.

Sometimes they did, but usually after he'd had too much medicine. "Medicine" was what he called the enormous quantity of beer he put away most days. Sometimes the "medicine" got his back pain into the "I don't give a shit" region.

But sometimes when he was drinking, he just got to feeling sorry for himself. "Why me?" he would ask at those times. "What did I do to deserve this shit?" There was no answer, of course, and it was when he was feeling most sorry for himself that he took out his frustrations on his family. Mostly he picked on his younger son, Jesse.

Randy couldn't pinpoint what he disliked so much about the boy. For one thing, he hated his younger son's eyes. They were too small and too close set, and sometimes they just seemed empty. The emptiness frightened Randy, and his fear was translated into anger, and in his anger, he often lashed out, striking the boy even though he was too old for physical punishment. Sometimes he was sorry afterwards, but usually he just figured the kid had it coming, that he'd done something bad he needed punishing for.

Occasionally, Randy would vow to treat the boy better, but then his son would look at him wrong or not bring his beer fast enough, and Randy would give the kid another whack or two. A few days ago, he'd had to whack him for lying.

"Where'd the bike come from?" he'd said. Father and son had been in the kitchen, Randy sitting at the table while the kid got him another beer from the refrigerator.

"Foun' it," he said, handing Randy a cold can of Bud. His eyes shifted, looking everywhere except directly at his father.

"Sit," Randy said, indicating the chair to his right. "Where'd you find it?"

"Uh, in the ditch back of the park. Me'n Brad was down there shootin' the shit, and there it was, all covered with mud." His son was smiling now, really getting into the lie Randy was sure he was telling. His son had never been a good liar. He always started grinning when he lied, and his son was grinning now.

Whap! Randy popped him a good one, and the grin disappeared. Tears started to the boy's eyes and just for a moment Randy was sorry he'd slapped him. Just for a moment. Cat-quick, he grabbed the boy's wrist, nailing him to the table.

"Where'd you think you was going?"

"Nowhere," he mumbled, easing back into his chair. He wiped his nose with his free hand. Randy released him.

"Let's try again. Where'd you get the bike?" Without taking his eyes off his son, Randy downed half the beer. His low-level backache was joined by a spearing pain down his left leg.

"At school," the kid had finally admitted, and Randy had made him promise to take it back. The bike was gone the next day.

CHAPTER 20

Vicki Ludlow smiled, thinking about her job. Was it the work she liked most or was it her boss? Mr. Childers, Hal, was very nice and sometimes she suspected he had a crush on her. This afternoon, for instance, when he had signed "H. Vicki" instead of his own name. Now that was a whatchamacallit—Freudian slip.

"What're you so happy about?" Bone said, setting his plate and utensils on the counter. Smoke from his after-dinner Camel fogged the kitchen.

"That you brought me your plate, Bone," Vicki said, and her husband smiled despite himself. In that smile Vicki saw something of the youth she had fallen in love with. How long ago? Eleven years?

They had been seniors at Harper High, Bone a football player, Vicki a pretty, shy girl in his English class. When he asked her out, she had been flattered. Bone was a real hunk in those days. He was big, 6'3", 220 pounds, and fast. He was still fast, and at 265, even bigger. But the extra pounds were mostly fat, the result of a meat and potatoes diet and no exercise. His belly was starting to make him look pregnant.

"You want me to stay home?"

"Of course not, Bone," she said. It was his bowling night, and these days Vicki rarely minded his going. She liked the opportunity to read a little, watch some television, and, perhaps, to daydream about her employer. "Just don't be too late." And don't come in drunk was her unspoken thought.

"I won't," Bone said, stubbing out his cigarette in the ashtray on the table. He left the kitchen.

Vicki stopped running her dishrag over the dishes and stared out the window over the sink. Growing dusk hazed her patio, softening the clutter of rotting lawn furniture, hiding the lawn mower in shadow. A slight frown creased her forehead. She ought to feel guilty thinking about Hal, but she didn't. Ever since she lost the baby, Vicki had felt restless in her marriage.

"Bye, Hon," Bone said, swinging wide to buss her cheek on his way to the carport door.

"Bye, Bone," she said, watching her reflection in the window. The door slammed, and Vicki smiled at herself, liking what she saw.

Maybe the baby would have brought them back together, but Vicki miscarried in her 6th month. Bone, looking forward to being a father, was disappointed with his wife—and unsympathetic.

"That's twice, Vicki," he had said.

"Do you think I did it deliberately?" she had asked.

Bone fidgeted under her glare, shuffled his feet, looked around the tiny room costing $90 a day. "I guess not," he said, but she hadn't been home from the hospital a week before he started hitting her.

Their lives could have been different. If Bone had been just a little bigger, he might have gotten a football scholarship to a university. But he wasn't quite big enough or fast enough for a scholarship, and with a pregnant wife he couldn't afford to go to college without one. So that left his job at the grocery.

"At least we won't ever be hungry, Vicki," Bone had said, "as long as I've got my job at the store." A package of gray ground meat lay on the kitchen counter between them, smelling almost rancid.

The sight and smell had been too much for the shy 18-year-old, newly pregnant and freshly married, and she rushed to the sink to vomit, then vomited and retched until she felt the pains in her abdomen signaling her first miscarriage. Remembering, Vicki turned from the window and strode to the wall phone beside the oven. She lifted the receiver and punched three numbers before she thought about what she was doing. She had been about to call Hal.

CHAPTER 21

H al sipped his wine, savoring its slightly effervescent sweet-
ness. The newspaper was spread across his thighs, but his
thoughts were far from the sports section. Under the paper,
he felt his growing arousal at the memory of Vicki standing over
him, her smell, the warmth of her body nearly touching his. What
must she have thought when he signed "H. Vicki"?

"Supper's about ready," Mary said from the kitchen, and Hal
started, coloring. Mary stuck her head through the door behind his
chair. "Would you tell the kids to come to the table?"

"Sure," he said. In a few minutes all were seated in the kitchen.

"How was your day, Dear?" Mary asked.

"Pass the salt, Dad," Sandy said.

"Okay," Hal said, handing his daughter the saltshaker. "We were
kinda busy this afternoon."

"We?" Mary watched her daughter dusting her plate with salt.
"Did you taste that first?" she asked.

"Mrs. Ludlow and I," he said.

"It always needs salt, Mom," Sandy said, instantly regretting the tone
of her reply. She wanted to ask her mother for some running shoes and
knew that any hint of smart-alecky behavior would hurt her chances.

"Since when do you call your secretary Mrs. Ludlow, Hal?" Mary
frowned at her daughter, then took a bite of her meatloaf. "Mmmm,
that's pretty good. Sure you won't have some, Bradley?"

"No thanks," Brad said. He took a last bite of his bread and sipped his milk.

"No wonder the kid's so skinny," Hal said to Mary, sidestepping her question about Vicki. "Is that all he's eating?"

"I guess so. Anything interesting happen at school today, Bradley?"

Her son shook his head, watching his sister wolf down her mashed potatoes. What a pig, he thought, and the image he'd had of her on the kitchen table popped into his head.

"Mom, can I get some running shoes?" Sandy said. "I wanna start running to lose some weight."

"Quit stuffing your face," Brad muttered.

"Did you hear that, Mom?"

"Not so loud, Sandy," her mother said. "That was totally un-called for, Bradley."

"She does eat too much," Brad said. "Just look at her plate."

"It's none of your business what I eat," Sandy shot back, wishing she hadn't taken so much.

"Aren't you going to say anything, Hal?"

Hal had been hoping he wouldn't be drawn into the squabble. "Your brother has a point, Sandy," he said, "but I think it's irrelevant to your question. You can get some running shoes."

"Just forget it," Sandy said, tears threatening to spill over.

Hal caught his son's triumphant smile. With his knife, he herded another bite of meatloaf onto his fork, then shoveled it mechanically into his mouth. He didn't care much for it, but he wasn't about to say it didn't have any taste.

CHAPTER 22

Noland heard the phone's ring and Sheritha's "Harper Police Department." He sighed, hand poised to take the call. What would it be this time, he wondered? What new rumor, clue, strange sighting would he have to add to the list that had grown steadily since the people of Harper opened their Tuesday papers?

His phone buzzed. "Hello, Chief Noland here," he said.

"Grady, this is Duane Glover."

"What can I do for you, Dr. Glover?" Noland sat straighter, unconsciously speaking faster, trying not to reinforce the stereotype of the Southern cop. Dr. Glover was the new president of the college, a man tall, silver-haired, and distinguished, a man equally adept at soliciting funds from the school's alumni and from state legislators. Dr. Glover was from Indiana.

"I saw the article in the paper, Grady, and wondered if you could give me any more details. Do you suspect foul play?"

"That's a possibility," he said, cautiously. "Have you heard anything out at the college?"

"Well, I called his department this morning, and the departmental secretary seemed to think Dewberry might have gone off with his female graduate assistant. Midlife crisis, she said."

"Uh huh," Noland said. He had the midlife crisis theory, which he doubted, on his list.

"Do you think there might be anything to it, Chief?"

"Not really," Noland answered, crumpling his doodle page and launching it toward the trash basket. The paper ball missed and rolled to join others under a bookcase.

"I see," Glover said. "Have you considered the possibility that Peter might have committed suicide? Gone off in the woods somewhere and killed himself?"

"It's been suggested," Noland said. "Do you know of any reason to suspect that?"

"Not really," Glover said. "It's just a rumor circulating."

"We're getting together a bunch of people this afternoon to search through the Lincoln Heights subdivision and the woods beyond," Noland said. An earlier caller told Noland he had seen a naked white man wandering dazedly through Lincoln Heights early Sunday morning. The naked man had a cut on his forehead.

"Crazy," the caller kept saying. Although there were a few private homes in Lincoln Heights, most of the area consisted of a low-income apartment complex known locally as the Projects. Noland drove by the apartments on his way to church: cars on jacks, unkempt lawns, broken screen doors, and graffiti, with unsupervised, unemployed, out-of-school teenagers hanging around. Dewberry would've been crazy to wander through the area, naked or clothed.

"Would you like to join the search, Dr. Glover?"

"Regrettably, no," Glover said, too quickly. "Meetings all day."

"Any way you could announce our effort? We're meeting at the junior high school at 2:00."

Dr. Glover promised to spread the word on campus and hung up. Noland was replacing the phone when the intercom buzzed.

"Someone to see you, Chief," Sheritha said.

"Send 'em in."

A man Noland guessed to be in his mid-40s and a teenaged boy entered. The chief recognized the boy from the picture he had gotten from Nancy Dewberry.

Danny Dewberry was blond like his mother, while he shared his father's cleft chin, full lips, and slender nose. The man with him was also blond, and Noland guessed correctly that he was related to Nancy Dewberry.

"Grady Noland," he said, standing and extending his hand.

"Roy Anderson," the man said, applying a firm grip. Danny's hand was damp, betraying his anxiety in the presence of an adult authority figure.

"I'm Nancy Dewberry's brother," Roy said, "and this is Danny Dewberry."

"Yes, I recognized him from the picture your sister gave me. Have a seat." Noland indicated chairs in front of his desk. "Can I get you anything? Coke? Coffee?"

"Co...," Danny began, interrupted by his uncle's "No thanks," answering for them both.

"What can I do for you, Mr. Anderson?"

"Call me Roy," he said. "What's happening with the search for Peter?"

"At the moment we're gathering information, getting leads from people who've seen the picture and story in the paper. Yesterday I sent one of my officers to the subdivision where your sister lives, to ask if anyone had seen Peter or the dog Saturday night. We've also posted flyers around town."

"I see," Roy said, and Noland thought his tone betrayed a hint of disapproval. "You mentioned leads. What kind of leads?"

"Well, one of the callers said he'd seen a white man walking through one of Harper's black areas, possibly Saturday night." Noland omitted the part about nakedness. Since he considered the sighting unlikely, he saw no need to add to Danny's distress with bizarre images of his unclothed father. "We're getting a search party together this afternoon to comb the area and some woods beyond. Would you like to join us, Roy? Danny?"

Danny nodded, and Roy said, "Yes. Where should we go?"

"Do you know where the junior high is?" Roy shook his head, while Danny said, "I do."

"Danny, just get you and your uncle to the school around 2:00."

"Yes, sir."

"You might want to wear some jeans and old shoes. We'll be looking through some fields."

"Do you know about Danny's bicycle?" Roy asked.

"Your sister mentioned Peter was looking for it over on Washington Street. Had y'all called us to report it missing?" he asked, looking at the boy.

Danny nodded.

"Do we have the serial number, Danny?"

"Nossir, but my dad gave a complete description."

"I see. Well, we'll recognize it if we find it then." Noland didn't think the bicycle figured into Peter Dewberry's disappearance, and, from his experience in Harper, stolen bicycles were seldom recovered. But he didn't vocalize his thoughts, as the bicycle was obviously important to Danny, if only because it took his mind off his missing father.

CHAPTER 23

Getting rid of the bike had been a piece of cake. Jesse had ridden it to school and parked it in the same slot where he found it. He didn't think anybody had seen him. He grinned to himself.

Mr. Hounsley, their English teacher, began class: "Today, we're going to continue with our reading of George Orwell's classic novella *Animal Farm*. As we go through it, I want y'all to be thinking of what the hidden meaning might be. Open your books to Chapter 4, and Jesse, I'd like for you to start us off."

Jesse smiled at this, because reading out loud was one of the few things in school that he liked to do. Struggling with only a few words, he read, "By the late summer the news of what had happened on Animal Farm had spread across half the county. Every day Snowball and Napoleon sent out flights of pigeons whose instructions were to mingle with the animals on neighbouring farms, tell them the story of the Rebellion, and teach them the tune of 'Beasts of England.'"

"Thanks, Jesse," Mr. Hounsley said. "Did anyone notice the word that seemed to be misspelled?"

One of the girls on the front row raised her hand, and a discussion of the British addition of "u" to words such as favor, behavior, and neighbor ensued. As the class continued, Jesse found himself thinking that he might actually read the book on his own, 'cause it looked interesting. He wondered if Brad had read *Animal Farm*.

At the bell, he was one of the first out of the room. He stopped at a water fountain and, slurping noisily, drank more than he wanted, mostly to bug the fat kid behind him waiting impatiently. Making sure that the kid was watching, Jesse touched his upper lip to the fountain. As he turned away, several drops fell on his Nike running shoes.

"What you lookin' at, fat boy?" he asked, thrusting his head forward, challenging the fat slug.

"Nothin'," the other said. He backed away, apparently deciding he wasn't thirsty after all. The bell rang, and suddenly the halls were nearly empty. Momentarily, he stood in front of the fountain, wondering where the break had gone. And then he sprang away, sprinting toward the stairs, the running shoes giving wings to his feet. He rounded a corner and ran into a student more delinquent than he, Russell Durr, a 19-year-old senior.

"Where the hell you goin' in such a rush, four eyes?" Russell said, grabbing him by the front of his shirt. Jesse tried to grin to show he wasn't afraid of Durr.

"And wipe that grin off your ugly face 'fore I knock it off." Durr shoved him against a bank of lockers. He felt a handle bite into his spine, and he cried out. Behind and to his right a door opened.

"You muthafucka," he screamed, drawing his knife and opening it in one swift movement. Durr's expression changed from hostile contempt to fear as Jesse charged. From behind he felt arms like tree trunks wrap themselves around his body, and he was lifted off his feet.

"Get out of here, Durr," his captor said, and the boy recognized the voice of Mr. Packard, his chemistry teacher. "And you, you and me are going to the principal's office." A few minutes later, unarmed, he left Harper High. He headed home, happy with his vacation even if it was for only 3 days. Now all he had to do was stay out of his father's way. The old man would have a shit fit if he found out he'd gotten suspended.

CHAPTER 24

Brad's stomach started hurting midway through his 10:00 class, and by 11 he was fighting nausea. His breakfast lay like lead in his stomach, and he remembered a time in fourth grade when he upchucked after lunch. They had had blackberry cobbler that day, and the sight and smell of Brad's puddle made Dottie Simpkins vomit in sympathy.

Now he feared he might make a similar puddle, and the fear surpassed his normal reticence about approaching teachers during class. Heads bent over their math assignment, few of his classmates even glanced up when Brad went to Miss Porter's desk. She looked up at him quizzically, slightly bloodshot brown eyes blinking myopically. Miss Porter had traded her glasses for contacts earlier in the semester. Brad often thought of telling her that she looked better in glasses than she did continually blinking from the irritation of the contacts. Brad was attracted to Miss Porter, seeing her the way he saw himself, as a socially crippled, extremely introverted, loser.

"Miss Porter," he whispered, trying not to get too close because he was sure his breath was awful, "I feel sick to my stomach."

Miss Porter opened her mouth to speak, probably to tell him he was excused, and Brad caught the glint of spittle in the crease where her upper lip met her lower. For an instant, he thought of holding the teacher, comforting what he perceived as her brokenness, wiping (or kissing) away that pearly drop.

"What was that, Brad?" Miss Porter said.

"Can, can I be excused? I feel like I'm gonna throw up." On the front row, Richard Palmer looked his way, and Brad blushed through his pallor.

"Yes, of course, Brad," Miss Porter said. "Do you need me to come with you to the office." She was solicitous now that she knew his problem, and Brad loved her for it.

"No, ma'am," he said. After easing the door shut behind him, Brad sprinted to the bathroom, making it just in time to dump the remnants of his breakfast into the first toilet. There it lay upon an unflushed, toilet-paper-covered, giant turd. Brad alternately flushed and retched until he was empty inside, and then he rinsed his mouth and blew his nose in a washbasin until he felt he wouldn't be too offensive to the office personnel. Only then did he call his mother to tell her to come get him.

CHAPTER 25

All morning Hal had surreptitiously watched Vicki–Vicki at the copier, Vicki talking on the phone, Vicki dealing with clients' minor needs. During slack periods, he had daydreamed about the two of them making love in the office, in the storage closet or on the floor beside his desk. Sometimes he imagined her doing things that Mary refused to do. Vicki might refuse too, of course; Hal saw her as at least as refined as his wife, and he didn't blame Mary for denying him. At 5 minutes to noon, Hal asked Vicki if she wanted to have lunch with him.

"Sure," she said, and her radiant smile made his heart skip a beat.

"Jesus," Hal thought, holding open the door for Vicki. "You would think I was a teenager again."

"How about the Holiday Inn?" he said. It was one of Harper's favorite dining places. Hal found it lacking in ambience and the food tasty but overpriced. The waiters were just slightly arrogant, so that he always felt he had to tip them big-city amounts.

"Holiday Inn would be wonderful, Hal," Vicki said, and 5 minutes later Hal pulled into the motel parking lot.

CHAPTER 26

"**S**hould I try to get you in to see the doctor, Bradley?" his mother asked. She signaled and turned right on Wallace Highway, a thoroughfare known to Harper residents as "The Strip." Over the years, fast food joints (rarely major franchises), video rental stores, combination filling stations/quick marts, package liquor stores, and auto parts or repair shops had sprung up along the road, producing the kind of urban blight multiplied a hundredfold in larger cities.

"Naw, I feel much better now, Mom," Brad said. In truth, he did feel better; perhaps it was the effect of cleaning out his insides in the bathroom or perhaps it was the increasing distance between Brad and school. Whatever the reason, Brad was actually beginning to feel hungry.

"We got any soup at home?" he asked, thinking that if they didn't, his mother could stop at Jitney Jungle. The store's parking lot began at the next intersection, just beyond a Holiday Inn.

"I'm pretty sure we do, dear," his mother said, applying the brake to stop for a changing light. Brad studied the motel parking lot, looking for new, sporty cars; his father sometimes made noises that gave Brad hope that one day he would have his own car. Of course, his father always talked about contingencies: "Brad," he would say. "You make some good grades, and I might consider looking around for something for you to run around in."

Imagining his father's voice, Brad watched as his father pulled into the parking lot. He glanced back at his mother, but she was concentrating on the traffic light. When Brad looked back at the motel, his father was opening the door for his receptionist, something he never did for Brad's mother. Brad felt their car beginning to move; Vicki was out of the car now, and the two of them were walking unhurriedly, smilingly, toward the motel's registration area. Brad couldn't believe it. In broad daylight, for God's sake. His mother was saying something that Brad hadn't caught.

"What's that, Mom?" he said, amazed that he could talk normally after what he had just seen.

"I said, 'Do you want me to stop and get some jello or pudding or something?'"

"No, thanks," Brad said. He felt slightly nauseated again.

CHAPTER 27

Danny glanced to his left, and his uncle nodded and smiled encouragingly. He trudged on in the late afternoon, staying even with the line of searchers, men mostly. To his right, Mr. Ellard from the bank had finally taken off his tie. Sweat glistened on the man's red forehead and plastered his white shirt to his back. Danny wondered when he would roll up his sleeves.

They walked through a field, the sun's last rays throwing shadows across the browning meadow grasses. Flushed, an occasional bird sped away, its alarm call trailing after. It was quiet in the field, as they had left the road noises behind a half mile earlier.

The search had been a lark at first, at least for Danny. He had gotten out of school, and the march through Lincoln Heights had proved interesting.

He had never been in the Projects, and he found its sights and sounds and smells fascinating. Little kids peered from torn screen windows at the sight of so many strangers in their neighborhood, while lean dogs barked and snarled menacingly. The chief knocked on one door after another, briefly questioning whoever appeared.

He usually said, "Did you see a white man come through here Saturday night?" to which the answer invariably was a head shake or "Sure didn't." Although he didn't see many people about in the Projects, Danny could feel them watching him and the other searchers. What would they think if they knew the search was for his father?

Danny and his uncle had looked inside a wheelless car on gray cinder blocks, a Ford LTD. His uncle said it was a 1965 model. Looking inside, Danny suddenly realized they were looking for his father's body, and the realization caused a sinking sensation in his chest.

"Face it, Danny," he told himself. "Sometimes Dad's a real pain in the ass." But pain in the ass or not, he didn't want to find his father's body, particularly not in the back seat or trunk of a rusting, immobile 1965 Ford LTD. And not in the field they had entered after leaving the Projects, either. He wondered if maybe he shouldn't have come.

Danny wanted to look up, to look way ahead of where he was walking, but he remembered his father's frequent reminders when the two looked for errant golf balls.

"Keep your head down, Danny," Peter Dewberry always said. "In high grass like this, you'll never see the balls looking away from your feet."

But we're not looking for golf balls, Danny thought. We're looking for something much bigger. Something that might fit inside the half-buried refrigerator ahead.

"Uncle Roy," he called. "There's a refrigerator in the grass." His uncle angled toward him, and the two met and stopped before the mildew speckled white chest. It lay on its back, door up, freezing them like the car had frozen them. It was one thing to walk between apartment buildings or through a field of meadow grass where there was little chance his father would be found and quite another to look inside an old car or an abandoned refrigerator. There might be something in the old Frigidaire even if it weren't his father. Mr. Ellard joined them. "Want me to open it?"

Roy nodded his head, looking closely at his nephew. "You okay, Danny?"

"Yessir," Danny said, heart pounding.

Mr. Ellard pulled the handle, and the door came up. A smell of mustiness escaped, but the box was empty; even the shelves were gone.

"Nothing inside," Mr. Ellard called, and the line of walkers, who had halted when the three gathered at the refrigerator, moved on.

Danny walked closer to his uncle than before. "What do you think, Uncle Roy? Will we find Dad?"

"I don't think so, Danny. Not out here, anyway."

They approached a small stand of trees and beyond that Danny could see a fence separating the field they were in from another. Chief Noland, three men beyond Mr. Ellard, called, "We'll stop at the fence."

"Do you think he's still alive?" Danny blurted to his uncle, finally voicing the question he had been struggling with all afternoon.

Roy hesitated, and Danny could almost see his uncle framing a comforting lie. The hesitation was answer enough, and he blinked back tears.

"I think we need to be prepared for the worst," his uncle said.

It was cooler under the trees.

CHAPTER 28

Roy pulled his car onto the grass beside his sister's driveway, stopping beside a huge Pontiac. He and Danny were met halfway to the house by a short woman with gray frizzy hair. Glasses the size of small saucers hid most of her wizened face.

"Hi, Daniel," she said, and Danny nodded, frowning slightly. Turning to Roy, she said, "You must be Nancy's brother." The woman had a quick, nervous way of speaking that Roy decided would drive him nuts if he had to listen to it very long. "I'm Mandy Murray, a friend from church."

"Roy Anderson," he said, shaking the woman's hand.

"Sorry you had to park off the driveway," she said. "I'm just leaving." Thank God, Roy thought, smiling. Mandy opened the door of her car and slipped inside, speaking to Roy and Danny through the opened window.

"It was so nice of you and your wife to come down so quickly, Mr. Anderson, but then, like I always say, 'Blood's thicker than turnip juice.'"

There's probably a message in that, Roy thought, but he was damned if he knew what it was. He smiled and nodded as though he agreed.

"We're all praying for your father, Daniel," she said, nearly yelling to be heard over the sound of the car's engine.

"Thanks," Danny said, unenthusiastically. Roy waved as the woman backed from the driveway.

"I'm sure glad she was leaving," the boy said, once they were inside the house. "Mrs. Murray really gets on my nerves."

"She gets on my nerves too, Danny," his mother said, sitting with her sister-in-law at the kitchen table, "but she means well." Roy could see that his sister had been crying.

Betty Anderson snorted. "I don't see how you can say that, Nancy, after what she asked."

Danny rooted in the refrigerator and found a Coke. "Want one, Uncle Roy?"

"No, thanks," Roy said. "Is there any more of that coffee, Nance?" When his sister started to stand, he added quickly: "Don't get up. I'll get it."

"There's probably another cup in the pot."

Roy poured a cup, then helped himself to sugar from a bowl between the two women. "What did she ask?"

Nancy looked at her sister-in-law, smiling slightly, tears threatening to spill over.

"She had heard all kinds of wild rumors and used the pretext of bringing food to pump Nancy about them," Betty said, obviously angry.

"What did she bring?" Danny asked, the talk of food attractive to his adolescent appetite.

"She'd heard Peter had made a large bank withdrawal Saturday morning," Nancy said.

Betty looked at Danny sipping his Coke, then at Nancy, touching her fingertip to her lips.

"It's all right, Betty," Nancy said. "He's going to hear these things at school anyway. Might as well get used to it."

Danny looked up, suddenly interested in the conversation. "Did Dad take any money out, Mom?"

"No more than he ever does on Saturday, Dear. Just some to buy gas and for your allowance."

"Oh."

"But why was he supposed to have taken the money out, Nancy?" Roy asked. "To ransom Danny's bike?"

"Oh, no, Roy. It was supposed to be much more than that. Do you remember how much, Betty?"

"Around $600. Something like that."

"Mandy had heard he was going to buy drugs with it."

"Good grief," Roy said.

"Dad doesn't use drugs, does he, Mom?"

"Of course not, Dear," his mother said. "Actually, one story going around is that Peter is an undercover narcotics agent with the Harper police." And another is that he dealt drugs, she thought, but she couldn't bring herself to tell that one in front of her son.

The four sat silently for a moment, Roy stirring his coffee while Danny drained the last of his Coke.

"What about the search?" Betty asked her husband.

He shook his head, frowning.

"We looked inside an old refrigerator, Mom," Danny said, "but Dad wasn't in it."

Nancy turned away from her son to stare blindly at her own refrigerator. She felt her brother's gentle touch on her arm.

CHAPTER 29

Ed's was quiet on Tuesday night. Eddie Lee, the owner, was behind the bar, wiping glasses and watching baseball on the wall-mounted Sony. In a booth in the darkest corner of the room, Jimmy Ivory was trying to make a move on Latoya Outlaw, his best friend Cecil's wife. Cecil was a campus security officer currently on the night shift out at the college.

"How come you're not home with Ida and the kids?" Latoya asked in her sexiest singsong voice. The light from the TV sparkled in her dark eyes.

Jimmy smiled at Latoya. "You seen Ida lately? That woman's big as a house."

"You got her that way, Jimmy Ivory, always poking her and filling her up with little Ivorys." She giggled at her joke.

God, I'd sure like to poke you, Jimmy thought. "You are some fine-lookin' woman, Latoya," he said.

Latoya just smiled and preened and sipped her sloe gin. They could hear the muted click of billiard balls from the back room.

In the back room, Charles "Stump" Watkins leaned over the table and aimed the cue ball for the right half of the seven ball, intending to cut it into the upper left pocket. He stroked smoothly, and the white ball rumbled toward the seven, catching it slightly left of where he'd intended. The seven circled the pocket but stayed on the table. "Shit," he said, backing away. Grinning, his brother took his place. The younger Watkins shot quickly, almost without aiming, setting in motion half the balls on the table. One of his stripes dropped.

"Hot damn," he yelled, leaning over to strike the balls again.

"Hold it down back there," Eddie called through the closed door.

"Take it easy, Bro," Stump said, quietly, grabbing the butt of his brother's pool cue. "You want Eddie to make us leave? He knows our IDs are fake."

"Let go, Stump," his brother said. "I'm okay now." He gave the balls another run around the table, but nothing fell this time.

Stump, studying the table to plan his next shot, said, "What'd you do to get kicked outta school?"

"It wasn't my fault, Stump. This guy in the hall calls me 'four eyes' and starts shovin' me aroun'."

Chalking his cue, Stump looked up at his brother. "So, what'd you do?"

"I pulled my knife on him." his brother said, diligently studying a roach on the next table.

"Then what happened?"

"Mr. Packard grabbed me and took me to the office."

"Goddammit, I thought I told you to cool it for a while. Not to get in trouble. What happened to the knife?" He was thinking how stupid his brother must be to take the murder weapon to school.

"Principal kep' it." He hypnotically watched his brother's bicep flex as Stump continued chalking his cue. He had replaced his confiscated knife already, but he didn't volunteer that information. Stump was mad enough as it was.

"You know they had a search party out looking for that guy you killed?"

"They fine him?"

"Naw," Stump said, bending over the table, carefully lining up a long shot. "They were looking out in the Projects and in that field past 'em."

"They'll never find him there."

Stump stroked the shot and made it. He walked to the other end of the table and squatted till his eyes were level with the table's edge. Studying the shape he had left himself. "No shit," he said.

"You reckon the guy's still in the dumpster?"

Stump stood, and his left knee popped. Sometimes he wondered about his brother. "What happens to the dumpster on Monday, Bro?"

His brother sat on a stool beside a talcum powder dispenser and watched Stump line up another shot. "They empty it," he said.

"So, what's that mean?" Stump asked. His try to cut the five ball into the side pocket just missed.

"The body's at the dump, I guess," he said, rising to take his turn. He put his cigarette on the side of the table with the burning end out toward the floor.

"Thas right," Stump said. "And somebody's gonna find it pretty soon is my guess."

His brother shot more carefully this time, but the result was the same; he missed. "Nothin' to connect us to it," he said, retrieving his cigarette.

"I hope ya right," Stump said.

CHAPTER 30

Hannah had found the mother lode of aluminum cans, and she muttered to herself as she pitched one after the other into her basket. "Lawsy, lawsy, Hannah. You done struck it rich this time." She picked up an Old Milwaukee can, shook it, and smiled at the sound and feel of the liquid inside. She sniffed. Beer. The warmth of it slid down easy. Empty, the can joined all the others.

"Sheeit," Hannah said. "They's $5 worth in there easy." She leaned over the open dumpster, shoved her scrawny arms under the cans, enfolded them, hugged them to her chest, tried to straighten up with her load.

Something held her back. Something circled her wrist, something cold and bony.

"Whaaa," she said, pupils dilating with shock. Her frizzled gray-black hair stood on end, and Hannah felt her heart thump in her chest. She released the cans and tried to pull away. The cans, clattering and clanking, bulged as though something under them was trying to get out.

"What's under there?" she screamed, eyes popping, liquid warmth spreading down her thighs to soak her rolled-down socks. "Keep the goddam cans, jus' lemme go." Cans rolled away from her wrist, and she saw what held her.

A hand. A bony, dead-white, maggoty hand. Another heave of the pile, and the owner of the hand sat up in the dumpster, turning empty sockets on the old woman.

Hannah shook her head dumbly, trying to will her mouth to work, screaming inside her head: "I didn' kill you, white man. You was already dead."

The man's blue lips parted, and a purple worm the size of Ida's breakfast sausages emerged. Hannah screamed and came awake. She stared at the dark ceiling, heart pounding. Her thin gown and the bed sheets were soaked with sweat and something else. She smelled urine. Ida would be hoppin' mad. Hannah fumbled in the dark for the butt of the cigarette she'd been smoking before she went to sleep, found it, and lit it, tilting her head to keep from setting her mustache on fire. The acrid, stale smoke calmed the old woman.

Since no one came into her room, she must not have screamed out loud. That was good; give her time to think. She sucked hard on the cigarette, its glow soothing in the dark. Smoke trickled from her nostrils, dribbled from her mouth. Hannah stabbed out the butt in the ashtray on the floor next to the bed. She linked her hands behind her head and looked toward the window where a pink light was growing.

What was she going to do about the dream? She'd had a different, equally scary, dream about the body the night before. In that one, the man had accused her of his murder. His voice had sounded like that cop, Noland. Maybe she would talk to Noland, tell him about the body. But not today; today she was going to walk away the dream, walk all over town if she had to. She would take her sheets with her, draped over her basket to dry in the sun. Ida would never know.

CHAPTER 31

Vicki looked at her husband's broad bulk in the bed beside her and was repulsed. She was repelled by his smell and by his lack of manners and by his ignorance. A long rumble broke the bedroom's silence, and Vicki scrambled out of bed, driven away by Bone's early morning flatulence.

The sound of the shower woke Bone. He rolled away from the noise, trying unsuccessfully to recover his dream. In it he had been a football star again, a juggernaut on the field and a tiger off. The rushing water had interrupted his sexual encounter with two cheerleaders. One was Vicki. Bone wished that Vicki was back in bed with him.

What time was it anyway? Bone cocked one eye toward the clock on the dresser on his wife's side of the bed. 5:35. Why was she up so early?

The water stopped abruptly, and Bone imagined his wife drying herself. If he weren't so sleepy, he would give her a hand.

Vicki studied her reflection in the mirror. Not bad, not bad at all. Hazel-green eyes, slender nose, generous mouth. She smiled. Her breasts weren't big, but then they didn't hang down like a pair of old sacks either. And her legs were nice and muscular and smooth. With a wry smile, she retrieved her panties and slipped them on, then dressed quickly.

"What do you want for breakfast, Bone?" she asked, stopping by the bed on her way to the kitchen.

"Umm, uhhh, whatcha get up so early for?" Bone rocked in the bed, pulled a handful of sheet over his ears so that only the top of his head showed. Lank hair fanned over a damp spot on the pillow where his mouth had rested.

"It's 6:45, same time we always get up."

"6:45? Shit, I just looked, and it was 5:35." He snatched the sheet away from his head and tried to raise himself enough to see the clock again.

"You must have read it wrong, Bone. Anyway, what do you want?"

"The usual, I guess. Wanna get back in bed for a quickie?" He flung back the sheet to reveal his piss hard.

Vicki tried not to show her disgust. "I've already had my shower, Bone," she said. "Maybe tomorrow." Maybe tomorrow she would run away with her boss. Maybe tomorrow she would cut off Bone's stupid prick and stuff it into his mouth. Give him a Mafia sausage for breakfast. "Want sausage or bacon with your eggs?"

"Bacon," he said, heaving himself out of bed. He entered the bathroom scratching and farting.

Fifteen minutes later Bone entered the kitchen, struggling with his clip-on tie. "Can you help with this, Hon?"

Vicki attached the clips to both wings of Bone's collar, holding her breath to keep from smelling her husband's cigarette and early-morning breath. "Is this a clean shirt?" A yellow stain on the pocket smelled like beer.

"Naw," he said.

Vicki returned to the stove, while Bone poured himself a cup of coffee. He added three spoonfuls of sugar at the counter before returning to his seat at the table. There he added Cremora until the coffee turned a light tan.

"Guess who I saw yesterday." Bone sipped his coffee, holding the cup with both hands while he rested his elbows on the table.

"Who?" Vicki asked. She slid two eggs onto a plate between two strips of bacon glistening with grease, then pushed down the lever on the toaster.

"That boss of yours. What's his name? Hal?"

"Oh? Did he come in the store?" She put the plate before her husband and handed him a napkin. "Want some more coffee?"

"No, this is okay." Bone dusted his eggs with salt, methodically going from one side of his plate to the other, back and forth. "Yeah, he came in. Must have been a little after 5. Probably gettin' something for supper. That guy smiles too much to suit me."

"He's just friendly, Bone," Vicki said, feeling a need to defend her employer. "He has to be to sell insurance." She started to tell her husband that he might try being a little friendlier himself, but she thought better of it.

Bone herded a piece of egg onto his toast and took his first bite. "Not bad," he said. "You gonna eat?"

Vicki turned and focused on her husband. He crunched noisily on a bacon strip. "I had a piece of toast and a glass of milk while you were getting dressed."

"Hmmm," he said. "How 'bout gettin' me the paper?"

CHAPTER 32

Grady propped the Wednesday newspaper, thick with ads, between the salt and pepper shakers and his bowl of oatmeal. He called the oatmeal "gruel," but he liked to have it at least once a week. Marge seemed to have settled on Wednesdays.

"What's it say, Hon?" Marge spread low-sugar jam on her piece of whole wheat toast, while Grady Jr. chewed his Crispy Wheats and Raisins loudly. "Chew with your mouth closed," his mother reminded him.

"Nothing much," Grady said after he swallowed. "Just that Dewberry's still missing." From the headline story of the day before, Peter's disappearance had slipped to a small quarter column piece on the front page. Most of the article was a rehash of how he had gone for a late-night walk with his dog and how the dog had returned without his master.

"Did he work for the department?"

"Where'd you hear that, Marge?" Grady said, looking up from his oatmeal.

"Grocery store. I saw the mayor's wife, and that's what she'd heard."

"May I be excused?" Grady Jr. said.

"Yes, Dear," his mother told him. "Take your bowl to the sink."

"And be sure to brush your teeth," Grady said. His son wore a pained expression on his way past his father, although he often "forgot" to brush on days he wasn't reminded.

"No, Dewberry wasn't an undercover cop and he wasn't having an affair and he didn't do drugs and he wasn't suicidal. As nearly as I can tell, he was just an ordinary guy walking his dog."

"Are you mad?"

Grady shook his head. "I'm just tired of all the rumors, Marge. Who starts 'em, anyway?" He sipped his milk.

"It's just small-town stuff, Dear. You oughta be used to it by now." She finished her oatmeal. "Through with this?" she asked, one hand on the tub spread.

"Yeah." Grady turned the paper to the sports page, folding it so that he could read an article about the high school's football team. Marge put away the spread and returned to wipe the table.

"You think he's dead?"

Grady nodded. They listened to the sound of the toilet flushing in Grady Jr.'s bathroom. "I just wish we would find Dewberry, Marge."

CHAPTER 33

"I'm not hungry, Mom," he said, pushing away the biscuits she had fixed.

"Can I have them?" Sandy asked, reaching.

"Do you really need them, lardo?"

Sandy colored and drew back her hand as if she had touched a hot stove.

"That wasn't nice, Bradley. Apologize to your sister."

"No way."

Mary turned to her husband for help. "Aren't you going to say anything?"

"What's that, Dear?" he asked, looking at her for the first time that morning.

"Don't you think Bradley should apologize to Sandy for calling her 'lardo'?"

"Certainly," Hal said, thinking there was a kernel of truth in the label. Sandy did tend to put on weight. Why couldn't she have taken after her mother instead of after his side of the family? His daughter reminded him of his youngest sister, Shirley. Thick and solid as a girl, Shirley looked like a bowling ball now. He didn't think it would hurt if Sandy passed up Brad's uneaten biscuits.

"I didn't give you permission to leave the table," Mary said when her son stood. "And you still haven't said you're sorry."

Brad turned at the door to the family room. "Sorry, fats," he said, grinning. He strode away, easily tuning out the chorus of angry sounds from the kitchen.

Brad entered the bathroom and locked the door. He turned on the water in the lavatory and studied his mirror image. "I wouldn't be half bad if I didn't have all these pimples," he muttered to himself.

"Don't pick, Bradley," his mother always told him. "You'll get them infected and that leads to scarring."

Ignoring his mother's warning, Brad put his forefingers on either side of a particularly swollen whitehead in the center of his forehead. He pressed. There was a moment of pain, a satisfying release, and a jet of pus struck the mirror. He squeezed again, and a drop of blood appeared. Fascinated, he stared at the reflection of the drop, and it seemed to spread until it covered the top half of his face. But no, it wasn't blood covering his face. It was a shadow, the shadow of something huge he hadn't seen in the mirror before. Something so close behind him that Brad could feel the heat from its body and smell its fetid odor.

Brad's heart kicked into another gear, beating so hard he was sure it was about to burst. Dimly seen at first, the menace behind him was becoming more sharply focused with each passing second. Many years earlier, Brad had watched an episode of "Space 1999" with his father. In the episode, the moon base was threatened by an energy creature that looked like a tall tree stump with whip-like tentacles around the top of its "head." He and his father had been deliciously horrified when the thing took a man into its "head" and extruded the remains of the man moments later in a steaming mass. The energy thing stood behind Brad now, and he knew that if he turned or moved a muscle it would lasso him with tentacles, take him inside its body, and reduce him to a steaming, stinking corpse.

"Help," he mouthed. "Help me."

Pounding on the door. "You gonna be in there all morning?" Sandy yelled. "Don't use all the hot water."

Brad blinked, and the thing disappeared. One moment it was there, and the next it wasn't. There was no fading out gradually the way it had come. The energy monster just vanished, leaving only the cold sweat on his forehead, a small drop of blood, and a pounding heart as reminders. Brad leaned over the lavatory and vomited into the running water.

When he was through, he splashed water on his face, rinsed his mouth and spat, and sat weakly on the toilet.

"Hallucination," his inner voice told him. "You had an honest-to-God hallucination. You're going crazy, kid." He heard Sandy just outside the door, talking to their mother, telling her that Brad had been in the bathroom much too long, even for him.

"I'll be out in a second," he called through the door. He flushed the toilet and turned off the light, standing for a moment in darkness before opening the door into the hall.

CHAPTER 34

Following a trail of aluminum cans and returnable bottles, Hannah walked across Harper. Draped across the side of her cart, her thin sheet dried in the morning sun and a fitful breeze that occasionally cooled her sweating face. For the most part, she walked in silence, buried in her anxieties and superstitions. A little after 10, Hannah's odyssey was interrupted by three white youths in a pickup.

"Whatcha doin', ole woman?" the driver called, slowing to match Hannah's pace.

"Even for a honky, you is ugly," Hannah muttered. After a glance, she resolutely kept her eyes on the sidewalk.

"Here's another can, granny," the young man in the truck's bed said, tossing a can at her. Hannah caught it and flipped it into her cart.

"Thanks," she said. "Jus' keep 'em comin', boys."

The boys in the cab laughed. They hadn't expected her response. "What's with the sheet, old lady? You sleep in that cart, too?" she heard the one in the back say.

"Know where I can get a pair of shoes like that?" Hannah heard a different voice say. Probably belonged to the one in the passenger's seat. She ignored the question and walked faster. She was approaching the entrance to one of Harper's older (and nicer) subdivisions. Her plan was to turn in and hope the boys wouldn't follow her.

They did.

Hannah's anger flared. "Ain't you boys got nothin' better to do than pick at an ole woman like me?"

In response, the driver revved his engine; winding down it back-fired twice, each time sounding like a gunshot. Hannah snuck another peek at the truck, which was now slightly ahead of her, taking in the three beefy, grizzled young men, noticing the gun on the rack across the back window and the Stars and Bars decal. "Jus' keep yore mouth shut, Hannah," she mumbled.

Hannah walked down a tree-shaded street, the sidewalk lifted and cracked at intervals by massive roots. Two-story houses, mansions to Hannah, sat far back from the street behind well-tended lawns. Hannah and her cart were anomalies in the subdivision, but then so were the young men in their pickup. They turned into a drive across the street from Hannah, reversed direction, and roared away, leaving behind a black cloud of unfiltered exhaust.

"Thank you, Lawd," Hannah said, crossing the street to head back the way she had come, back to the main street and the trash along it. She could tell she would find no cans in the subdivision. Hannah rooted through her skirt pocket for her longest cigarette butt. Time to celebrate. She lighted it and drew the acrid, stale smoke deep, exhaling with a cough that ended in a spit. Hannah turned back onto the thoroughfare.

Near noon, Hannah sat in the shade of an abandoned filling station and ate the sandwich she had brought from Ida's. It was an onion and tomato sandwich with bread made soggy by tomato juice. Afterwards she smoked the rest of a Virginia Slims butt she had found the day before, her lips covering the lipstick print on the filter.

She had walked steadily since early morning, her slow pace eating the miles until she now found herself on the outskirts of Harper. A hot breeze carried the odor of rotting garbage, and Hannah knew she was near the city dump. She often searched the dump, continually amazed at the treasure people threw away. She had found several watches (a few working), empty wallets and purses, good pairs of shoes that she took home to Ida's kids, books that she threw back since she didn't read, and many things she would like to have taken that were too big to carry. Why would people throw away bikes and vacuum cleaners, she wondered, walking faster now that she had a destination. Why would they get rid of good baby buggies and lawn mowers?

A garbage truck passed her, and the black passenger waved. Hannah knew the man, Winston something-or-other. She was glad the truck was leaving.

At the dump, Hannah skirted the ramp where the trucks unloaded and picked her way carefully down a path beside the garbage. Although most of the city's trash was in black bags, some of it, the stuff from the dumpsters mainly, was loose. Hannah hoped there was some that hadn't been picked over by the kids she'd seen on other visits.

"They all in school, Hannah," she told herself. She retrieved a broom handle to poke piles of trash. She could also use it to hit any rats or snakes she might see. Hannah rattled on, stopping occasionally to toss an empty can into her cart. Flies buzzed around rotting organic matter, and the stench was almost unbearable. Hannah lit a cigar butt she had saved for a visit to the dump, puffing until a small cloud of blue smoke masked the rotten smells. She headed for a dumpster pile that looked promising; maybe some of the cans still had paint in them. She could ask Ida's oldest daughter, Chanté, to paint her room. It had been years since Hannah had had a freshly painted room, and the idea of it brought tears to her rheumy eyes.

As Hannah neared the pile, she could see it was mostly building materials: broken two by fours with nails sticking out, pieces of brick, paint cans. Some of the stuff seemed to have been burned. She poked a can with her stick, then slipped the stick's end through the can's wire handle. "Too light," she muttered. Empty. She poked another can. This one wasn't round like a paint can; it looked more like the cans Ida sometimes bought cooking oil in. And it wasn't empty.

Tossing her cigar butt, Hannah lifted the can, unscrewed the lid, and sniffed. The contents smelled good and sweet and pungent and almost familiar. It wasn't paint, but Chanté could use it. Hannah put the can in her cart and turned back to the pile. Watching out for splinters, she wrapped her hands around a piece of 2 x 4 and pulled, dislodging it. Two brown rats the size of small cats skittered away, stopping just out of reach of her broom handle. Facing her, they hissed, tails thrashing. Hannah had never seen them act that way. She waved her stick, and the animals scampered away, disappearing into separate holes.

"Brave suckers," she muttered, wondering what they had been chewing on. The sickly sweet smell of death rose from the pile of paint cans and boards and bricks. Hannah pushed her pole between two cans, right into the spot where the rats had stood. Something yielded to the pole's tip, something like foam or a mattress. Or flesh.

Hannah caught a hint of something under the pile, a grayish white something with a ragged hole in it. Near the hole gleamed a watch. Hannah leaned closer, pushing cans away with her pole. She still couldn't see what the watch was attached to, but it didn't matter. She wanted the watch. This one was so bright and shiny it was bound to work. All the others had been digital watches, the kind that sold for $3.97, the kind with plastic bands and batteries, the kind people threw away when the batteries died.

Hannah knelt and saw that the watch was strapped to a piece of meat. A piece of meat that ended in a hand. A cold, gray, very dead white hand with a gold ring on one finger.

Hannah's scalp tightened, giving her the look of a fox. She felt the skin crawl on the back of her neck, and, despite the afternoon heat, goosebumps peppered her papery-dry brown skin. She knew whose arm she was looking at, knew as surely as she knew her name that the body under the junk was the subject of her nightmares. But she had to see.

Hannah batted away cans, pulled two by fours unmindful of splinters until she had uncovered the body's mashed head. On the side nearest her, maggots were down to the skull and the white man's teeth gleamed from his polished jawbone. He seemed to be grinning at the old woman.

"You," she whispered. "You was already dead." Hannah backed away from the sight, bumped into her cart, pushed it aside, and ran, heart thudding in her chest, out of the dump and back along the thoroughfare. She didn't stop until she came to a store with a pay phone. She inserted a quarter and dialed 911. She asked for the police, and when the police dispatcher answered, Hannah asked for Chief Noland.

CHAPTER 35

While there had been no repeat of his bathroom hallucination, Brad had felt peculiar most of the morning. Somehow, he had come unglued in his second period class. That was the way he would have put it if anybody had asked him. In his mind's eye, he saw himself as Peter Pan's shadow—detached from his body. It wasn't an altogether bad feeling.

He could see himself sitting in class, stupidly grinning; that in itself should have alerted his classmates that Brad was deeply disturbed. Brad never grinned in class, although he smiled occasionally when he was with Jesse.

Although Brad wouldn't know it and wouldn't have cared if he had known it, the kids sitting around his grinning figure on the first day of Jesse's suspension would talk later about how they had noticed how strangely he was behaving.

"He seemed almost peaceful-like, you know," Peggy Batson would tell Wanda Turner, and Wanda, nodding, smacking her gum, would say, "Like he was, you know, in a trance or something."

"I thought he was high on something, man," Tommy Lee told a reporter, and Tommy Lee should have known, since he was nearly always at least half stoned himself.

But hindsight is 20/20, and on that Wednesday, no one noticed or said a thing. Brad saw himself, still grinning, leave his seat when the lunch bell rang, walk normally out of the room and into the hall, accompany the crowd down the hall to the cafeteria, stand patiently in line, get the tuna casserole, jello, milk, and a roll, and take a seat next to Maria Sanchez. He saw himself eating, chewing normally, and swallowing, but there was no feeling of the texture of the food and no sensation of taste. It was as though he were chewing and swallowing air. Maria said something to him, and his head nodded and his smile broadened. Maria giggled; perhaps she had told him a joke.

Brad left the cafeteria then, sure that his body would follow, and it did after a short delay. He assumed that the part of himself on autopilot had taken his tray to the conveyor belt that carried dirty dishes and utensils to the huge steaming sinks behind the serving lines. Although he hadn't heard it, Brad could easily imagine the clatter of plates, the clinking of silverware, and the chatter of the dishwashers coming through the square opening the conveyor belt passed through.

"Me...and...my...sha...dow," Brad hummed in his mind, recalling catchy lyrics from a song he had heard in an old movie on television. "Strollin' down the a...ve...nue." Or maybe it should be "my shadow and I" doing the strolling. Whatever, Brad thought, wondering what it would be like to rejoin his body. Still on autopilot, it was heading straight for the bleachers, straight for a rendezvous with his good buddy, Jesse. Brad knew, while his body apparently didn't, that Jesse wasn't under the bleachers today, that he had gotten kicked out yesterday. He had heard all the details in his first period class, back when he was still in one piece.

CHAPTER 36

Rejoining his body was almost as easy as slipping out, and instead of going under the bleachers, Brad climbed them instead. He sat and stared out at the track and the practice football field. A couple of guys were running laps. It made Brad tired just to look at them.

The knowledge that he could detach himself from himself gave him a certain feeling of security. He could see himself detaching whenever his parents fussed at him or whenever he wanted to tune Sandy out or whenever Mr. Packard tried to embarrass him.

"Brad," he heard someone say and seeing no one in front, he looked behind him. Nobody there either. Was he having auditory hallucinations now? He had read somewhere that they were the most common kind.

"Brad," the voice came again, and it sounded just like Jesse. At least this was better than the energy monster he had seen in the mirror. Should he talk to it or just listen quietly to what it had to say? He felt something tug his shoe.

"I'm under here, dummy," Jesse said.

"Damned if you aren't," Brad said. "I thought you got kicked out, Jesse."

"I did. C'mon under, and I'll tell you about it. I got some cigarettes we can share."

Brad joined Jesse and the two smoked companionably in silence. Brad heard the bell ring and easily ignored it; he had decided on his way under the bleachers to cut his first afternoon class.

"Why are you under here, Jesse?"

"Hell, Brad, can you imagine what my ole man'd do if he knew I got kicked out? He'd beat the livin' shit outta me."

Brad digested Jesse's statement. He couldn't imagine not telling his parents if he got kicked out of school. But then he couldn't imagine doing anything that would get him kicked out.

"So what happened yesterday, Jesse?"

Jesse told him, embellishing the story only a little when he described how scared Durr was of his knife. "Well, he shoulda been scared, after what I done with it Saturday," Jesse said.

"What was that?" Brad asked, casually, like he didn't care if Jesse told him or not.

"Can't say," Jesse said, clamming up. "Stump'd kill me if I tol' you."

"What if I tell you something really weird that happened to me this morning, Jesse? Would you tell me then?"

Jesse shrugged.

Brad told his friend about the energy monster and even threw in how he had dissociated his mind from his body all morning.

"That's pretty weird, awright," Jesse conceded.

"So what'd you do Saturday?"

Jesse studied him, seemed for a moment about to tell, but then he looked away and busied himself extracting another cigarette from the pack in his shirt pocket. "Stump'd kill me," he repeated, almost to himself.

Brad cast around in his mind, searching for something really awful he could share with Jesse, something that would elicit a secret so profound that Stump would have a shit fit if he found out Jesse had told it. Not that Stump would ever get Jesse's secret out of Brad. Maybe if he swore to that, Jesse would tell him.

"You can tell me, buddy," he said. "No way Stump'll know."

Jesse just shook his head.

Brad's eyes widened, and his smile broadened. He had it. Sex, Jesse was always interested in sex. "Listen, Jesse," he said. "Know what I saw yesterday when my mother picked me up?"

"Naw, what?"

"I saw my old man taking his good-looking receptionist to a motel, an' you know what that means?"

"Naw, Brad," Jesse said, "spell it out for me."

If Brad hadn't known Jesse better, he would've suspected his friend of sarcasm, but what Jesse really wanted, Brad was sure, were graphic details of what probably happened at the motel between his father and Vicki. So he supplied them. At some point during the "details," Jesse's eyes got that faraway look that frightened Brad, the look that said Jesse would do, say, or try anything.

"What you gonna do about it?" Jesse said, when Brad wound down. "You gonna slip him some of that stuff you talked about gettin' from chemistry lab? You ain't got it yet, have ya?"

Brad shook his head. He took the cigarette Jesse offered and lit it with Jesse's lighter.

"Tell you what, Brad," Jesse said, and his face had that saturnine look that both frightened Brad and attracted him at the same time. "I'll tell you my secret and help you get the poison if you'll promise to use it."

"I don't know, Jesse. He's my old man, for chrissakes."

"I knew you was chicken. All talk, Brad, that's what you are. Probably didn't even have that, what'd you call it, vision or whatever this morning." Jesse flipped his glowing butt at the underside of the descending bleachers. Sparks showered where it hit.

"Go ahead and promise, Brad," he told himself. "You don't really have to go through with it, and you'll get to find out Jesse's big secret."

"Okay, Jesse," he said. "I promise I'll get the arsenic and use it." Although maybe not on his old man; maybe on Sandy. "What'd you do Saturday?"

"You know that guy from the college they lookin' for?"

"Dr. Dewberry?"

"Whatever. Stump held him, and I fixed him with my knife. Only took one little poke," Jesse said, grinning from ear to ear.

I'm not hearing this, Brad thought. I'll dissociate like I did this morning, so I don't have to listen to Jesse anymore. He felt he was going to lose his lunch listening to how Jesse had mashed the man's head, how Jesse and Stump had put Dr. Dewberry in a dumpster and then tried to burn his body with some turpentine they found in the trash. But Brad heard it all, unable to distance himself from a single gory detail. And through it all, Brad was thinking how much he had liked Dr. Dewberry, how Dewberry had been his scout master for all those years before Brad dropped out of the Boy Scouts.

"These are the man's shoes, Brad," Jesse said, pointing to the nearly new Nikes he was wearing.

"Jesus," Brad breathed. "You really did it."

"Fuckin' A," Jesse said. "Now here's how I'm gonna help you get the arsenic."

CHAPTER 37

Brad tried to concentrate on Mr. Packard's lecture, but it was no use. His mind kept worrying over the same thing, circling back to it whenever he managed to think of something else. Ruminating, that's what he was doing. He had read that somewhere, and now he truly understood what it meant.

"I won't think of it anymore," he told himself, and 5 seconds later the images started again, the image of Stump holding Dr. Dewberry and Jesse stabbing him. The image of Jesse crushing Dr. Dewberry's head with a brick because the man's legs were still moving. The image of Stump and Jesse carrying the body to the dumpster. Grinning, Jesse had told Brad that Dewberry's flattened head bumped along on the grass and the sidewalk. "But he was past hurtin'," Jesse said, as though that made it okay.

Brad had only himself to blame. Although he figured Jesse probably wanted to tell someone, Jesse wouldn't have told if Brad hadn't been so insistent. "You just had to know, asshole," he berated himself. And now that he knew, he would never be the same again.

What should he do with the knowledge? Should he tell his mother? His father? Call the police? Go to the office and tell the principal? What would happen if he turned Jesse in? Of course, he mustn't forget about Stump. Stump was guilty, too. Stump had held the man while his brother stabbed him.

What if he ratted on Jesse and Stump, and they managed to get away from the police? After all, his parents were always talking about how incompetent the Harper police were. He could see the brothers being picked up for questioning and then released because the police had screwed up the evidence or failed to read them their rights or something else equally stupid. It had happened before in Harper.

They would know who told. Brad thought about Stump Watkins, former star Harper lineman. He remembered the broad back, the massive upper arms that strained the cotton of Stump's t-shirt, the neck broader than the head, and he knew that Stump would pound him and break all his bones while Jesse, his former friend, cut him into little pieces.

But could he live with the knowledge? He didn't think he could. Maybe the answer was to get the arsenic and kill his whole family, himself included. How bad could it hurt to die from arsenic poisoning? From what he had read, it wasn't a fun way to go.

What if he leveled with his parents, told them what Jesse had told him, and let them make the decisions? Forget all about the arsenic. Why had he ever become so obsessed with that stuff anyway?

Brad knew exactly what Jesse was going to do and when he was going to do it, but when it actually happened, he was just as startled as the rest of the class.

"Okay, everybody," Mr. Packard said. "Line up behind me, and we'll file out in an orderly manner. Last one out close the door behind you." And Mr. Packard was gone, with the rest of the class hurrying behind. Brad (and everybody else) knew the teacher was supposed to go last—that's what they had always done in their practice fire drills—but Mr. Packard knew this wasn't practice, and he didn't want to be trapped if there really was a fire. Last in line, Brad closed the door like Mr. Packard said, but he closed it in front of him, not behind.

Fear of Jesse's ridicule, the greater fear of Jesse's wrath, the thought that he was going crazy, and the bloody images of Dr. Dewberry he couldn't seem to stop propelled Brad through the back door of the classroom into the adjoining laboratory. In the dim light from the windows, he saw that somebody from the previous class had failed to lock the cabinet behind him. Just my luck, he thought, as he opened it and extracted the As jar. He couldn't take the whole thing; Mr. Packard would be sure to notice that. What could he put some of the stuff in? He thrust his hands into the front pockets of his jeans, rooting frantically for some kind of container. He felt his chapstick, keys, some change, a nearly empty package of Juicy Fruit gum. No help from any of that. Brad's heart triphammered, sweat dotting his forehead. Time was hurtling by, and any moment he expected Mr. Packard or one of his classmates to come through the door.

"Arnold," Mr. Packard would say. "What are you doing in here? Why didn't you come out during the drill? You know anything about the false alarm?"

"C'mon, Brad, there's got to be something you can put just a little bit of the arsenic into. You don't need much, according to the books," said Brad's inner monologue. But he needed something to put it in, something he could close and slip into his pocket, something like—like—the gum package.

With shaking hands, Brad emptied the sticks of gum into his shirt pocket. He could almost fill the container with the powder and seal it by rolling over the top. All he had to do was open the jar of arsenic.

The lid was on too tight.

"Goddam that Mr. Packard and his weightlifting," Brad felt like screaming. The sonofabitch had pumped himself up and then screwed on the lid of the arsenic jar so tight that only Stump Watkins could open it. He'd probably done the same thing with all the poisons just to foil someone like Brad.

Silence. The alarm had stopped.

Brad tried the lid again. This time his hands were so damp from his fear of being discovered that they slipped, and he nearly dropped the jar to the floor.

"Fool," he berated himself. "At least put the jar over the counter so it won't break if you drop it." Brad pulled his handkerchief out of his back pocket and wrapped it around the lid. He grasped the lid again, squeezed as tightly as he could, and tried to turn it. Muscles in his forearm quivered and sweat clouded his vision, but the lid refused to turn.

"Shit, shit, shit," he whispered, his heart thudding in his chest. He heard voices from students back in the building. He had only a few moments more before his chemistry class came back and he was discovered. He would have to tell Jesse he had tried to get the arsenic, but he couldn't get the lid off. Surely Jesse would accept that. He would give it one more try, but that was it. He could probably put the jar up and get back to his desk without anyone knowing he had been in the lab. He would pretend he had dozed through the whole drill. So what if Mr. Packard made an ass of him.

To his eternal regret, this time the seal broke.

Brad scooped some of the white powder into his gum package, spilling a few grains onto the counter. He crimped the top of the package and slipped it into his pocket. Working feverishly now, he herded the spilled arsenic back into the jar, the thought crossing his mind to lick the heel of his hand where some of it stuck. Brad fumbled the lid back on, cross threading it, twisting it as tightly as he could. He closed the cabinet and slipped to the lab door. The classroom was still empty.

Brad threw himself into his desk and put his head down on his crossed arms. He closed his eyes and tried to still his breathing. He had to look like he was asleep.

CHAPTER 38

The room was cold. Overhead a fluorescent light flickered and hummed. The smell of death overpowered the carbolic acid odor and Roy felt sick.

"Yes, that's him," he said, looking at the "good side" of his brother-in-law's ruined face. There was enough intact skin and facial structure to convince him of the body's identity. Besides, the left hand was relatively intact, and Roy remembered Peter telling him about a childhood accident that had cost him the last joint on his ring finger.

Still, the chief had said it was bad, but Roy had never imagined it was *this* bad. Peter's head was flattened and blackened, like it had been beaten and then burned, and the skin on one side of the face was mostly gone. Thank God Nancy had not had to see this. Let her last memory of her husband be of him leaving the house, alive, whole.

"Are you sure?" Noland had tried to prepare Roy, but the condition of the corpse was unimaginable. Although he didn't want to look, he felt his own gaze drawn inexorably to the table.

"I'm sure," Roy said with a finality that begged for the sheet to be replaced.

Noland pulled the sheet back over the fire-frizzled hair. "Let's go back to my office," he said.

————•((•))•————

"Do you want some coffee?"

"Thanks," Roy said, taking the cup mechanically. He still felt slightly queasy, and he knew the image of Peter at the funeral home would haunt his dreams. At the funeral home he had wanted to ask the chief how he felt about Peter's murder, but the look on the chief's face told him all he needed to know. Horror, disgust, and anger had been plainly visible as Noland stared at the body.

"How's she taking it?" the chief asked.

"Nancy? She seems pretty calm, but then she's been expecting this since he didn't come back." He sipped the coffee. "Probably in shock."

"You won't tell her how he looked," Noland said flatly, more a command than a question.

He shook his head. "Thanks for asking me to identify the body."

Noland toyed with a pencil. "Preliminary indications are that he died instantly."

Roy nodded. He took another sip of the coffee, tasting it for the first time. It was pretty bad and not nearly as hot as he liked. He sat the cup carefully on the chief's desk. "From head injuries?"

"No, the doctor who first saw him at the hospital said he had a stab wound that probably punctured his heart. Maybe his killer or killers thought smashing his face would make him unrecognizable."

"Which probably tells you something about their intelligence."

Noland nodded.

Roy thought of the conversation he and Betty had had with Nancy the night before. He had noticed his sister spoke of Peter in the past tense, even before they got Noland's call. "He was a good husband and father," Nancy had said, tears drifting down her cheeks. As Roy thought of his sister in her living room, reciting her husband's qualities, gently crying, he began to weep.

Noland looked away, not sure how to respond. Even though he had not known the victim, he felt moved by the family's loss, by the senseless tragedy of it. After a few moments, he wiped his eyes and cleared his throat.

"Although it's not much consolation, we'll find who did this," he said.

Roy extracted a handkerchief and wiped his eyes. He folded it carefully, letting his concentration on the task bring his emotions under control. "Who found the body?"

"A black woman," Noland said, "Hannah Green. Hannah's the closest thing to a street person in Harper. Roams around pushing a shopping cart." They sat in silence for a moment listening to the muffled sounds of the dispatcher taking calls and communicating with the patrol cars.

"Was Peter killed at the dump?"

Noland shook his head. "Turns out Hannah found your brother-in-law's body twice, Roy, today and early Sunday morning. Sunday the body was in a dumpster in the woman's neighborhood."

Roy leaned forward. "Why didn't she call you then?"

"Afraid of the police, mostly. You've got to realize we're the enemy to most of the black community, even though half our patrolmen are black. About the only time most of Harper's blacks have any contact with the police is when they're arrested." Noland started to tell Roy that he had talked to Hannah Monday but decided not to.

"So why'd she report it today?"

Noland smiled. "Superstition, I suspect. When she called, she kept babbling something about a dream she'd had that Peter figured prominently in." The odd expression on Roy's face prompted Noland to add, "You don't mind if I call your brother-in-law Peter, do you? We never met, but from the contact I've had with the family I feel I know him."

"No, no, that's all right," Roy said. "I know my sister's grateful for the concern you've shown, Chief." Roy studied his fingernails, then nervously began to chew on one. He caught himself and stopped.

"You think Peter was killed near the dumpster?"

Noland nodded. "It's not a bad neighborhood," he said, "but they're some bad elements in it." Like the Watkins brothers. Charles had stayed out of trouble since he dropped out of school, but Jesse had a growing record of scrapes with authority. The chief had learned about the brothers from Sergeant Lemon Johnson, one of Harper's black cops. Lemon was short for Lemonjello, which had a Spanish pronunciation, Lee-MON-julow. Lemon had a twin brother named Orangejello, pronounced O-RON-julow.

"I've got men checking the area now, looking for anything that might be related to the crime." As soon as he could, Noland was going to take a drive down Washington Street. Have a talk with Larraine Jackson, the grandmother Sgt. Johnson said the brothers live with.

CHAPTER 39

Emmett Watkins' three-bay garage could easily be mistaken for a barn by someone leaving Harper. Other than a small sign on the side farthest from town that read "Watkins Auto Service" and the line of to-be-serviced cars parked near the highway, there was nothing to differentiate Emmett's garage from real barns in the area. Using word-of-mouth advertising, Emmett Watkins got just enough business at the garage to support his family, an older mechanic, and his nephew, Charles "Stump" Watkins. Stump had been working in the garage since he dropped out of school. He was just starting to change the oil on a 1981 Toyota Corolla hatchback on the rack in the last bay.

"They foun' the body, Stump," Jesse said, watching his brother trying to loosen the drain plug. Stump put more pressure on the ratchet, and the bolt gave all at once.

"Shit," he said. "Shit, shit, shit." He dropped the ratchet and stared balefully at a knuckle on his right hand where blood oozed and mixed with grease and oil. He turned the same look on his brother.

"Why're you grinnin', Jesse?" he demanded. "I just knocked the crap outta my han', and you telling me they foun' the body and you stand there with a stupid grin on your face? You fuckin' crazy."

Jesse's grin broadened, almost including his eyes. "Thanks, Bro," he said, and he meant it.

"Hi, Jesse," Emmett said. Concentrating on each other, neither brother had heard his approach. They exchanged guilty looks.

"Hi, Uncle Emmett," Jesse said.

"How you comin' on that car, Stump?" Emmett asked.

"Fixin' to drain the oil."

"You need to be finished by 5," his uncle said.

"Yeah, I remember." Stump pushed a pan on a tall stand under the car and loosened the drain plug all the way. Oil as black as tar and almost as thick spilled into the pan. Stump stepped back, wiping his hands again on the oily rag. For a moment, the three stood staring at the gushing oil as though mesmerized by it.

"Did I hear you say somethin' 'bout a body, Jesse?"

Jesse grinned, and Stump was afraid of what he might say next. "That guy from the college they been lookin' for," he said, before Jesse could answer. When his uncle looked blank, he added, "That black cop Lemonjello come 'round here tryin' to get us to help look."

"Oh, yeah, I remember. Where'd they find him?"

"At the dump," Jesse said.

"Hmmmm," said Emmett, clearly not interested in further details. "Jesse, you let your brother get on with his work."

"Just another couple of minutes, and I be gone," Jesse said. "The oil's gotta drain anyway."

Their uncle hesitated a few seconds, looking from one brother to the other, the one grinning like a Cheshire cat while the other grimaced as he wiped his hands with an oily rag. "See you boys later, then," their uncle said. He left.

"Where'd you hear about 'em findin' the man?" Stump asked when he was sure their uncle was out of earshot.

"On the radio." Jesse had been listening to his favorite station when the DJ broke in with the announcement. Pissed him off.

"They say who foun' the body?"

"Hannah Green, the old lady with the cart who rattles aroun' in our neighborhood."

"What else they say on the radio, Jesse?"

"That the police didn't have any leads."

"Man, I'm glad to hear that," Stump said. "I jus' hope it's true. What'd you do today anyway?" Stump asked, wiping his hands again. That was the thing he hated about this job; he could never get his hands completely clean. No matter how much time he spent scrubbing them with Lava soap, there was always some remaining black in the creases of his knuckles and under his fingernails. The ooze of blood had stopped.

"Went to school, jus' like I always do," Jesse told him around the cigarette he was lighting. "Then hid under the bleachers all day." He blew a perfect smoke ring and then followed it with another.

"You talk to anybody?" The oil had slowed to a trickle, and Stump wiped the threads before starting to screw the drain plug back in. He tightened it with a couple turns of the ratchet, then moved the oil drain pan away from the car.

"Brad." Jesse said, wafting another set of rings in his brother's direction.

Stump nailed him with a look. "You tell him anythin'?"

"Naw," Jesse said, hesitating an instant too long and grinning a tad too broadly.

"Lying sonofabitch," Stump said, grabbing the back of his brother's neck. Jesse squirmed, but he was trapped. "What'd you tell him?"

"Nothin', Stump," Jesse said. "I swear it. You're hurtin' my neck."

"I'm gonna do worse than that if you don't tell me the truth, Jesse." Stump gave his brother the look he reserved for opposing linemen when he was trying to intimidate them before a play. Stump increased the pressure on Jesse's neck.

"He guessed it," Jesse said, tears starting to his eyes. Stump eased the pressure.

"And you tole him everythin', I suppose."

"Just that I stuck the guy, Stump, thass all. And I didn't mention your name, honest."

Stump wasn't sure he believed his brother, but he freed him. He pulled a lever, and the car started to descend. "And what you gonna do if he starts tellin' all his friends or the po-lice?"

"First of all," Jesse said, taking another drag on his cigarette, "I'm the only frien' he's got."

"With friends like you, who needs enemies," Stump thought, but he didn't say it. Just kept his opposing-lineman stare focused. With a finishing hiss, the rack settled to the floor.

"An' he ain't goin' to the po-lice, Stump," Jesse babbled, little puffs of smoke accompanying each word.

"And why not?" Bending over the car's engine, Stump wrapped his hand around the oil filter. Pretending it was his brother's skinny neck, he started unscrewing it.

"He's plannin' to off his whole family with some poison he stole from chemistry lab."

"And when did Brad steal the poison?" At the end of the threads, Stump held his oil rag under the filter that he inverted to keep from dumping any remaining oil onto the garage's floor. His uncle liked to keep his garage as clean as possible.

"Durin' the fire alarm." Jesse dropped his cigarette on the floor and crushed it underfoot.

"Pick that up and put it in the trash barrel, Jesse." As his brother was bending over, Stump said: "Did you have anythin' to do with the fire alarm?"

Again the hesitation, the quick grin, and Stump pictured his brother breaking the glass and pulling the lever. A chill passed over him then, and he felt his scrotum shrivel, and he knew it was just a matter of time before Jesse did something so stupid the police would come pounding on their door. Numbly, Stump began to screw on the new filter.

CHAPTER 40

Roy entered, walked straight to his sister, and held her. Just for an instant he had seen the question in her eyes. Was it really Peter, she had been about to ask, still hoping when hope was gone. His action gave her the answer.

"How did he look?" Nancy asked, when all were seated in the living room.

"Pretty bad, Nance," Roy admitted, "but it wasn't really Peter in there. I mean, it was his body all right, but the real Peter, the Peter we knew and loved, was gone."

"Do you think he suffered, Roy?" Betty asked.

"I'm sure he didn't. Chief Noland said he died instantly from a stab wound to the heart."

Nancy nodded, as though the thought of her husband's instant death made the whole thing more palatable. "Thank God for that."

"Thank God for that?" Danny echoed. "How can you say that, Mom? I mean, God let Dad be killed, and you're grateful it was quick?" He stood, angrily rubbing his eyes, then started for his room.

"Danny," Nancy called, and started to rise, but her sister-in-law stopped her with a touch on the arm.

"Let him go, Nancy," she said. "He's got to work through this just like we all do."

The front doorbell rang. "I'll get it," Betty said, already on her way.

The phone rang, and Nancy rose, weary already. "Ghouls," she said.

Roy stood and hugged his sister again. "Just remember they're hurting too, Nancy. They want to help, to say anything to make it better, but there's nothing that'll do that." Only time, he thought, watching his sister walk to the phone in the kitchen. Time and the arrest of the scum that killed Peter.

CHAPTER 41

B rad had tossed and turned all night, alternately sweating and freezing. Although he tried to convince himself that he was physically ill, in his heart of hearts he knew it wasn't true. Lurking behind every normal thought that he tried to force through his consciousness was another, the certainty that he had lost control of his thoughts. The feeling of loss of control was scarier even than some of the thoughts that proved it.

So Brad had lain in bed, heart hammering, thoughts racing along two paths he found equally disturbing. Over and over, he saw Jesse stabbing Dr. Dewberry. Sometimes Stump was in the picture, and sometimes he wasn't. At times Dr. Dewberry's face quivered and dissolved and became that of Brad's father. Brad felt like crying when this happened.

When he wasn't obsessing about Peter Dewberry's murder, Brad's thoughts centered on the white powder in the gum package in his pocket. Sometimes he thought of replacing the poison or throwing it away. He would flush it down the toilet, and only Jesse would ever know he had taken it. But other times he saw himself putting the powder in something his family would eat. He saw his father puking until there was nothing left to puke, the toilet water stained red with blood when he tried to disgorge his stomach. Thoughts like this almost sent him into his parents' bedroom to awaken them, to tell them everything, to beg them to take him somewhere he could be locked away, where they would be safe from him, and he would be protected from his thoughts. Maybe there was something he could take that would purge him of his insanity. And thinking this, he would know what it was—the arsenic!

Morning had finally come, and Brad had dragged himself out of bed. It was all he could do to eat a bowl of cereal, and his mother fretted that he was getting so thin, and why did he have such dark circles under his eyes? Wasn't he getting enough sleep? Glancing up from the paper, his father had said that maybe he was getting too much sleep, and Brad had fled into the bathroom, away from the rationality and sanity of his family. There he held his face under the tap and ran cold water into his eyes to try to wash away the gritty feeling. When Sandy knocked on the door, Brad dried his eyes, combed his hair, and surprised his sister by leaving before she even had a chance to complain to their mother. In fact, she was so startled that she said "Thanks" with a quizzical look. Unsarcastically, Brad had muttered "You're welcome."

Like a zombie, Brad had sat through his first two classes, eyes boring holes through the heads of first Patsy Sartor and then Jason Moss. Now he was in biology, a course he was repeating, and things had definitely taken a turn for the worse.

The light flickered and hummed, emitting bluish rays only he could see. Mrs. Simmons' voice waxed and waned in her lecture on the feeding habits of *Drosophila*.

"When the fly encounters a *sugar* solution," she said, "*sensors* on its feet trigger it to *lower its proboscis*."

The class was a sea of bent heads, with Brad's head like the prow of a ship above water. Fascinated, he stared at the giant fly behind the teacher. It reminded him vaguely of the creature Jeff Goldblum had become in *The Fly*.

Why couldn't Mrs. Simmons see it or smell it or hear it rustling? Or maybe she could. Maybe it was a class demonstration. The "fly" was just another student dressed up in a costume that the teacher had brought in as a visual aid. Mrs. Simmons was a good teacher, he had to admit.

And a nice lady. A sweet person. So sweet Brad saw the fly lower its proboscis toward the top of Mrs. Simmons' head. He wanted to cry out, to warn his teacher of the pale pink, sticky horror approaching her hair. Droplets of fly spittle splattered Mrs. Simmons, but she was oblivious to them.

"Distension of the fly's foregut tells it when to stop feeding," Mrs. Simmons said, as the thing behind enfolded her in its "arms."

"Mrs. Simmons," Brad whispered, mouth dry as chalk, and Brenda Furman in the desk in front of his stopped writing, turning halfway in her seat. Mrs. Simmons stopped lecturing.

"Yes, Bradley?"

The fly disappeared.

"Nothing," he said, feeling flushed and foolish. Twenty-five pairs of eyes speared him, and he could feel their pricks tingling on his face, neck, and hands. Mrs. Simmons gave him a long look, and Brad sensed her concern. She probably thought he was crazy. He *knew* he was crazy.

Heads bowed again as the teacher continued her lecture. Brad looked down at his notebook page covered with doodles, spirals, and triangles in which a single word was repeated.

"Poison."

Was that an omen? Had his unconscious made the decision for him? If he did it, when would be a good time? It couldn't be tonight. Tonight, Sandy was sleeping at a friend's house. The whole family had to be together.

He needed to put the arsenic in something they would all use if they ate a meal together.

The saltshaker? Everybody used salt but probably not enough to do the trick. What about in the milk? That wouldn't work, because sometimes his father drank a beer or a cold drink with his meal. Something they all used, something like ... salad dressing. That might work. His mother had fixed salads a lot lately, and the whole family used a buttermilk dressing mix she made. All he had to do was empty his gum pack into the jar of dressing, shake it around until it all dissolved, and the Childers family would be history. But timing was important. He had to wait until they were all going to eat together. And have salads.

CHAPTER 42

Bone had a headache. It had started an hour earlier, around 10:00 when his boss, Wilbert Small, caught him in the produce cooler guzzling a brew.

"Goddam, Ludlow," Small had said. "I expect to catch some of the sackers in here or maybe Curly and Irene but not my produce manager."

"Sorry, Will." Bone tried to look contrite with half a buzz. He was on his fifth Bud that morning. As the manager stood in the doorway, glaring, Bone had wondered if he should finish the can he was working on.

"Did you pay for the beer?"

"Yessir," Ludlow had said, hoping Small wouldn't ask the checkers.

Muted Muzak competed with the sound of beeps from the checkers' scanners. Bone's stomach churned from the sickly sweet smell of overripe bananas. Holding his breath, he grabbed a stalk of black-speckled bananas and stuffed it into a plastic sack. He scribbled 25c on a label, stuck it on the side of the bag, and then tossed the sack onto a stack of similarly labeled fruit.

"Are these grapes seedless, Mr. Ludlow?" a tall, skinny woman in motorcycle boots asked. Bone recognized Miss Lanelle Davis. Miss Davis was on the far side of 65, but except for all her lines and wrinkles, she might have been a teenaged "old lady" to some crazed biker. Over her shoulder, Bone could see her Harley through the storefront window.

"Sure are, Miss Davis," he said. "How's life treatin' you?"

"Not bad," the woman said, selecting a stalk of grapes. She smiled at Ludlow, a sly, secret smile, and Bone remembered the stories he had heard about Miss Davis when he was in high school. She was younger then, not nearly so wrinkled, and some of the guys said she liked to make it with high school boys. Give them an around-the-world, whatever that was. If he hadn't already been screwing Vicki, he would've taken a trip with Miss Lanelle.

"You hear about that teacher over at the college, the one got killed last weekend?"

Bone had seen something about it in the paper. "Awful," he said, as Miss Lanelle moved away from the grapes. The wobbling front wheel on her cart caught his eye. He watched Miss Davis strut down the aisle, twitching her blue jean clad hips in some ghastly parody of eroticism, her old buns nonexistent.

He turned back to the banana display, intending to fill in the space he had created by replacing the nearly spoiled fruit with some green bananas from the cooler. Laughter at one of the check-out counters caught his attention, and he looked in the direction of the sound. Just above the counter, Mr. Small stood in the manager's cage, watching Bone.

Ludlow colored, dropped his gaze, and snatched a bunch of bananas from a box on the produce transport cart. He wondered if Vicki had to put up with a boss staring over her shoulder all the time.

CHAPTER 43

It had been a slack day at the insurance agency. The phone had rung a few times, and Vicki had dealt efficiently with the calls. A few people had stopped by to drop off payments, but Vicki had spent much of the morning staring out the window at the highway in front of the office, hoping to see Mr. Childers' (Hal's) car. He had left early for some meetings with clients on campus.

Vicki wondered if she should tell him again how much she had enjoyed their lunch together Tuesday. Maybe he would think she was fishing for another invitation. But she did want another invitation, didn't she? And hadn't she thought of what they might have done there at the motel after lunch?

When she thought of *that*, Vicki pictured Hal doing the things Bone had done before she let him "go all the way." She saw her employer holding her, caressing her cheek, telling her how nice she smelled, whispering "sweet nothings" in her ear. She saw them making love, not having sex. Her years of marriage to Bone had convinced her that love and sex were not synonymous. She was enough of a romantic to believe that Hal knew the difference.

Hal pulled in at 11:30, parking in the back, so all the places in front would be for customers. Vicki gave him a radiant smile when he appeared at the door separating his office from her work area. He had taken off his suit coat, and she could see damp circles under his arms.

"Pretty busy this morning?" he asked.

"It's been about like this," she said. "How did it go out at the college?"

"Pretty good," he said. "This thing with Dr. Dewberry has gotten some of the professors out there thinking life insurance, and that's bound to be good for business." Hal slouched on a cheap sofa across from Vicki's desk. Its cushions were covered in material sporting large brown, orange, and yellow imitations of sunflowers. Hal loosened his tie and yawned.

"Speaking of Dr. Dewberry, did you remember that he had a life insurance policy with us? You said something about calling his wife this afternoon."

"You think it's too soon? Maybe I should wait until after the funeral." Hal sat up and tightened his tie. A car had pulled into one of the spaces in front of the office.

"That would probably be best," Vicki said, watching an elderly man get out of the car and walk around to open his wife's door. She found that so touching she almost felt like crying. "I'll put it on your calendar for Monday. The paper said he'll be buried Friday." Vicki pushed her chair back and stood, smoothing down her skirt with a reflexive motion. Hal went into his office. She walked to the front door and opened it for the couple making their agonizingly slow way up the brick steps. They reminded her of her grandparents, the man with a full head of white hair and a dowager's hump, the woman slender and fragile. Again, she had an urge to cry.

"Come in, Mr. and Mrs. Parkhurst," she said, smiling. She felt the contrast between the coolness of the air-conditioned interior and the heat outside.

"It's so hot out there," Mr. Parkhurst said, stepping gratefully and gingerly over the threshold.

"But it's cool in here," his wife added.

CHAPTER 44

Noland knocked on the screen door. From just inside he could hear a television set. Its light flickered bluely in the darkened room. Springs creaked as something huge rose from a sofa facing the flickering screen. Noland listened to the slap-slap of slippers on a bare floor. A large black woman filled the door.

"Yeah?"

"Grady Noland, Chief of Police," he said, holding out his badge.

"So?"

So this is going to be tough, he thought. "Are you Mrs. Larraine Jackson?"

On the other side of the screen, the woman nodded.

"Charles and Jesse Watkins' grandmother?" Another nod.

"Are either of the boys here, Mrs. Jackson?"

"Nope," she said, folding her arms across her enormous bosom. Signaling rejection. She reminded Noland of an older Ida Ivory.

"May I come in? I just want to ask you a few questions."

"About what?" Larraine opened the door, allowing Noland to enter.

"About something that happened Saturday night." Larraine flopped onto the couch, pulled her shift over knees too plump to stay together, fixed a wary eye on Noland. Reflections from the TV moved over her face. Noland sat gingerly on a Naugahyde-covered recliner. The house smelled of salt pork and cabbage. A small fan buzzed on a table next to the sofa. None of its breeze reached Noland who felt a trickle of sweat start down his back.

"Where were your grandsons Saturday night around midnight?"

"Both here, as far as I know." Larraine looked away from Noland. Something on TV was more interesting.

"Jesse's the youngest?"

Larraine nodded.

"Is he in school today?"

"Far as I know," she said, her voice expressionless. Noland had learned from the high school principal that Jesse hadn't been in school all week.

Noland watched Larraine closely. Time to spring his big question. "Mrs. Jackson, did Jesse bring home a bicycle from school about a week ago?"

No reaction. Larraine Jackson shook her head.

"I can check with your neighbors," he said.

"Check all you want," the woman said, her eyes glued to the TV. "Jesse ain't foun' no bicycle."

"Looks like another blind alley," Noland muttered to himself, pulling away from the house. He was sure he would have gotten some reaction if Jesse had brought home a bicycle.

CHAPTER 45

Ronny had watched the bicycle from his classes all day. He could see it just outside the window of his last-period government class, parked in the rack's last slot. Unlocked, dirty, abandoned—Ronny wanted it.

Ronny Gadsden wanted a lot of things he would never have. Like a house he wouldn't feel ashamed to bring a friend to visit. Or, better yet, a friend.

"Gadsden, you 'bout through with that test?" Mrs. Kopecky stood over him, frowning.

"Yes'm," he said, marking several answers randomly. His teacher moved away, and Ronny sneaked a look out the window again. The bicycle hadn't moved. Maybe he would take it home. But what would he tell his mother?

"I found it by the side of the road, Mom," he might say. If he were lucky, she would be so preoccupied with his father's latest medical crisis that she wouldn't give his explanation any thought.

Ronny's feelings for his father were mixed. He was disgusted by his father's helplessness, angry that his father was so sick he couldn't work, and ashamed of his own lack of sympathy. Why doesn't he go ahead and croak, Ronny thought sometimes, particularly after his father had kept him awake all night with his coughing and choking.

How old was his dad anyway? 48? How could he be dying of congestive heart failure at 48 when he didn't even smoke? A congenital defect, his mother had told him, as though that meant something. Like, was it inherited? He sure hoped not, but if it was inherited maybe his brother would get it and not him.

He hated his brother. How could the little geek sit on the bed beside their father all the time, reading to him, emptying his bedpan, helping him with the oxygen mask? Was it Ronny's fault that the sickroom smells made him want to vomit?

But he would soon have something his brother didn't have. A 10-speed bike. Ronny looked out the window again as the 3:00 bell rang and kids bolted out a side door, blocking his view of his bike.

"Turn in those papers," Mrs. Kopecky yelled over the general din of desks moving, backpacks being zipped, and students talking.

Ronny threw his paper onto the teacher's desk and reached the hall in three strides. He weaved his way around clots of milling kids, dodged outstretched arms reaching into opened lockers, and burst through the side door nearest his sixth-period class.

To find? "His" bicycle gone! Stolen!

———— ◈ ————

Unknown to Ronny, someone else had spotted the bicycle that day, its rightful owner, Danny Dewberry. As soon as he saw that the bike was back in the rack, Danny had asked the teacher to be excused. At the moment Ronny burst out the side door, Danny was halfway home on his bike.

Unfortunately, he was not allowed to keep it. When he showed it to his mother, she called Chief Noland and told him about the bike.

"That's great, Nancy," Grady said. "I'll send someone to pick it up so we can check it for fingerprints. Tell Danny he'll just have to wait a bit longer to have his bike back for good."

CHAPTER 46

Except for revivals and Easter Sundays, the sanctuary of Oakwood Baptist was as full as Noland had ever seen it. Chairs lined the raised platform to the right of the pulpit, and Noland, one of the first panelists to arrive, perched on one as though poised for flight. He felt terribly self-conscious at the front of the church, while the man to his left, Reverend Benny Conklin, appeared as cool as a rock in a mountain stream.

"Good turnout," Conklin said to Noland, his voice steady, his breath Binaca fresh.

Noland nodded, remembering the minister's earlier call. "There are all kinds of wild rumors going around, Grady," he had told the chief, "and a town hall meeting will help us clear the air in Harper. We can have it at the church."

"You think anybody will come?"

"I'll spread the word, Chief. We'll fill the sanctuary."

The minister had certainly kept his promise. Mayor Homer Wainwright eased his bulk into the next seat and effusively greeted the college president, Dr. Duane Glover, on his right, before reaching across to shake the chief's hand.

"How're you doin', Grady?" the mayor said. His bald head gleamed as though he had polished it before coming.

"Just fine, Mayor," Noland said, recoiling slightly. The mayor's breath was redolent of garlic and oregano. The chief mopped his brow with a limp handkerchief. Marge smiled encouragingly from the front pew, while their son concentrated on the book he had brought.

The mayor leaned across Noland to greet the minister. The chair beyond Conklin was still empty, reserved for one of Harper's black leaders, Dr. Anthony Griffin. Dr. Griffin was a general practitioner whose payment from Medicare alone was more than three times Noland's salary. The doctor drove a new Cadillac with a personalized license plate that read "MED 1."

Wainwright leaned across Noland again, and the chief toyed with the idea of swapping seats with the mayor. "Should we go ahead and start without Dr. Griffin?" the mayor asked.

Brother Conklin shook his head. "He said he would be here, and we definitely need his presence on our panel."

Wainwright settled back as several black people came through the rear doors, Dr. Griffin leading the pack. The doctor continued as one by one his retinue found seats in the pews. The physician shook hands with Brother Conklin, spoke to the mayor and to Dr. Glover, and nodded at Noland before taking his seat.

Brother Conklin stood and strode confidently to the pulpit. "May I have your attention, please?" Without amplification, his voice easily filled the room. The minister thanked the people for coming and then began the session with a short prayer. When this was over, he came straight to the point.

"Last Saturday night, Dr. Peter Dewberry took his dog for a walk. Dr. Dewberry never came home. Yesterday his brutally abused body was found at the city dump. I think it's fair to say that this murder has shocked and outraged our community." There were murmurs of assent and nods from the crowd.

The reverend continued. "My purpose in calling this meeting is to discuss this event rationally, factually, and to try to clear up some of the misconceptions I know are troubling our community. Our panel consists of myself, President Duane Glover, Mayor Homer Wainwright, Police Chief Grady Noland, and Dr. Anthony Griffin." Each man nodded as his name was called. "Robin Grant, principal of Harper High School, is unable to attend the meeting.

"Now I know there are lots of rumors about this murder. I think that's to be expected in a small town. I'll begin with a question to Chief Noland." Noland's heart rate immediately doubled. "Was Dr. Dewberry associated with the police force in any way?"

Noland cleared his throat. "I've heard that rumor," he said, aiming his response at the minister, "and there's no truth to it."

A hand went up, and the minister nodded to a large, red-faced man in his mid-30s. The man stood.

"Is it possible that Dr. Dewberry was an undercover narcotics agent, working for the FBI or something?" The man sat down.

Noland saw several people nod, and he caught whispered phrases like "yeah, a pusher" and "big drug buy" and "dope peddler." He thought about saying "anything's possible" but decided against it.

"Peter... I mean Dr. Dewberry... was not a policeman or an undercover agent or a drug pusher or a drug user. To the best of my knowledge, he was a credit to Harper and to the college, where he was employed."

"I'll second that," Dr. Glover said.

"May I say something?" Dr. Griffin asked.

"Of course," the minister said.

The doctor stood in front of his chair. As always, Noland was impressed with the man's quiet dignity, due, in part, to his appearance. He was tall and slender, and something about the way he carried himself always reminded Noland of Sidney Poitier, the actor. Dr. Griffin's close-cropped hair had just a touch of gray at the temples. He spoke with that quiet assurance often found in successful members of the medical profession.

"Several of my patients today expressed concern that this terrible crime would lead to a return of the kind of racial tension Harper hasn't had for several years." Noland saw the nods and heard the sounds of agreement. "My question for the chief is whether or not this murder was racially motivated." The doctor sat down.

Before Noland could reply, the mayor spoke. "During my administration, Harper has been exemplary in race relations, and we don't need any outside agitators stirring things up at this time."

There was a clamor from the audience as several people tried to speak at once. Noland stood. He felt slightly queasy.

"I would like to answer the doctor's question," he said, speaking louder than normal to be heard over the din. He paused, and in a few moments the audience fell silent. "As far as we know at the present time, there's no evidence that Dr. Dewberry's murder was racially motivated." They didn't even have any suspects, black or white. Noland sat down.

"Helen," the minister said, recognizing a well-dressed woman near the front. Noland recognized her, too: Helen Borden, reporter for the *Harper Daily News.* Helen was in her late 50s, and her coal black hair (chemically refreshed, Marge later told him) and unwrinkled skin gave her a youthful appearance. A wart on her upper lip spoiled her looks, and Noland had often wondered why she didn't have it removed.

"I don't really have a question," she began in a soft voice. "I just ..."

"Speak up," someone yelled from the back. "We can't hear you."

"Uhhh, I don't have a question," she repeated, louder this time. "What I want to say is I feel there's been a loss of innocence in our town, if you know what I mean."

"That's right," an elderly woman said, and Noland saw Marge nodding. There were other signs of agreement.

"One of the advantages of living in a town like Harper is that there's not much crime," Helen continued. "I've always felt safe living here. You don't have to worry about locking your doors or being mugged or things like that. At least you didn't have to worry about such things before this happened." She paused, smiling ruefully. "That's what I meant about a loss of innocence. I guess the danger was always there; it just took something like this to make us aware of it."

"Like Paul Harvey says, 'You can run, but you can't hide,'" the mayor blurted out.

"Now, hold on a minute," Noland said, rising again. "As terrible as this is, I don't think you should blow it out of proportion. We've still got a safe town here, folks. It's not perfect, that's true, but it's not Chicago or L.A. or Detroit, either." To a chorus of "Amen," and "Right on, Chief," Noland sat down.

Behind Marge, Leslie Pang stood. Ramrod stiff, Pang wore a khaki shirt and trousers that just missed being a military uniform. On the right lapel, he sported an American flag pin, while a stars-and-bars pin graced the left. A soft khaki cap adorned with another flag pin covered his crewcut. Pang drove a shiny black Oldsmobile adorned with bumper stickers that read, "The South Shall Rise Again," "America, Love It or Leave It," and "God, Guns, and Guts Made America Free." Pang frightened Noland.

"I know we've got to kowtow to the darker element in our town," Pang said in his peculiarly high-pitched voice, looking pointedly at Dr. Griffin, "but I think what we've got here is an example of what happens when you try to mix the races."

All around Pang there came the sounds of disagreement and derision, and several of the panel members tried to speak at once. "Ridiculous," said one, and "The man's insane," said another.

"Thank God there's no support for your position, Mr. Pang," Brother Conklin said, but Noland wasn't sure there weren't some who agreed with Pang. Mickey Ludlow came to mind.

"You did a good job, Grady," the mayor said when the meeting was over, and there were just a few groups of people still standing around.

"Thanks, Mr. Mayor," he said, greatly relieved it was over. Marge stood at his side with Grady Jr. tugging his trousers. "I think once we lock away whoever did this, people will realize things are no different than they've ever been." Of course, for Nancy and Danny Dewberry things would never again be the same.

CHAPTER 47

He could see the looks, the expression changes as he walked by. They all knew. It was as though Mr. Grant, the principal, had announced over the loudspeaker: "Danny Dewberry's father has just been killed. Let's let him know how we feel."

It was obvious how they felt. Shocked. Stunned. Curious. He could see it on the averted faces, hear it in the whispers behind his back. Sometimes curiosity won, and someone made contact.

"Hi, Dan, sorry to hear about your dad," Cheryl Dawkins said, her features expressing just the right amount of concern.

Danny was surprised when Cheryl spoke, as she'd never spoken to him before, and he didn't even think she knew his name. Cheryl was in the drama club and aspired to be an actress, and Danny could imagine her practicing her sorrow face in front of a mirror until she had it just right. He nodded, twitching his lips in what he hoped passed for a brave smile. Cheryl dropped back, rejoining her friends. Danny passed through the milling students like a drop of oil through water.

"You don't have to go to school today," his mother had told him, but he had wanted to go. School was better than home and the incessant phone calls and visitors. At least here at school the sympathizers were mostly his age. At home they were all adults.

Danny dreaded the funeral. He would have to dress in some monkey suit to hang around awkwardly and be hugged by relatives and his parents' friends. Why had his father gone and gotten himself killed anyway? What an awful thought that was.

Danny slipped through the bathroom door, nearly colliding with an older student on his way out.

"Watch where you're goin', fella," the youth said.

"'Scuse me," Danny muttered into his shirt collar. He reflexively squinted at the glare of the fluorescent lights on floor-to-ceiling white tile. Keeping his head down, Danny walked to the urinal, where he stopped, unzipped, and aimed a stream at a soggy butt. Next to him, a slender kid unsheathed a dong that seemed twice the size of Danny's. Danny finished, zipped up, and took a step back, his right heel mashing someone's toes.

"Clumsy fuck," a voice behind him said, and the voice's owner gave him a shove. Danny sprawled against the kid next to him, jamming him against the porcelain back of the urinal.

"Sheeit," the boy said, whirling.

Danny noticed four things at once about the kid he had accidentally pushed into the urinal: His jeans were wet, he wore thick glasses, he was grinning; and ...

"Where'd you get those shoes?"

Jesse, about to attack the sonofabitch who shoved him, froze at the question.

"Those are my father's shoes," Danny shouted, tears streaming down his cheeks.

Jesse looked down at the shoes and thought about how mad Stump would be at him for wearing them. "They're just Nikes," he said, suddenly on the defensive. "Anybody can have Nikes."

"Not Nikes with a spot of blue paint on them," Danny cried. He could see his father smearing the blue spot with turpentine, berating himself for wearing his new shoes to paint. Behind Danny, a crowd was growing. The bathroom was silent except for his shouting and the other boy's heavy breathing.

"Fight," somebody whispered, and the word was repeated over and over until it was out the door and into the hall. A passing girl heard the word and ran for the office.

"You fuckin' crazy," Jesse said, in the unusual position of trying to defuse a fight before it got started. How would he ever be able to tell his father he had gotten suspended again on his first day back? And how could he get this kid to stop carrying on about the shoes? "These ain't yore ole man's shoes. I got this spot on 'em today in Art." Jesse was proud of himself for coming up with this lie, because he had never gone near an art class.

"You killed him," Danny yelled, charging.

Jesse fell back against the urinal, then reflexively shoved Danny away. "Keep him the fuck off me," he yelled to several boys Danny fell against. In response, they pushed Danny back toward him.

Jesse had to get out. If he stayed in the bathroom with this wild-assed kid, they would both be sent to the office, and Mr. Grant would kick him out again, this time calling his father first. Worse, they might check on the shoes and have some way to know that they'd belonged to the guy he and Stump killed. He sidestepped Danny's charge, tripping him neatly with one of the Nikes. With Danny on the floor and for the moment just bawling, Jesse pulled his knife, whipped open the blade, and swished it at arm's length at the gawkers.

"Outta my way," he yelled. The crowd parted, some scrambling out the bathroom door, while others less lucky sought refuge in the stalls. "Goddam," Jesse thought. "I'm actually gonna get out of this." Without breaking stride, he brushed the blade closed against his pants leg and slipped the knife back into his hip pocket. He hit the door on the run. Expecting resistance, he was surprised when the door to the hall opened abruptly. Off balance, he tumbled onto the cold tiles and found himself looking up at Mr. Packard. Standing behind Packard was Mr. Grant.

CHAPTER 48

Noland put down the autopsy report. Peter had died instantly from a stab wound to the heart. Person or persons unknown had then used a brick on his face, and fragments were still embedded in the burned flesh. Both the beating and the burning were probably attempts to prevent recognition of the body. His phone rang, and he picked up.

"I've got a call here from Mr. Grant at the high school you might want to take, Chief," Sheritha said. "Danny Dewberry's in the office claiming a kid has on his father's shoes."

Noland leaned forward, his heartrate accelerating. "Put 'em on," he said.

There was a moment's pause, and then Noland heard the mellifluous tones of Robin Grant, principal of Harper High School. He could picture the man: large, florid face, pencil mustache, squinty eyes, usually smiling. "Is that you, Grady?"

"Yessir," he said.

"How's life treating you, Grady?"

"Just fine, Robin. Sheritha said something about Danny Dewberry."

"That's right, Grady," Grant said, and Noland remembered one of the things he didn't like about the man: Robin Grant used his name in nearly every sentence. "Danny attacked a kid in the bathroom he said was wearing the shoes his father had on the night he was killed."

"Now hold on, Grady," Noland told himself. "This kid might have found the shoes or Danny might be mistaken." Or the kid might be Peter's murderer. "What's his name?" he asked Grant.

"Jesse Watkins, Grady," Grant said, "and he's a bad apple from the word go. Today was his first day back at school after he got suspended for attacking an older boy in the hall with a knife."

"You say he used a knife in the first attack?"

"Sure did, Grady, and I've got it right here in my desk. Took it away from him Monday, but he had a new one on him today."

"Don't let Watkins out of your sight, Robin. I'll send someone to get him and the knife. Send Danny home, but tell him I'll try to get by to talk to him this evening."

<hr>

"You read him his rights?" Noland asked the patrolman who'd brought Jesse to the station. Sgt. Lemon Johnson nodded.

"He say anything on the ride over?"

"Naw, Chief. The kid just sat in the back seat grinning. That's one weird dude."

Noland stepped through the door into the tiny interrogation room. There were two chairs in the room, one on either side of a well-worn table. A slender youth with feral features sat in one of the chairs, leaning it back against the wall; Noland eased himself into the other. He studied Jesse for a moment and realized he recognized the boy from previous scrapes with the law. He turned his attention to the boy's school record.

Noland learned that Jesse was nearly 18 (he looked younger), in the 11th grade (he'd failed once), and had received at least five 3-day suspensions each of his last 3 years in school. Most of his trouble had come from fighting, although vandalism and smoking at school were mentioned.

Noland closed the folder, then leaned back in his chair, steepling his fingers in front of his mouth. He didn't say anything, just stared at Jesse. Is this the new breed of killer, he wondered? Jesse didn't seem hostile. The boy returned Noland's stare with a grin; thick glasses magnified his eyes, making him look vulnerable.

"Do you want a lawyer?"

"Naw," Jesse said.

"Do you know who I am?"

Jesse shrugged. "Some kinda cop."

"That's right. I'm Chief of Police here in Harper. Grady Noland." Noland held his identification where Jesse could see it, but the boy plainly wasn't interested. "Wanna tell me what happened at the high school today?"

"Not really."

"Let me rephrase that, Jesse. Tell me what happened at school that got you sent here." That's right, Grady, he told himself. Show him the brass knuckles in the glove.

"I was takin' a leak when some guy I never seen before knocked me into the john. I wasn't lookin' for trouble, with it being my first day back at school and all."

"So what happened, Jesse?"

Jesse shrugged. "Kid kept chargin' at me, and somebody said 'fight,' and I ran out of the bathroom to get away from the crazy kid. Mr. Grant was out there, and he thought I been fightin' again, I guess."

"I see. So it really wasn't your fault at all. You were just trying to get away from Danny."

"Who?"

"Danny Dewberry, the boy who kept trying to pick a fight with you."

"Thass it," Jesse said. "I was just tryin' to get away from Danny. Can I go now?"

"Not just yet, Jesse. We've called your father, and he'll be here shortly."

Jesse's grin departed at this news. "Oh, shit, my old man'll have a shit fit for sure."

"Did Danny say anything before he charged you?"

Jesse blinked at this question, and a sly smile crept over his fox-like features. "Naw," he said, after a slight hesitation.

"That's not what the principal says, Jesse."

"He might've said something, man, but I couldn't make it out."

"Could Danny have been saying something about you stealing his bicycle?"

The front legs of Jesse's chair hit the floor with a clatter. "Paydirt," Noland thought. "He thought I was gonna ask about the shoes.

"Bicycle? I don't remember him saying nothin' 'bout a bike." Jesse's forehead was damp, although the room was cool.

"You didn't happen to take a bike home from school recently that didn't belong to you, did you?"

"Naw," Jesse said.

"I can ask your father, Jesse," Noland said. He had noted Jesse's response when he said he'd been called.

"Maybe I did find a bike at school, but that kid never said nothin' 'bout no bike."

"Where's the bike now, Jesse?"

"I took it back."

The grin was back. Time to knock it off. Noland pushed his chair back until he could see under the table. "Those are nice shoes, Jesse. Where'd you get 'em?"

"I foun' 'em," Jesse said. "In the dumpster back of the shoppin' center near my house."

"Mighty nice shoes for someone to just throw away, don't you think?"

"I guess so," Jesse admitted. "Man, is it hot in here."

"We're just about through, Jesse," Noland said. "I've just got a couple more questions." There was a discreet knock on the door, and Noland felt like chewing out whoever it was interrupting him. He was certain that Jesse was about to crack. He smiled at Jesse. "Be back in a second," he said, and then he snatched open the door and squeezed through it before anyone could enter. The anyone turned out to be Detective Buster Mixon.

"You better have a good reason for interrupting me, Mixon," he said softly. The younger man's insolent grin disappeared.

"Uh, just wanted to tell you the boy's father is here, and he's hoppin' mad. Wants to know what Jesse's been up to this time. He smells like he's about half potted, Chief."

"Hmmm. So, he's not talking about getting Jesse out of here, then."

"Hell, no. If anything, I think he would be glad for us to just keep Jesse here permanently."

Noland smiled. That was good news. "Get him some coffee or a cold drink, Mixon, and tell him I'll be out to talk to him in a few minutes." He squeezed back through the door.

"Is my ole man here?" Jesse asked before Noland sat down.

Noland nodded, and Jesse paled. "He seems pretty mad, Jesse. Do you want to spend the night here, so maybe he'll have time to cool off? I'll tell him you pulled a knife during a fight at school, and we want to ask you more questions tomorrow. How does that sound?"

"Yeah, that would be great," Jesse said—so eagerly that Noland almost felt sorry for the boy. Almost.

"One more question, Jesse: Did Danny say anything about the shoes when y'all were in the bathroom? Like they were his father's or something?"

"I don' remember." Jesse seemed to shrink, to pull into himself.

"There were several witnesses, Jesse. I suspect they heard what Danny said. Besides, Danny'll remember."

"He mighta said somethin' like that."

"Did you hear about Peter Dewberry, the man who was murdered last weekend?"

Jesse stared at his shoes. Noland felt he could almost read the boy's thoughts. At the moment he was probably thinking how stupid it was to be wearing something belonging to a man he'd killed.

Jesse shrugged. "I heard somethin' about it. Not much."

"Peter was Danny's father."

"So?"

"So, what were you doing last Saturday night?"

Jesse squirmed in his chair. "Gotta take a leak."

"Answer the question."

"I ain't sayin' nothin' else," Jesse said, standing.

Ah, but you will, Noland thought, closing the door behind him. A little more pressure and Jesse Watkins would crack like an egg.

CHAPTER 49

Stump stared at the building, trying to screw up his courage to go in. Even now it might be too late. Jesse might have spilled his guts already. But if he hadn't, Stump would lean on him, tell him to keep his mouth shut, or else. Buy himself a little time. Earlier, his uncle had told him about Jesse's latest trouble.

"You hear about Jesse?" his uncle said, and Stump had taken the wheel off and rolled it to the back of the car. For a moment, he hoped his uncle was going to tell him that Jesse had gotten killed. Struck by lightning. Run over crossing a street. Stabbed in a knife fight. Shot. Anything that would silence his little brother forever.

"What about him?"

"They got him down to the police station."

"Oh yeah?" Stump said, pretending he didn't care. He lifted the back wheel he'd already brought to the front of the car and, grunting slightly, mounted it. "What'd he do this time?"

"Got in a fight at school is what I heard. Your old man's fit to be tied."

Stump started screwing the lug nuts on. "So, why've they got him at the police station if he jus' got in a fight at school?"

His uncle hadn't been able to answer that question, but the answer was obvious to Stump. The police suspected Jesse of something far worse than just fighting at school. But what was there to tie him to Peter Dewberry's murder? He had to know, and he had to know before Jesse ratted him out.

Although Stump had been a big man at Harper High, he knew he wouldn't be so big in prison. He was old enough to be tried and sentenced as an adult, but young enough to be "fresh meat" to old cons. And a gang rape in the shower was something he wanted to avoid in the worst way.

So, Stump Watkins was planning to run if it looked like Jesse was going to give it all away. But he had to be sure, and to be sure he had to enter the lion's den. He stepped off the curb and crossed the street.

Stump had picked a good time to visit the police station. Friday night after 10, almost everyone on duty was out on patrol. Maximum visibility, it was called. Keep the high school and college kids under control. Corporal Brian Jones, the dispatcher, looked up from his magazine when Stump walked through the outer doors. Cpl. Jones had graduated from Harper High a couple of years ago, and Stump knew him to speak to.

"Hey, Stump," Jones said.

"Hey, Brian," Stump said. "You got my brother in here?"

"Hell if I know. Lemme see." He picked up a phone and punched two numbers. "Jerry, you awake back there?" There was a pause, and Jones laughed at Samuels' response. "You keepin' Jesse Watkins outta mischief?" There was a longer pause when Jones glanced at Stump from time to time. Stump tightened his fists and tensed, ready to run.

Jones replaced the phone, carefully. Smiling, he said, "You can go on back. Samuels will let you in."

"Thanks." Stump started down the hall leading to the lockup. He knew his way around the station. Every year Coach had taken the whole team to see the jail, to show his boys where they might wind up if they didn't stay on the straight and narrow. Stump figured Coach might have been a preacher if he hadn't discovered coaching.

Jones leaned his head out the window of the dispatcher's cage. "Jesse's in a heap of trouble, Stump," he said. Stump didn't turn around.

Corporal Jerry Samuels sat at a desk to the right of a locked metal door. The door's small window had wire mesh in it. Samuels had played center for Harper High a few years and 200 pounds ago. When Stump had been in junior high, Samuels had been his idol. Now his ex-idol's sausage-shaped fingers held a huge ham sandwich. Juices from it dripped onto a paper plate. He nodded at Stump. When he spoke, his voice was distorted by the food in his mouth.

"Haven't seen you in a while. Whatcha been up to, Stump?"

"Not much," Stump said. "Tryin' to keep outta trouble. I see you're still eatin', Jerry. Keepin' your weight up?"

Samuels laughed, several chins quivering. "You wanna see Jesse?"

"Yeah, Granma wanted me to come see how he is."

"Shit, Stump," Samuels said, putting down his sandwich. He wiped his hands on a filthy blue shirt. "Jesse can't get in no trouble down here." Samuels heaved himself up, panting slightly. Stump moved back to give him room to maneuver. Samuels unlocked the outer door and motioned for Stump to follow.

"Pretty empty tonight," Stump observed as they walked past vacant cells.

"It'll fill up later," Samuels said, shuffling along. He walked on the outsides of his feet, and the heels of his shoes were worn flat there. With all the metal, the lockup was cold and damp. Underneath the strong disinfectant smell, there was a hint of vomit and urine.

At the end of the row, two cells were occupied. In the one on the right, an elderly man snored loudly. Jesse stood at the bars of the other, grinless for once.

"Step back, Jesse," Samuels wheezed, "and I'll let your brother in." Stump squeezed into the cell, and Samuels locked it behind him.

"Just call when you're done," Samuels said, and he left them alone.

Before he said anything, Stump took another look at the man sleeping in the other cell. He hadn't stirred. Stump spoke softly to his brother, although he would rather be yelling. "I oughtta beat the shit outta you, Jesse," Stump said, scowling at his brother. "Why the fuck you go and get in a fight your first day back?"

"Believe it or not, I was tryin' not to get in a fight, Stump. The kid kept chargin' me in the john. He was yellin' I killed his ole man. Kep' lookin' at the shoes."

Stump looked at Jesse's feet, saw the Nikes, and slapped his brother, all in one motion. "Stupid shit," he hissed. "I thought I told you to get rid of the shoes."

Jesse, glasses askew, started to blubber. "They were so new, Stump," he said. "I ain't had no new shoes since ninth grade."

Stump stared at his brother, clenching and releasing his fists, wanting to hit Jesse again, but fearing that if he did, he would keep hitting him until he had beaten him to a pulp. Jesse took off his glasses, folded them carefully and put them into his shirt pocket. He wiped his eyes with his palms. Watching him, Stump felt his anger evaporate. He looked over at the old man. Still sleeping soundly.

"What'd they ask you, Jesse?" he whispered.

"You know, 'bout the fight and all. Why I got in it."

"So what'd you say?"

"I said that other kid kept pushin' me into the john, that I really didn't wanna fight him."

"Anythin' else?"

"The head cop aksed 'bout the bike, if I took one home that wasn't mine."

"Jesus," Stump said. "They know about that?"

Jesse nodded miserably. His nose was running, and he wiped it with his sleeve.

"Well, give it all to me. Did the man ask 'bout the shoes, too?" Again, there was the miserable nod. Talking to his brother, Stump was beginning to wonder if they were going to let him leave the station. He could see Brian Jones calling the cop who had questioned Jesse. He had to know if Jesse had mentioned his name to the man.

"Was my name mentioned in anything you said?"

Jesse shook his head emphatically. "Naw, you're in the clear, Stump, but I think they suspec' I had somethin' to do with that guy's murder las' weekend."

"Well, I wonder what gave 'em that idea," Stump said, unable to resist the sarcasm.

Jesse gave him a quick look, and just for a moment Stump recognized the faraway look his brother had in his eyes when he stabbed the man Stump was holding. The look gave him goosebumps.

"Lots of things, I guess," Jesse said, not responding to the sarcasm. "The shoes, the bike, what more does they need? At the end, the man wanted to know what I was doin' Saturday night."

"What'd you tell him, Jesse?"

"Nothin', Stump. I didn't tell him nothin'." Jesse tried to grin to show his brother how brave he had been, but his grin was lopsided, mostly just a grotesque twitch of the right side of his face. "You think he'll aks me more questions 'bout the knife?"

"You can count on it," Stump said. "My advice is jus' keep your mouth shut, Jesse. Don' tell 'em nothin' else." He didn't think it really mattered if Jesse kept quiet or not. He was pretty sure the cops already knew, and what they didn't know, they strongly suspected. Jesse might have kept his name out of it today, but tomorrow was a different story. And that was why tomorrow would find him long gone from Harper.

CHAPTER 50

They were in the tiny room again, Jesse sitting in the chair he'd occupied the afternoon before. Breakfast had been better than his granma ever fixed, so Jesse had about decided that jail might not be too bad after all. He knew he stank, but they hadn't let him take a shower.

"Would you like a lawyer, Jesse?" Noland asked. "We can get you a court-appointed attorney at no charge to your family."

Jesse shook his head. He kept his eyes on the table edge nearest him, avoiding the looks of the two policemen.

"What about your father and grandmother? They can be here with you during questioning to provide advice."

Again, the head shake.

"Mind if we tape?" the younger cop asked. Jesse thought his name might be Buster something or other.

"No, sir." Lying awake through the long night, Jesse had decided that showing some respect might be the best game to play.

The younger cop started the recorder and spoke softly into the microphone. Jesse heard his name and the date and the names of his questioners. Mixon was the detective's last name.

"What'd you do last Saturday night?" Noland said.

"Went to bed."

"What time was that?" Mixon asked.

"'Bout 10." Jesse tried to pick his nose surreptitiously. He rolled the result between his thumb and forefinger.

"Stump with you?" Noland said.

Jesse hesitated, weighing his answer. He nodded. At the same time, he rubbed his finger on the underside of the table. He felt a hardened piece of gum.

"Ten o'clock, you say?"

"'Bout 10, yessir."

Noland nodded to Mixon. "We talked to your father yesterday evening, Jesse," the detective said. "He wasn't sure of the exact time, but he was sure you came in after midnight. He couldn't sleep because of the pain in his back."

"He's lyin'," Jesse said.

"Why would your father lie, Jesse?" Noland asked, speaking softly.

Jesse shrugged. "He never liked me." *That* was certainly true.

Noland looked at his notes. "Yesterday you said you found the shoes you're wearing. Is that right?"

Jesse nodded.

"I talked to Danny Dewberry last night, and he was certain the shoes were the ones his father was wearing when he was killed. He said he identified them by a smudge of paint, and he remembered you told him in the bathroom that you had gotten paint on them in Art. Did you tell him that?"

"I might've said that."

"You've never taken Art, Jesse."

Jesse nodded with what he hoped was an apologetic expression. His forehead felt damp, and he wanted to wipe it on his sleeve, but the cops would notice it for sure if he did that.

"So, why'd you lie to Danny?" Noland asked.

"To shut him up. Like I said yesterday, I wasn't lookin' to get in no fight."

"That makes sense," the chief said. "Where'd you find the shoes again?"

Jesse felt his heart skip a beat. He'd told so many lies recently that he couldn't remember what he'd said about the shoes. He wanted to say he'd found them in the church dumpster, but that was where he and Stump had put the body, so surely he hadn't said that yesterday.

"We're waiting, Jesse," the detective said, pressuring him.

"In the ditch back of my house," Jesse said, hoping that was right. He'd often told his father that he found things in the ditch, things he'd really stolen.

Noland looked at him sharply, and Jesse figured he'd guessed wrong. "In the dumpster at the church, I meant to say."

"Well, which is it, Jesse? Dumpster or ditch? You've got a 50-50 chance of telling the truth," Noland said.

Jesse gave up. "I don't remember what I said yesterday. All I know is I foun' 'em."

"But were they lost?" Mixon asked.

Noland leaned toward him. His breath smelled of coffee, and Jesse felt slightly nauseated. "I'm going to level with you, Jesse," the man said. "So far you've told us nothing but lies. You said you went to bed about 10, and we know that's wrong. You said yesterday you found the shoes in the dumpster, then today you tell us you found them in the ditch back of your house and then try to change that lie when you saw the way I looked at you. You told Danny you got paint on the shoes in Art when you've never taken an art course. You told me yesterday you didn't find a bicycle, but that wasn't true either. Why don't we start over and see if you can't come up with the truth this time?"

"If I tell, what's gonna' happen?"

"How old are you, Jesse? 15? 16?" said Mixon.

"17, almos' 18," Jesse said.

"That old? Well, he'd still be tried as a minor if he's 17, wouldn't he, Chief?"

Noland nodded.

"This is the first time you've done anything this serious, Jesse. The judge'll probably consider that," Mixon reassured him.

Jesse stared at the table.

"So, what really happened Saturday night?" Noland asked.

Jesse sighed. "Me an' Stump were in the backyard talkin' when we heard somethin' from the front of the house, near the carport."

"What time was this?" Mixon asked.

Jesse shrugged. "Dunno," he said. "Late."

"Go on," Noland said. "You heard something ...."

"Stump said, 'Let's check it out.' He went one way an' I went the other, and we foun' this guy messin' with the bike I got at school."

"The bike you stole?" Mixon asked.

"Yessir," Jesse said, noting the look the chief gave the detective.

"Go ahead, Jesse," Noland said. "We won't interrupt anymore."

"Well, Stump came up behin' the guy and grabbed him. The dog was barking like crazy." Nearing the good part, Jesse felt his growing excitement and knew he mustn't let it show. These two cops might have known the guy he killed. Jesse could never remember the guy's name.

"With Stump holdin' him, the guy couldn't move. I had my knife out just to scare him, but he started cursing me and saying he was gonna get the police 'cause I stole his kid's bike an' that was when I did it." Jesse said this all in a rush, hoping it would sound like the man at least halfway had it coming to him.

"Did what exactly?" Noland said.

"Stabbed him," Jesse said, trying to restrain his grin. "He'd peed on hisself he was so scared."

Noland pinched the bridge of his nose, frowning. "If he was so scared, Jesse, why did he start cursing you?"

"Uh, uh, how should I know?" Now Jesse regretted having said—Dewberry, that was the guy's name—had cursed him. He could see that didn't fit. "Maybe he wasn't cursin'. It's hard to remember."

"Yeah," Mixon said. "That was all of a week ago."

"Detective," Noland said, fixing the younger cop with a hard stare. Jesse had seen that look; his father used it on him often enough. It meant, "You better stop what you're doing right now, or I'm going to beat the living shit out of you." Jesse didn't think Noland would do to Mixon what his father did to him, though.

"So, then what happened?" Noland asked.

"Stump let him go, and the guy fell on the ground. It looked like he was tryin' to run."

"What about the dog, Jesse?" Noland asked. "What was the dog doing all this time?"

"Barkin' like crazy. I threw a brick at him, but I missed. He took off."

"So the dog ran away. Then what happened?"

"Does it matter? I already said I stabbed him."

"That's true, Jesse," Noland said, "but sometimes people confess to things they didn't do. They get some kind of kick out of it. You don't look like that kind of person to me, but we need the details to be sure."

Jesse couldn't read Noland's expression. At first, he'd sensed anger from the cop, but now he thought the guy was just tired. It was something in his speech. Mixon seemed excited more than anything else.

"I hit the guy with a brick," Jesse said, "to put him outta his misery."

"Were you trying to fix Dewberry so we wouldn't recognize him?"

"Not with the brick. I was just tryin' to stop his legs."

Noland nodded. "Then what?"

"Me an' Stump carried him to the trash bin back of the church. Man was he heavy. Stump said it was bein' dead made him heavy like that. We put the body in the trash, and I foun' some paint stuff to pour over him and Stump lit it with his lighter. He went up like a torch." Jesse remembered the sight and particularly the smell of Dewberry's burning flesh. It was awful. He knew he should feel sorry for what had happened, but mainly he was just sorry he'd gotten caught. The guy deserved to be killed, snooping around at night in Jesse's yard.

"Stump took the shoes," Jesse said, as though that made his brother as guilty as he was.

Noland stood. "Detective, get Sheritha to transcribe Jesse's statement, and he can sign it. Take him back to his cell for now."

Mixon nodded.

Jesse smiled at the chief, but Noland left without looking back. He again had the thought that prison might not be so bad; he would be away from his father, the food would probably be at least as good as he was used to, and he could smoke as much as he wanted. They might even have grass in prison. He was pretty sure he had heard that. Come to think of it, he and Brad might be able to room together after Brad offed his family with the poison.

CHAPTER 51

Stump wasn't home, and his father and grandmother hadn't seen him since late Friday night. Randy Watkins stood just inside the front door with Noland just outside. They were talking through the screen; Noland hadn't been invited in, but that was okay with him. He was eager to get away to continue his hunt for the missing brother. Besides, he found the heavy smell of bacon grease sickening.

"He came in late," Randy Watkins told Noland, "rooted aroun' in his room awhile, and then said he was goin' out. He didn' come back."

"Any idea where he might have gone?"

"Naw," Watkins said. "Are y'all still keeping Jesse down to the jail? Is he still there for fightin' at school and pullin' a knife?"

"No, it's more than that, and he really needs a lawyer. Do you want to get him one, or do you want to use a court-appointed attorney?" He also ought to see the morning paper, because there was a large article on the front page about his son's arrest for the murder of Peter Dewberry.

"What's the little shit done this time?" Watkins said. Noland noticed a slight twitch of the man's right eye.

"He's being questioned about the murder last weekend," Noland said. He saw no point in telling him that Jesse had already confessed. He would find out soon enough.

Randy looked like he might explode. "Jesus H. Chrise," he said, halfway to Noland and halfway to himself. "I always thought the boy was rotten, but I didn't think he would ever kill nobody. Steal? Yeah. The sumbitch'll take anythin' not nailed down. Did I tell you about the bike he stole from school, Chief? I made him take it back the day after I saw it here."

"Does Stump have a girlfriend?" Noland said, getting back to the purpose of his visit.

"Nobody special," Watkins answered. "I think he probably used to screw some of the cheerleaders, though." Noland detected the pride in the man's voice at the thought of his son's conquests. He felt sure the man had lived vicariously through his older son while despising the younger boy.

"Other relatives in town or nearby?"

"Charles works for my brother at his garage," Watkins said.

Noland had gotten directions to the garage, and that's where he and Sgt. Johnson were headed now. Johnson was driving.

"You know this Emmett Watkins?" Noland asked.

"I know some people who use him, Chief. He's okay from what I hear. Charges fair prices, does the work."

They were driving along the strip now, or at least what passed for urban blight in Harper. They passed service stations, fast food restaurants, package liquor stores, and every now and then a few houses as reminders that this had once been a residential area.

"What they puttin' up over there, Chief?" Johnson pointed to a recently cleared area where workmen were pouring a gigantic concrete slab.

"A Wal-Mart," Noland said.

"No kiddin'. Man, we done finally got our own Walmark. I'll be glad to see that open."

"Me too."

Just past the Wal-Mart site, the four-lane narrowed to two lanes, and Johnson pulled into Watkins Auto Service. A solidly built man who reminded Noland of Randy Watkins detached himself from a three-way conference in front of the opened hood of a fairly new Honda Accord. He strolled unhurriedly to the police car.

"What can I do for y'all?" he said, crossing his arms and leaning against the driver's side door.

Noland leaned toward the man. "Are you Emmett Watkins?"

"Sure am, and you're Chief Grady Noland unless I miss my guess. I seen you ridin' with the mayor in the Christmas parade." Watkins thrust his right hand towards the chief, who pumped it with his own. Johnson leaned his head back so the two men would have less of his presence to contend with.

"We're looking for your nephew, Mr. Watkins. Stump, or Charles. You seen him today?"

"Sure haven't, Chief, but then he don' come in on Fridays." Watkins pulled a red rag from his back pocket and mopped his forehead with it. "Why don' you two get out and join me in the office for a Coke or somethin'? It's too hot to be out here in the sun."

"Sounds good to ...," Johnson started, but he was interrupted by his boss.

"We appreciate your offer, Mr. Watkins, but we're kinda in a hurry. Any idea where Stump might've gone?"

"You went by his house, I suppose?"

Noland nodded. "Your brother said he hadn't seen him since he left late last night."

"What's he done, anyways? Stump's always struck me as a pretty good kid, not like that brother of his. Man, I don' trus' that Jesse atall."

"We just want to ask him a few questions, Mr. Watkins," Noland said, wondering if anybody read the Saturday paper.

"Actually, I would like to aks him a few questions myself," Emmett Watkins said. "Like if he knew anything 'bout one of the cars left here last night. The car's gone, and the keys are missin'."

Noland and Johnson looked at each other. "Could the owner have picked it up, Mr. Watkins?"

Watkins shook his head. "I called him first thing when I noticed it was missin'."

"You thinking what I'm thinking?" Noland asked Johnson.

"Yeah, Chief," Johnson said.

Emmett Watkins looked from one cop to the other. "I can't believe Stump would've took it," he said. "He's a good kid."

CHAPTER 52

Mary squeezed the tomato. Too firm. She put it down, frowning over the display. The summer tomatoes were gone, replaced by fall's pale, hard, tasteless variety. The sign said, "Vine ripened," but she didn't believe it for a minute. The things were hothouse grown, picked green, and injected with a gas that turned them a sickly pink. She had read all about it in a magazine. Oh well, the salad dressing would give it some taste. She put a couple into a plastic bag.

Mary moved on, stopping at the cucumber bin. She selected the smallest one she could find, put it into a plastic bag, and dropped it into her cart. To Mary, the cucumbers were only marginally better than the tomatoes. Huge, too green, so slick they looked waxed and probably were. Greenhouse cucumbers had about as much taste as the tomatoes.

Face it, Mary, she told herself, pushing her nearly empty buggy past carrots and celery and mushrooms, you're sick of grocery shopping. She was sick of being a homemaker, if the truth were known. More and more lately, Mary felt guilty for not working. Other than some of the doctors' wives, she didn't know any of her friends who weren't employed outside the home. Maybe she would talk to Hal about it. She could always work as his secretary/receptionist like she'd done when they were first married, before Bradley was born.

Mary paused at the banana display, searching for a bunch that was just right, a stalk with a hint of green at the top and no dark spots.

"I've got some greener ones, Mrs. Childers," the big man said. "In the back."

Mary stared at the man, blinking myopically, wishing she had worn her glasses. He looked familiar.

"My wife works for your husband," he said, as though reading her thoughts. Although he was smiling, Mary instinctively didn't feel comfortable near him. He was too large, stood too close, and his breath smelled warmly of beer.

"These are fine," she said, putting the bunch she had been about to reject into her cart. She moved carefully away, making a conscious effort not to walk provocatively. Mary felt Ludlow's eyes burning through her slacks.

She wondered what Hal's secretary saw in the man. Vicki was so attractive, clean and neat, while her husband was such a slob. If he was drinking at work on a Friday afternoon, he also had an alcohol problem.

Hal certainly had his faults, but drinking wasn't one of them. Mary smiled to herself, thinking about her husband. Last night had been wonderful, one of those peak sexual experiences they had so seldom had in the last few years. What had come over him?

She stopped at the meat counter and selected a package of lean ground meat. She planned to have lasagna, garlic bread, and a large salad for dinner, a meal the whole family liked.

CHAPTER 53

"**N**o," he said, "that's not true." But it was like talking to a brick wall. The voice went on, accusing, berating.

On the bed, Brad drew his legs closer to his chest, wrapped the pillow tighter around his head, and chanted "No, no, no," but the voice continued. Before, the words had come from inside his head, and he had recognized them as his thoughts, part of his stream of consciousness, but now they came from outside, from his radio. He had unplugged the radio, but that hadn't stopped the voice.

The voice had a deep, raspy quality like the voice of a smoker. It sounded like Jesse at times, like his father at other times.

Jesse. All the bad thoughts were Jesse's fault. Jesse had encouraged Brad to steal the arsenic and had even emptied the school to give him the opportunity. Now Jesse was in jail; Brad had heard about the fight in the bathroom. He had also heard that Danny Dewberry had said Jesse was wearing his father's shoes. Brad knew why, and if he had any guts, he would tell his parents about it.

"You're bad, Brad. Evil, sinful," the voice said. He remembered the time he had looked up "masturbation" in his grandmother's old dictionary. The synonym was "self-abuse," and the rest of the entry said that the practice could cause insanity.

Was that what had happened? Had he abused himself until his mind went? Well, at least he wouldn't have to listen to the voice much longer. With his mother shopping, his sister out, and his father still at work, Brad had finally put the arsenic into the salad dressing.

CHAPTER 54

R oy squeezed her arm, then held the door as she climbed into the funeral home's limousine to sit beside her son. Danny looked pale in his dark suit, sitting slightly hunched forward on the seat. Nancy's mother sat next to Danny on the wide seat, while Roy sat across, on the jump seat. Peter's parents and his brother followed in a second limousine

Nancy leaned her head back on the seat and closed her eyes. One thought randomly followed another, nothing sticking except for one thing: Peter was gone. When this was over, she wouldn't have him to comfort her.

The car eased forward. "You all right, Mom?" Danny said. She nodded and felt a tear begin a familiar journey. Another tear? After all the ones in the past week and in the funeral home last night and in the church this afternoon?

She had never seen so many people in the church. Surely a quarter of Harper had turned out for the funeral. The pews were overflowing, chairs lined the aisles, and people stood in the door-way and in the hall leading to the Sunday School wing. If you could only have seen it, Peter, she thought. But maybe he had seen it. Maybe he was watching from somewhere, from some higher plane of existence. If she could only hold on to that thought.

"I think there were more people at Peter's funeral than at your father's, Dear," her mother said.

Nancy nodded, thinking it was like her mother to count heads. Form's not important, Mother, she wanted to say, not when Peter's dead.

The limousine moved on, slowly, rocking gently over the rough surface of Harper's streets. A loose strand of hair fluttered in the car air conditioner's breeze, and Nancy wondered why air conditioning was necessary. She had felt slightly cold all day. She felt Danny's hand under hers, and she linked fingers with her son, taking comfort from his strength.

"We're almost there, Mom," he said, and Nancy felt the car turn and start up the long slope she remembered from other burials. This couldn't be happening. If she could only fall asleep in the car, she might awaken to find it had all been a horrible dream. Or, maybe she wouldn't awaken at all. Maybe she would just fall asleep and be wherever Peter was. More tears, and the limousine was stopping.

With a shudder, Nancy opened her eyes. Outside, the driver approached her door. In moments he would open it, help her out, and she would have to carry herself through more of the necessary ritual. Part of the separation procedure. Put Peter's coffin in the ground where she could see it and know he was really gone. But she hadn't seen him in the coffin; she hadn't really seen his body. Maybe it wasn't Peter in there. Maybe it was all some ghastly mistake, and Peter was alive somewhere. Perhaps he was at home, doing some mundane chore like cutting the grass, wondering where everyone was. Perhaps she was losing her mind.

Nancy stepped out of the car, leaning on the driver, a gaunt man smelling of aftershave lotion, and stood, chin up. The cool air under the trees smelled fragrant with the odor of freshly mown lawn. Muffled by distance, she heard traffic sounds. Closer, the crunch of tires on the gravel drive reminded her of something she hadn't thought of in years. Her parents had owned a pecan orchard and a pecan cracking machine that sat in the garage, surrounded by shells. Walking on the shells made a sound like tires on gravel.

The first limousine's passengers stood just off the drive, on grass close cropped and achingly green, waiting for the rest of the family.

Wordlessly, the family gathered and began the slow trek up the slight incline toward the grave site. Nancy, bracketed by her mother and son, led the way, while Betty and Roy, holding hands, followed. Looking frailer than Nancy remembered them, Peter's parents were close behind, trailed by John Dewberry, Peter's younger brother, who lived with them. Nancy listened to the sound of birds in another part of the cemetery and to the whump and thunk of dozens of closing car doors. She listened also to her inner voice saying that even though she felt like falling, she wouldn't. "One step at a time, Nancy," the voice counseled. "Take it one day at a time and even though your empty tomorrows stretch to the end of your life, you can make it. Others have." Small consolation.

They were directed to their seats under the bright canvas tent by the owner of the funeral home, a cadaverous man who looked enough like their driver to be his brother and probably was. Although the man called Nancy by name, she didn't know him. Roy (thank God for Roy) had made all the arrangements. She had a sense of people moving behind her, crowding closer, straining to hear the preacher's soft words. Nancy, in the best position to hear, heard sounds with no meaning. Life's meaning for her was in the coffin behind the minister, so near that three steps and she would be able to touch it.

Touching. That was the best part of afterwards. She stood bravely, hugging and being hugged, hearing without hearing the comforting words, storing away impressions, random thoughts, that in other times she would have told Peter and now she would never be able to share with anyone.

She watched as the police chief took Roy aside and spoke passionately to him, all the while glancing at her, and she knew he was telling her brother something connected with Peter's murder. She wanted to tell the chief that it didn't matter now, that arresting the killers wouldn't bring Peter back. And then someone who looked vaguely familiar stopped to tell her something important.

"I'm so sorry, Mrs. Dewberry," the man said. "I just wanted to let you know that you don't need to worry about your husband's life insurance policy."

She nodded, and the man wandered away. Nancy supposed that thoughts of life insurance policies must be comforting to some widows and perhaps one day she would find the money Peter had left a comfort. But not today. Today she would search for solace in sorrow.

Later, riding home from the cemetery, Nancy asked, "What did the policeman tell you?"

"Noland? He said they know who killed Peter and that one of the murderers is already in jail."

"Was it that kid with Dad's shoes?" Danny asked.

His uncle nodded. "Jesse Watkins," he said.

CHAPTER 55

J esse stood at the front of his cell, arms hanging through the bars. The openings were too narrow to stick his head through, but with his face pressed against the metal rods, he could just barely see the man in the next cell.

"What you in for, kid?" the man asked.

"You know that guy got hisself kilt last Saturday? Me 'n my brother iced his ass," Jesse said, playing the tough now that he had confessed.

"Man, you in some deep shit. Wanna smoke?"

"Yeah," Jesse said, taking the cigarette his neighbor offered. "Thanks." He lit the cigarette and took a deep drag, exhaling slowly.

"My name's Jesse Watkins," he said. "What's yours?"

"Jimmy Ivory."

"What'd you do, Jimmy?"

"Got caught shoplifting," Jimmy said. "I tried to swipe a necklace from K-Mart."

"For your wife?"

Jimmy laughed. "Naw, for my girlfrien'. They don't make necklaces big enough to fit aroun' my old lady's neck." He laughed again, and Jesse laughed with him.

"Say, Jesse," Jimmy said. "My mother-in-law foun' the body of the man you killed."

"Hannah Green?" Jesse asked, remembering the woman's name.

"That's her. Man, she's a crazy old bag. Goes all aroun' town with a shoppin' cart she fills with all kinda junk she finds. Too bad she foun' that body."

"No shit," Jesse said. He took another drag of his cigarette before saying, "Hell, Jimmy, if she hadn't foun' it somebody else would've. Can't keep somethin' like that secret in this heat." He laughed, thinking how bad the body must have smelled after a few days in the sun.

"Man, you got a crazy sense of humor," Jimmy said.

Jesse grinned in his cell. While he was a nobody at Harper High, here he was somebody. Here he was Jesse the murderer, Jesse the killer, and nobody could take that away from him. It didn't occur to him that nobody would want to take it away. Jesse tapped his cigarette and watched the gray ash flutter to the concrete floor. "Jimmy, you been in here before?"

"Coupla times," Jimmy admitted.

"What you think they're gonna do to me?"

"You tell 'em you killed the man?"

"Yeah," Jesse said, wishing now he had kept his mouth shut like Stump told him to. He hoped they would put Stump in a different cell.

Jimmy whistled.

"They said the judge might not be too hard on me since it's my firs' bad mistake," Jesse said, looking for some comfort.

"Who said that, your lawyer?"

"One of the cops said it. Don't have no lawyer."

"He say it before or after you told 'em you killed the man?"

"Before," Jesse said.

"Shit, Jesse," Jimmy said. "They'll tell you anything to get a confession. After they get that, your ass is grass and the judge is the lawnmower." Jimmy laughed.

Jesse's breakfast lay heavy in his stomach. Jail didn't seem like such a good place anymore, and he wished he could talk to his granma. "What if I tell 'em I made it all up?" he said.

"Too late for that," Jimmy answered. "They got your confession now. You jus' better hope they don't start talkin' about fryin'."

Jesse backed away from the bars and flopped onto his cot. He stared at the peeling plaster on the ceiling. What if he told them Stump killed the man? He could say Stump stabbed him and then beat his head in and then told Jesse to say he'd done it or Stump would kill him, too. If they fried Stump, then he wouldn't have to worry. He wondered why Stump hadn't been arrested.

CHAPTER 56

Stump hadn't been arrested, because he'd gotten an early start and had kept moving. He got on I-65 not far from Harper and headed south, reaching Birmingham early Saturday morning. From there, he took I-20 to Atlanta, pulling into a rest area off I-75 just past the city. Stump rolled up the windows, locked the doors of the stolen Buick, and slept until dawn's light and his growling stomach set him in motion again. The Buick gave him a bad time at the rest area, almost refusing to start, but cursing and kicking and playing with the sparkplug wires finally did the trick.

Stump left the interstate at Cordele, Georgia, where he spent $21.35 to fill the car's gas tank and another $3.77 to fill his stomach at McDonald's. Luckily, he'd had a little money put aside from his job at the garage, but at the rate it was going, he would be broke in a couple of days. It was nearly 10 when he re-entered I-75. Back in Harper, Jesse was just starting his confession.

As Peter Dewberry's funeral was concluding, Stump Watkins left I-75 and headed southeast on the Florida Turnpike. The Buick was running fine, purring along at 65 (Stump had been carefully obeying the speed limit) when he bypassed Orlando.

"Stump, this is a goddam good car you got," he told himself, not once, but several times along the way. He was going to hate to have to abandon it when he got to Miami.

Stump's "goddam good car" let him down near Port St. Lucie. He felt the steering wheel lug to the right even before he heard and felt the bump, bump, bump of the flat. He eased off the interstate, pulling as far onto the shoulder as he could. Luckily the flat was on the right side. Stump put the car in Park, killed the engine, and set the parking brake. He stretched when he got out, and then walked to the trunk.

The spare was flat.

"Sonofabitch," he said, staring in disbelief. "Goddam sorry bastard had a flat for a spare. I'll kill the muthafucka."

He stood cursing awhile longer, then kicked the rotten Buick several times. While he was kicking, he saw the highway patrol car go by.

"Jus' keep on goin'," he breathed. "I don't need your help." The patrol car slowed, spun across the median, and headed back his way.

"Oh, shit," he said, trying to decide whether to run. The car eased up behind Stump's Buick on the shoulder. The driver got out, adjusted his gun belt, and then walked unhurriedly to where Stump stood.

The man was at least 6 foot 3, and he wore silvery sunglasses that reflected whatever he looked at. At the moment, Stump was mirrored, and he saw himself as the patrolman saw him: a kid with lots of muscles wearing clothes that he'd slept in. The cop's mouth was a narrow slit below a slender nose and invisible eyes. Stump didn't think the man smiled much.

"Having problems?" the man said, his lips barely moving.

Stump, mouth as dry as the powdered shells lining the interstate, could only nod.

"What seems to be the trouble?"

"Flat," Stump said, resisting the urge to be sarcastic, "and the spare's flat, too."

"Mmhmm," the trooper said, beginning a slow walk around the Buick. Standing in the Florida sun with the only breeze from the occasional passing of a truck, Stump thought of trying to overpower the trooper. Hit him with a tire iron, maybe. Take his gun and his big car and burn up the road between here and Miami. But what if he missed? What if he didn't put the guy down right away? The gun strapped to the man's hip would put a hole in him big enough to poke a fist through.

"May I see your license, please?"

Stump handed the cop his license, and the man held it under his sunglasses for a moment before handing it back. "Insurance?"

"Insurance?"

"Proof of insurance. In Florida, you're supposed to carry it in your car."

Stump swallowed hard, thinking quick. He decided to go with something close to the truth. "The car isn't mine," he said. "I borrowed it from my uncle."

"I see," the trooper said. He was Trooper First Class Edward H. Snodgrass, according to the strip of metal pinned to his immaculate uniform. Stump wanted to tear the man's glasses off, but he was afraid of what he would find underneath: empty sockets or eyes so cold they'd freeze his heart.

"Just wait right here, Mr. Watkins, while I call for a wrecker." The big man turned and walked his slow walk back to the patrol car.

Stump knelt behind the Buick, watching as Snodgrass talked to his home base. Aimed at Stump, the silver goggles never wavered. Time passed so slowly it seemed he and the patrolman had been locked in the tableaux all afternoon. Finally, the patrolman finished his call. Stump watched him leave his big car, still idling, and begin his return stroll. Halfway to the Buick, the trooper drew his big gun. Stump Watkins had caught a one-way ticket back to Harper.

CHAPTER 57

"How was the funeral, Dear?" Hands full of salad fixings, Mary pushed the refrigerator door closed with her elbow. She released her load onto the counter and bent to retrieve salad bowls from a cupboard below.

"Okay," Hal said. "The church was really packed." He sipped his wine, making a face at the liquid's bite. He always found Chianti better with a meal. Hal sat at his place at the kitchen table, watching Mary preparing dinner. "I did say something kinda stupid, though."

"What was that?" To concentrate on her cutting, Mary unconsciously stuck out the tip of her tongue.

"I told Mrs. Dewberry she didn't need to worry about her husband's life insurance policy. Shoulda waited 'til Monday, like Vicki said."

Mary sliced some cucumber into the first bowl, cutting toward her thumb with a skilled motion. "She probably didn't hear anything anybody said, Hal."

He took another sip of wine. "You're probably right." Hal felt tension in his shoulders and released it. A few more sips of the wine, and he would really be able to get into the room's ambience. The kitchen smelled delightfully of garlic, onion, tomato paste, and oregano. Hal always loved his wife's lasagna.

"What're the kids doing?"

"They're both in their rooms, as usual. Sandy's watching MTV, and Bradley was writing something when I asked what he wanted in his salad."

"Maybe he's doing some homework for a change," Hal said. "I sure hope so."

CHAPTER 58

What do you put in a suicide note, Brad wondered, crumpling another effort and lofting it toward his trash can. He opened his desk drawer and slipped out a fresh sheet of looseleaf paper. At the top he wrote:

Why I Did It
by
Arnold Bradley Childers

Why am I doing it, he wondered. He had felt pretty good all afternoon, with none of the hallucinations that had plagued him in recent days. Brad smiled to himself and sat tapping his teeth with the bottom of his pen. It was like going to a doctor and having his symptoms disappear in the waiting room. Now that he knew the end was near and had relaxed and accepted it, his insanity had vanished.

He put down his pen and spread his hands on the desk to study them. Pale. Too slender. His long fingers reminded him of something from *E.T.* or maybe from *Close Encounters of the Third Kind*. Some science fiction movie, anyway. The outside edge of his left hand had a dark smudge like it always did when he wrote with a pen or a pencil. Just another thing he hated about being a southpaw.

Brad put a carat between and below the "I" and the "Did" in his title, and above the two words he added the word "Almost." "I almost killed my family because my dad's such a prick," he wrote, and then scratched through the sentence. That was part of it, all right. He had planned to kill his family, because his father was screwing his secretary and didn't deserve to live.

Carefully, he folded the sheet of paper in quarters and then tore it savagely into dozens of pieces. He sprinkled the pieces into the trash can.

He looked at his left hand as though seeing it for the first time. What was wrong with it? Why did it look so funny? Blood vessels snaking across the back seemed to describe a pattern with meaning just beyond Brad's grasp. He poked his hand with the tip of his pen hard enough to create a depression surrounded by wrinkles. When he took the pen away, the wrinkles disappeared, but the pit, now with a black dot at its bottom, stayed. He rubbed the dot but nothing happened. He rubbed it harder, desperately.

The dot was still there.

"What does it mean?" he whispered. "Why won't it go away?" His eyes danced, striking and bouncing off familiar objects on his desk, extracting no meaning. Until they lit on the scissors.

"Should I snip it off, make a little fold there and clip off the part with the spot? Or should I poke it with the points, jab it out, gouge it out?" The line "Out, out, damned spot" spun through his mind. He knew it was from some play they had studied in school, but it seemed to have acquired new meaning, a meaning only he could discern.

The scissors flashed up and then down, impaling the spot. "Unnhnnn," Brad breathed, mentally screaming. He dropped the scissors. A pond of blood appeared. Brad snatched a handful of tissues from the box on his desk and pressed them to his wound. Fascinated, he watched red soak through the center of the tissue wad and spread, gradually devouring more and more of the tissues.

"Supper's ready," his mother called from the kitchen.

CHAPTER 59

"What happened to your hand, Bradley?" his mother asked.

"Hit it on the corner of my desk," he said, thrusting his hand between his legs. Out of sight.

"Want some more wine?" His father topped off his glass and held the bottle over his mother's glass.

"Just a little," Mary said. Her cheeks were flushed from the oven's heat and from the previous glass she'd had. Brad thought she looked wonderful.

"Pass the Parmesan cheese, Mom," Sandy said. She began to cut her lasagna into pieces an inch square.

"You look pale, Dear," his mother said to him. "Don't you think he looks pale, Hal?"

"Yeah, I guess so," his father said, glancing his way. "Why don't you go ahead and use the salad dressing, Hon?"

His mother, still looking at him, shook the bottle and poured. "Darn," she said. "Now look what I've done." A few green pieces swam in a white sea.

Brad felt like he was going to faint. Sweat dotted his forehead, and his stomach churned. Pour it out, Mom, he wanted to say. For God's sake, don't eat it. His mother took a bite.

"Let me have it before you use it all, Mom," Sandy said, reaching for the bottle.

"I feel sick," he said, eyes glued to his mother's salad.

"Well, go on to the bathroom if you think you're going to throw up, Son," his father said, frowning. He took another sip of wine and took the dressing Sandy offered.

"Can I have his lasagna?" he heard Sandy ask before he entered the hall bathroom.

"I'll save it for tomorrow," his mother answered.

Brad turned on the light and shut the door. He squatted on the floor and rested his head against the cold porcelain of the toilet. It's not too late, he thought. Nobody's gotten sick yet. I'll tell them what I did, and they can throw up or take an antidote.

Did I eat any of it, he wondered. He stood and peered at himself in the mirror, finally sticking out his tongue to see if it was coated white. No, it was purple, purple like a giant worm. As he watched, his tongue writhed and twisted and reeled out of his mouth to circle his head, thrusting its tip into his nostril. He could feel it forcing its way up through his nasal cavity, seeking his brain. Brad closed his eyes, and when he opened them, his tongue was normal again. He flushed the toilet, cut off the light, and staggered to his room to lie on the bed, face to the wall. He fell asleep.

CHAPTER 60

"I feel really awful, Hal," Mary said on her return from the bathroom. She flopped onto the couch next to him and closed her eyes. Hal touched her pale forehead and found her skin cold and clammy.

"Maybe you've got what Brad had at supper tonight," he said, remembering how pale his son had been and how he had complained of nausea. Hal swallowed, aware of a burning sensation in his throat. Heartburn, he decided.

"Could you get me some water? I feel incredibly thirsty."

Hal stood and that's when the first cramps hit, low, rumbling, foreshadowing worse to come. The first wave passed quickly, and he hurried to the kitchen to get Mary's water before they returned. When he reentered the family room, his wife was gone. He started down the hall.

"Watch out, Dad!" Sandy yelled, nearly colliding with him after bursting from her room. She dashed into the hall bathroom and slammed the door.

"What's your problem?" he said to the closed door. The unmistakable sounds of vomiting gave him the answer.

"What's going on here?" he muttered, entering the master bedroom. Mary lay on the bed, breathing slowly, shallowly, her skin so pale he could see a vein throbbing in her neck. His stomach knotted, and he felt bile rising in his throat. He choked it back, set

Mary's water glass on the chest, and hurried to the bathroom. He barely made it.

After, he sat on his side of the bed, holding his wife's hand. "Food poisoning, Mary," he said. "Do you think I should call the doctor?" When Mary didn't respond, he felt for her pulse. Looking at the sweep second hand on the nightstand clock, Hal started counting. With twenty seconds to go, he was already over 100. He picked up the phone and dialed 911.

CHAPTER 61

"**D**id you lock the door?"

"Yeah," he said, watching his wife's preparations. Naked, she was totally unselfconscious, and Grady found that exciting. He felt like a voyeur observing an unsuspecting neighbor.

Grady lay on his back on the bed, hands interlocked behind his head, wearing only black socks. "My stag movie hero," Marge whispered, nuzzling his neck.

He kissed her then, deeply, holding either side of her face in his big hands, delighting in the feel of her bath-warm body on his. Her breath was a sweet blend of peppermint and Colgate.

Grady turned her over, kissing and nibbling.

The phone rang.

Marge snatched the phone before it could ring a second time and wake their son.

"Hello." Marge listened for a moment, then said, "Hold on a second." She handed him the receiver.

"Yeah?" he said, feeling his desire fading.

"Jack Strong here," the voice at the other end of the line said. "Sorry to call so late, Chief." But the doctor didn't sound sorry.

"That's all right, Dr. Strong," Grady said, sitting up. "What is it?"

"You know Hal Childers?"

"State Farm agent? Sure. What's the problem?" The bed moved as Marge rolled out and headed for the bathroom to put on her gown.

"He and his wife and daughter have been poisoned."

"Poisoned? You gotta be kidding."

"I wish I were. Looks like arsenic, but we'll have to do some tests to be sure."

Grady heard the toilet flush. "Any idea who might have done it?" he said, starting to feel awkward talking to the doctor naked.

"Looks like the son, Grady. Kid's nuts if you ask me. We've got him here at the hospital, and you might want to hear what he has to say."

"What about the victims, Doctor? How are they doing?" Marge slipped back into bed and opened the paperback she was reading.

"Hal's okay, and Sandy—that's the daughter—should recover. It doesn't look good for the wife, Grady. She was comatose when Hal called the hospital, and we've got her in Intensive Care now, trying to get her stabilized."

"I'll be right down."

Grady hung up and kissed his wife's cheek. "Sorry, Hon," he said. "Rain check?"

Marge nodded, grinning. "I just hope we don't forget how."

CHAPTER 62

C hief Noland drove carefully through Harper's nearly desert-ed streets. Waiting for a light, he snapped on the radio and rotated the dial slowly, searching for a station broadcasting high school football scores.

The one-story hospital spread like a tumor on a lot across from a funeral home. Noland hoped the bond issue would pass, and the town could build a new hospital. Preferably in a new location. He pulled into his reserved parking slot next to one marked with a cross, killed the engine, and sat for a moment listening to the pop-ping sounds of the engine cooling and to cricket song.

What in the hell's happening in Harper, he wondered. Why all the misery? First, he'd had to listen to Jesse's gruesome confession, and then go to the funeral of the boy's victim. And now this. A whole fam-ily poisoned by the teenaged son. With a sigh, he left the car.

Noland got Hal's room number at the front desk and pushed through swinging doors guarded by a "No Visitors" sign to enter a long corridor. Dim fluorescent lighting guided his progress along a familiar route. The hospital was very quiet, only the muted sounds of air conditioning or a TV or a toilet flushing indicating the pres-ence of life. He knocked gently on number 139, heard a muted "Come in," and entered.

Hal Childers was sitting up in bed, sucking a piece of ice, staring listlessly at the TV. Noland thought he looked awful.

"Hi, Grady," Childers said. They shook hands.

"How do you feel?"

"Drained," Hal said with a wan smile. "Have you seen my boy?"

"Not yet," Noland said, thinking it was strange Hal asked about his son first.

Tears sprang to Hal's eyes, and Noland wanted to look away but didn't. "He kept saying he was sorry, over and over, all the way here."

"Wanna tell me about it?" Noland pulled a chair close to the bed and sat. A nurse poked her head through the door, saw Noland, frowned, and disappeared.

Hal closed his eyes, put another piece of ice in his mouth, and sucked for a moment. When he spoke, his voice was soft and slightly distorted by the ice.

"Not much to tell, Grady. Mary got sick maybe 30 minutes after supper, vomiting, diarrhea, that kind of thing. I had a burning sensation in my throat that I took to be heartburn. By the time it really hit me, Sandy was sick in the bathroom and Mary ..." His voice broke. "... Mary was like passed out or something. She was so cold I thought she was dead, but I could feel her pulse racing, so I knew she was still alive. I called 911."

"What about your son?"

Hal cut off the TV with the remote control. "Brad had said he was sick at the supper table. I knocked on his door, but he didn't respond. That really scared me, so I went on in."

Hal's door opened and the same nurse from before steamed in, a young doctor in her wake. "You're going to have to leave immediately," she hissed, indignation in every rigid feature.

"Sorry, Chief," the doctor said, recognizing Noland. "We didn't know it was you." He started backing out, beckoning the nurse to follow. She stood, hands on hips, looking angrily from Noland to the doctor. Visitors after 10:00 were clearly more than she could handle.

"I won't be long," Noland said, soothingly. "But I will want to see Brad, too." With a long sigh of exasperation, the nurse followed the doctor.

Hal smiled wanly. "I hope she's on duty if my mother-in-law comes to visit."

"What about Brad?"

"His room was dark and had a funny smell, but that might have been because I had just been vomiting. Anyway, he was all curled up in a ball like when he was a little boy." More tears were flowing, but Hal continued. "I called his name, and he turned over and looked at me framed in the light from the hall. 'I'm sorry, Dad,' he said, and then he held his arms out for me to hug him." Hal hugged his chest as though trying to recapture the moment with his son. "Then he said, 'Don't eat the salad. Tell Mom not to eat the salad.' I was sick again, and when I was through, Brad was standing in the bathroom door saying he would drive us to the hospital."

"What about the ambulance?"

"Out on another call. Brad carried his mother out to the car, Grady. Put her in the back seat, tears streaming down his cheeks. I mean, there he'd poisoned us all, but it wasn't meanness or hatred made him do it."

Noland stood. Impulsively, he clutched Hal's hand and squeezed it. He felt close to the man although he didn't know him well.

"What's gonna happen to him, Grady?"

"I really don't know, Hal," he said. "How old is he?"

"Sixteen, no, 17. He just had his birthday." Hal covered his eyes with his forearm, and Noland could hear his sobs as he slipped out the door. He paused for a moment to wipe his own eyes with a handkerchief.

The nurse waited outside Hal's room, her arms folded over her ample bosom.

"I need to see the son," Noland told her. He followed her glance at the clock over the nurses' station. 10:35.

"No more than 10 minutes," he said.

"143." Her voice was flat and hard.

"Thanks." There was no response.

Noland rapped softly and entered Brad's room. The boy lay on top of the sheet, facing the door, his knees drawn up to his chest, his left thumb in his mouth. His eyes were open but unfocused. The reading light was on over his bed, and Noland was struck by how much the son resembled the father, in a pale, thin way.

"I'm Grady Noland," he said, "Chief of Police." There was no sign Brad heard him.

"I've just been talking to your father, and he's okay, Brad."

No response.

"Can you hear me?"

"Kill me," the boy said.

"What was that?"

Louder. "Kill me."

"Nobody's going to kill you."

"Behind you," Brad said, pointing. "Don't you see it?"

Noland looked where Brad indicated and saw only a clothes locker and beyond that the closed door. "What is it, Brad?"

"It's gone now."

"Have you been seeing things?"

Brad nodded, thumb back in his mouth, and Noland remembered Dr. Strong said he thought Brad was crazy.

"Are they dead?" the boy asked.

"Who?"

"Sandy and my father."

"No, they're all right."

"Mommy."

"Your mother's pretty sick, but we hope she'll be all right, too."

"Jesse made me do it," Brad said.

"Jesse? Jesse Watkins?"

Brad nodded, and Noland was momentarily stunned. How in the world was Jesse involved in this? He was about to ask when Brad said, "Don't eat it, Mommy." His voice was flat, emotionless. Then he screamed.

Noland shivered, goosebumps peppering his arm, hair on the back of his neck rigidly erect. For an instant he was back in 'Nam, and Harry, his buddy, was hit and screaming just this way. Mindlessly, a scream that would last forever. Or until he died, which Harry did in his arms a couple of minutes later. Noland wanted to hold Brad, to do anything that would stop the scream, but he couldn't move. Behind him, he heard the door open.

"Out, Chief," the nurse said, shoving him brusquely toward the door. Noland stumbled from the room, the sound of Brad's scream ringing in his ears, still loud out in the corridor with the door shut. Dr. Strong swept by, his white coat unbuttoned. The doctor carried a syringe like a knife.

Long minutes later, the screaming stopped, and the doctor emerged.

"What brought that on, Grady?" The doctor didn't look accusing, just tired.

"The boy said something to his mother, like he was giving her a warning, then he started screaming."

"Interesting," Strong said. "His mother just died."

CHAPTER 63

Heat waves shimmered on the road ahead, and Grady turned up the fan on the car air conditioner. Pines by the roadside were dusty, and the grass was parched and brown. Grady felt the heat and drought like an open hand pressing down. Suffocating.

"You're awfully quiet, Grady," Marge said. "Whatcha thinkin' about?"

Grady glanced in the rearview mirror at the sleeping form of their son, then looked back at the road. "The heat," he said, "and my father."

"Your mother's in good spirits, considering."

"Yeah," he said, remembering his mother in the hospital. "Maybe manic is more descriptive." He caught Marge's nod from the corner of his eye.

"I just hope she calms down before they take your father home." Marge rooted through her purse. "Want a piece of gum?"

"Sure." Grady slipped the white rectangle into his mouth. He chewed, listening to the swish of the tires and the steady hum of the engine.

"What did you notice most about Dad?"

"He looked awful," Marge said.

"Yeah, that's true, but I meant more specifically."

"Well, I thought he looked pale and kinda drawn around the mouth. His face just looked thin, I guess."

"Didn't you notice how small he looked? Like he'd shrunk or something?" Even though Grady was taller than his father, he had always thought of him as a giant, a burly man with a booming voice and an easy laugh. The man in the hospital bed had been a querulous, fragile, wizened stranger.

Marge nodded. "I guess so."

Grady chewed his gum mechanically, thinking of his father. William Michael Noland, Mike to his friends, had moved to Birmingham around the time Marge was pregnant with his grandson. Going where the action was, he'd told Grady. His father sold drugs for a pharmaceutical house.

"How's Dad been doing with his sales?" Grady had asked his mother in the hospital.

His mother shook her head. "Not so good, Dear. He says all the young salesmen have college degrees, and he feels like he can't compete."

"Can he retire?"

"Maybe he'll have to now," his mother said. "The problem is the company's retirement plan is a joke, and we don't have any savings."

"What about Social Security?"

His mother's face registered her disgust. "Your father's not quite old enough to start getting it, and the last time I checked it wasn't very much anyway. I've told him I could get a job, but he won't hear of it. You know how your father is."

Stubborn. Proud. Afraid of getting old. Grady had wanted to assure his mother that he would help financially, but he and Marge didn't have any extra money. Being a policeman in Harper didn't pay much, even if you were the chief. The town couldn't even afford a new jail.

"You know the Watkins brothers are still in Harper?" Grady cracked the window and tossed his tasteless piece of gum.

"Watkins? Oh, you mean the ones who killed that college professor. What made you think of them?" Marge extracted a tissue from her purse, tore off a piece, wrapped her gum in it, and put the wad in the waste bag hanging from the cigarette lighter.

"Long train of thought," he said. "They shoulda gone to the state pen, but it's too full." If Grady had had his way, Jesse would have been electrocuted by now, not living at the expense of the state's taxpayers.

Initially charged with capital murder, Stump and Jesse had pleaded guilty to the lesser charge of robbery and murder to avoid the death penalty. Each received a sentence of life plus 25 years.

Unfortunately, life didn't really mean life, and Grady feared that they would be eligible for parole at some point during his life. He just hoped there would still be enough interested parties around to argue effectively against their release.

Actually, he could see Stump being released early for good behavior. In his heart of hearts, Grady tended to see Stump as almost as much of a victim as Peter Dewberry. He saw Jesse as the instigator of what had happened and figured Stump just went along out of the necessity of dealing with a man's body.

He just longed for the day when the state penitentiary would have room for the two still in Harper's antiquated jail.

CHAPTER 64

"Why won't you do it, Jerry?" Stump said. Samuels, the turnkey, hesitated outside the Watkins' cell, holding their supper tray. Fried chicken, mashed potatoes and biscuits steamed.

"Sheeit, Stump. You don' know what you're askin', man." Samuels slipped the tray through the slot where Jesse grabbed it.

"Move down a little, Jerry," Jesse said. "You're blocking the TV." He sat on the end of his bunk, tray across his knees, eyes glued to a rerun of "Night Court." On the show, Judge Harry Stone was about to sentence a man accused of breaking and entering.

"All you hafta do is forget to lock it one time after we have our showers. We be gone, outta your hair," Stump said.

Samuels laughed, quivering all over. "Ain't got no hair, Stump," he said, running a meaty hand over his nearly bald head. On the TV, Dan was making a joke about Bull's shaved head.

Stump, who had lost his sense of humor in the months he and Jesse had spent in jail, felt like strangling the fat man in the corridor. He took a deep breath and tried to force his features into the semblance of a smile. "You know what I mean, Jerry," he said.

"Yeah," Samuels said. "You be outta here, and I be outta work. Enjoy your supper, boys." He shuffled away, baggy pants scrunched up in the crack of his behind.

Stump turned away from the front of the cell when the outer door clanged shut behind Samuels. "Give me some of that chicken, Jesse."

"You're wastin' time with Jerry, Stump," Jesse said, passing his brother the tray. Stump took a greasy drumstick.

"Don't you want to get outta here?"

Jesse shook his head. "Naw. This ain't so bad. We got TV, and I don't havta go to school." And he didn't have his father picking on him all the time. He just wished Brad was in with them. He'd never thought the kid would really do it, poison his family, and he grinned every time he thought about how he was at least partly responsible.

"Yeah, I know. And the food's not so bad either," Stump said sarcastically, looking in disgust at the grease running down his fingers.

"Better'n anythin' Granma ever made," Jesse said.

CHAPTER 65

B rad felt the bright, sharp pain as the needle entered his arm. There was a warmth at the point of his impalement. He was spreadeagled on the bed. Crucified. He screamed.

"How long has he been like this?" the sandy-haired man asked, his voice fading in and out like a distant radio station.

"Since last Sunday," the woman in white said. Brad saw her intestines writhing like gray snakes, starkly visible against the broad expanse of her skirt. "His father and stepmother came for a visit, and when they left he went into a stupor."

Spittle from the woman's mouth drifted slowly down. Brad wanted to dodge but couldn't move. Spikes through his hands and feet and now his elbow held him in place. He screamed again, but the man and woman pretended not to hear. A sweetly bitter taste filled his mouth.

The bald man turned pages in a manilla folder. To Brad the rustle sounded like a forest fire; each turned page was an exploding pine.

"We've tried 'em all, Alma," the man said. "Chlorpromazine, Trifluopromazine, Haloperidol, you name it. His chart looks like a pharmacopeia for treating schizophrenia."

The words drifted through Brad's mind, dropping off into odd places, triggering strange associations. Faintly scented, cooled air, pain from the inserted catheter, rumbling from his lower bowel, the vision of the nurse's intestinal snakes; all competed with the words for his attention. His mind was roiling confusion.

"Can I make a suggestion, Doctor?"

"Please do," the doctor said, closing the manilla folder.

"Forbid any visits from his relatives. He was doing pretty well before this last visit."

CHAPTER 66

"Why'd I let you talk me into it?" Hal said.

Vicki closed her book, marking her place with a finger. "Into what, Hal?"

"Into going to see Brad."

Vicki sighed. She slipped her bookmark into place and put the book on the nightstand beside the bed. "You still worrying about that?"

"I can't get the screams out of my mind," her husband said.

Stark terror, that's what Vicki had seen in the boy's face. But he hadn't seemed to be afraid of either his father or her. When he started screaming, he was staring at something behind them. Vicki had turned involuntarily to follow Brad's gaze, but there was nothing to see.

"You think it was my fault, Hal?" she said.

"Not really," Hal said, with just a moment's hesitation. Like maybe he did blame the scene they had witnessed on her presence. "I just wish we hadn't gone."

"How could we have known?"

The letters they had gotten from the doctor spoke of progress and remission. In light of the Brad they had seen, the letters seemed self-serving. Vicki turned off her light and turned to kiss her husband good night.

Hal kissed her and rolled away, but Vicki knew he would have trouble falling asleep. He loved his son; she had seen that in his anguished expression as the orderlies held Brad for the injection that finally stilled the screams. She had heard the love in Hal's recounting of that awful night back in the fall. Vicki wished she could solve her husband's problem as he had solved hers. Freed after divorcing Bone Ludlow, Vicki felt guilty to be so happy when Hal was in pain.

CHAPTER 67

B one squeezed. Click. The muzzle had an oily, metallic flavor, reminding him vaguely of the taste in his mouth some mornings when he woke after a heavy drinking session. The front sight was hard against his upper palate. He squeezed again. Click.

Why didn't he just load the gun and be done with it? Or maybe he would put one round in a chamber and play Russian Roulette. He remembered his morbid fascination with scenes from the movie *The Deer Hunter*. Maybe he could re-enact them.

Click.

Bone sat at the kitchen table; empty, crushed beer cans littered its top. Some had fallen to the floor. The room stank of beer and dried sweat and stale smoke.

Click.

Bone wondered why he was crying. Was he crying because Vicki left him? He had halfway expected that. After all, she'd threatened to leave often enough. The only surprise was how quickly she'd married her boss after the divorce.

Why then? Was it because he had gotten fired? Naw, he had hated his job. Small had done him a favor that day in the meat locker.

Small, standing in the locker doorway, face livid, had said, "Ludlow, I told you if I caught you again what I was gonna do. You're fired."

"You can't fire me, you little shit," Bone had said, trying hard to sound sober. "I quit." He had chugged the last of his beer and hurled the empty at his ex-boss. Surprised, Small ducked too late, and the can caught him on the side of the forehead. In seconds, blood dyed his white shirt red.

Yeah, great scene. Only the beginning was wrong. Sometimes Bone changed the beginning. Before Small opened his mouth, Bone yelled, "Take this job and shove it!" Then he hurled the beer can with a little beer still in it. Yeah, that was even better, not that the way it really happened hadn't been good. Bone particularly liked all the blood and the yelling that followed.

Click.

Maybe he would load the pistol and take a ride by the store. Show Small what he really thought of his pissant job. Blow the little fucker away after he robbed him. Bone had already spent nearly all of his share of the savings.

Click.

Darkness deepened in the kitchen without taking away the heat. What time was it anyway, Bone wondered. Without a job, he had lost track of time. He lowered the pistol and held up his watch to the moonlight filtering in through the kitchen window. Bone peered at the watch face, shadowing it with his head.

"Shit," he muttered, extracting his lighter and flicking it on, blinking in the sudden flare of light. 10:34. His stomach growled, protesting its emptiness.

Bone dowsed the lighter and stood, swaying slightly, momentarily blind in the greater darkness after the light. His head hurt, and the taste in his mouth was indescribable. For comfort, he slipped the pistol into the top pocket of his overalls.

Working by feel, Bone found the refrigerator and pulled it open. The sour odor of rotting food greeted him, and Ludlow backed away, leaving the door open. Waste of time to close it with the electricity off.

Tomorrow he would pay the bill. "Damn Vicki anyway," he said, remembering as he opened the carport door how good she had been about paying bills. Fresh tears sprang to his eyes, and he wiped them away with the palm of his hand. All her fault, her and that goddam boss of hers. Mighty convenient, if you thought about it, how that goddam son tried to kill the whole family but got only his mother.

He eased into his car, sitting for a moment with the door open to savor the interior light. The motor started quickly, and Bone set off for McDonald's. After he ate, he might just swing by the Childers' house. See what they were up to.

CHAPTER 68

Bone belched, and the taste of tartar sauce and fish filet reminded him of McDonald's. Could he help it if he had forgotten his wallet? That greasy shit wasn't worth $3.73 anyway. He had snatched the sack from the girl's hand, peppered her with all the change he could root out of his pocket and the car pocket, and then sped away. Thank God she couldn't see his license number because he had forgotten to turn his lights on.

He turned into the subdivision where Hal and Vicki lived, driving slowly down their street. Most of the houses were dark at this time of night, and the sound of his car was loud in the silent neighborhood. Bone had seen the hole in his muffler and knew he should get the muffler replaced.

There was a rise before the street curved to the right, and Bone took his foot off the accelerator to coast down on the other side. Vicki, his Vicki, lived in the red brick house with the Toyota and the Oldsmobile in the driveway. He drifted by, spitting contemptuously at the street number painted on the curb. The house was as dark as its neighbors'.

Bone stopped two houses down and killed the motor. He sat in the hot darkness listening to the popping of his cooling engine and to the chirping of crickets. He pulled a cigarette from the pack in his overall pocket and lighted it with his faithful Bic. Bone smoked for a while, occasionally glancing in the side mirror at Childers' darkened house. The cigarette's glow was soothing, and his thoughts drifted. Memories floated in and out of his mind, mostly memories of times with Vicki. One stuck, scalding him in its intensity. It was another summer night, in the dark front seat of his car, Vicki beside him. Remembering, he stiffened, and hot tears spilled over. "Shit," he said, and took a last deep drag before flicking his cigarette butt into the street. Briefly glowing sparks fanned over the asphalt.

With nothing in mind, Bone left his car and walked back to the red brick house. He felt like whistling but didn't. A dog barked in the yard behind him, tentatively at first, then with more gusto, settling into the kind of rhythm that could go on all night. From the sound, Bone pictured a large dog with a barrel chest. He crossed the street to put more distance between himself and the animal. The barking continued.

Bone looked around and saw no one. The street was empty. He straightened, clenching and unclenching his fists, flexing the muscles in his arms and shoulders. "Let's check 'em out, Bone," he said, talking to himself like he did more and more since Vicki left. He lit a fresh cigarette before setting off briskly across the dry lawn.

Bone slipped around the side of the house into darkness where streetlights didn't reach. Ivy carpeted the ground, muffling his footsteps. From the street, the house looked completely dark, but up close Bone saw there was a light in the rear bedroom. A light-blocking shade prevented him from seeing inside. He hesitated, sucking his cigarette for comfort, standing still with a large pine between himself and the carport of the house next door. The crickets were deafening. He hunkered down and crept around to the back of the house.

CHAPTER 69

Vicki undressed slowly, languorously, drawing out her movements as Hal watched. After letting her blouse slip silently to the floor, she began removing her other clothing. Before her divorce from Bone, Vicki had found herself undressing quickly in the bathroom and donning her nightgown hurriedly before he got to the bedroom and took her movements as an invitation. In truth, she had begun to find Bone disgusting, his slovenliness a complete turnoff.

Nearly to the end, Vicki turned to face Hal as she reached behind her back to unfasten the button on the back of her skirt. With this and her final garments on the floor at the end of the bed, Vicki joined her husband in bed, both basking in their closeness.

And that was when they heard the noise from just outside the window.

CHAPTER 70

The click startled Bone. What was he doing with the pistol in his hand outside the Childers' bedroom? He didn't remember taking it out, but it must have happened during . . . .

Goddam bitch, Bone screamed in his mind, imagining what Vicki and her fricking husband were doing. He stumbled away from the window, shuffling through ivy that clung now instead of muffling his footsteps as before. He sprinted down the driveway of the house next to Vicki's, and at the street he made a cut his old teammates would have been proud of. Breathing heavily, he jerked open the car door and hurled his body under the wheel. The engine roared, and Bone sped away into the night, not even stopping to light a cigarette until he was well out of the Childers' subdivision.

In his own carport, Bone cracked the car door and sat in the dim light, smoking and cursing his ex-wife. He held the pistol again, and with each curse he pulled the trigger.

"Goddam bitch," he said.

Click.

"Sorry sack of shit quit undressing where I could see her sorry ass!"

Click.

But truth be told, that sorry ass was looking damn fine now that she was with that hairy sumbitch she had married. What the hell has he got that I don't have?

Well, a job for one thing, his inner voice told him. And money. And a nice house. And all the things he thought he and Vicki had once had.

And now he had jack shit.

He should just load his pistol and get it over with.

Or maybe he would load the pistol and take them both out before he blew his brains all over their nice, clean bedroom. That would show 'em.

CHAPTER 71

B rad opened his eyes to the darkness of the room. Moonlight cast a pale glow over the end of his bed. In shadow, the rack holding the glucose solution looked like a stick figure.

His arm ached dully, but Brad lay still, ignoring it. A bandage covered the needle stuck into the vein in his elbow, tethering him to the rack. How long had it been since he'd heard the voices? A week? For the past week he'd slept and feigned stupor, lying passively while he was cleaned and his bed linen changed. He hadn't struggled even when his urine catheter was removed, discarded, and replaced. For all *they* knew, Brad was his normal insane self.

Where were the threatening, warning, commanding voices that had filled his consciousness for the past months? They were gone but not forgotten. It was like the time Brad had had a terrible sore throat. He awakened one day to its absence, but he spent most of the morning swallowing heavily to see if the pain would return. Brad spent most of the time he was awake searching his mind for the sounds he had sometimes known were hallucinatory.

Brad listened to the ward sounds, to the sigh of the air conditioning, to the soft snores of the men in the few occupied beds. Mr. Douglas was unusually quiet in the bed nearest to his. Perhaps he was more sedated than usual.

In one of his lucid periods, Brad had heard why Mr. Douglas shared the ward for the criminally insane with him. After months of hearing voices telling him to do horrible things, Mr. Douglas had finally listened to them. The event that finally sent him over the edge was when he came home one day to find his wife in bed with his best friend, or at least with the man he had considered his best friend. Without a word, he had gone across the hall into the spare bedroom and retrieved the pump 12-gauge shotgun he kept under the bed. He came back to find his wife and his former best friend scrambling to get dressed. When they saw the gun, they begged for mercy, but three shots later, they lay in pieces on the floor and bed, their blood soaking into the carpet and mattress.

Brad had heard one of the nurses say that Mr. Douglas didn't have long to live, and the staff checked on him so frequently that it was almost more than Brad could bear. He had come close to revealing his consciousness several times during the past week because of Mr. Douglas.

Why was he faking the stupor? It would certainly be more comfortable without the needle in his arm and the tube in his bladder. But every time he started to reveal himself, something held him back. This way he was invisible, the catatonic schiz on the ward.

"You think he'll ever come outta it?" the nurse named Marta had asked Bruce. Bruce always came with her when it was time to replace the catheter. Although Bruce was gentle, Brad mentally cringed when he heard the man's tread.

"Naw, I've seen 'em like this before," Bruce answered. "This dude done burned all his wires."

Another day Brad heard Bruce ask Marta, "You know what he's in here for?" Marta didn't know.

"He poisoned his whole family. Killed his mother and sister, I heard."

Sandy didn't die, he had wanted to say. She was too heavy. But to tell the truth, he was glad he hadn't killed his sister. Maybe she would come see him someday.

Brad heard the lock and watched the shaft of light widen on the ceiling. Midnight inspection. He closed his eyes and settled his breathing, listening to the squeaky tread of rubber-soled shoes.

They stopped, and he sensed the flash of light aimed at the face of a sleeper. The light winked out, and the squeaking started again. Another stop and another light flash. Walking sounds again, nearing his bed. Brad's heart rate skipped into another gear. He felt the attendant's presence at Mr. Douglas' bed, and the spot of light reddened the inside of his eyelids. Any moment now and the light would wink out, the tread would start and stop, and the light would be on his face. Could he fool the attendant? Would his palpitations give him away?

Something was wrong. The attendant was taking too long checking Mr. Douglas. Brad wanted to look, to crack his eyelids and, squinting, see the reason for the delay. But he didn't, fearing that the moment he opened his eyes, the flashlight would stab into them like a spotlight, and he would be discovered.

The light winked off, and the squeaky tread began again. But it was moving away this time.

Fast.

Brad turned his head toward Mr. Douglas' bed, peering into the shadowy darkness. The man was half out of his bed, his head and shoulders hanging off, one hand brushing the floor. The ward door burst open, and two white-garbed men came toward Brad, walking swiftly. He turned his head back and closed his eyes, praying they hadn't seen him.

They hadn't.

"You were right, Al," one voice said, after the two stopped. "He's deader'n a mackerel."

"Shit," said the other. "Why'd the fucker have to go on our shift?"

They walked away, unhurriedly this time. Brad listened for the sound of the lock. It didn't come.

A chance? After all, he was invisible, the nut in a stupor. If he could get out the door, out of the building, hide somewhere on the grounds, maybe he could get away in the excitement over Mr. Douglas' death.

But where would he go? What would his father say if Brad came home? Brad knew his father still loved him, perhaps more than before. Maybe his dad would shelter him, not make him come back.

Brad moved then, hoping he had a few minutes. First, he ripped off the bandage and slipped out the IV needle. There was a momentary sting that was quickly replaced by the familiar dull ache.

Next, he pulled out the catheter. It made him need to pee, but he squeezed back the urge. He slipped out of bed and stood, tottering momentarily, weak from lack of exercise. His stomach churned, and he broke into a cold sweat. Fighting nausea, Brad thrust his pillow lengthwise under the sheet. To a casual glance the bulge might be his sleeping body.

Brad was almost to the door when he heard voices approaching. He flattened himself against the wall. The same two men entered, one pushing while the other guided a gurney.

"What'd the doc say?" asked the pusher, whispering.

"He said to get the body outta the ward. Keep the loonies from being scared by it." They stopped at Mr. Douglas' bed, both with their backs to the door. Brad slipped through it into the brightly lit hall outside.

Squinting against the light, he padded softly on bare feet down the deserted corridor to where it intersected another. Brad was already panting from exertion and fear. His legs quivered, and he prayed he could make it out of the building. At the intersection, he turned right, guided by an exit sign.

An endless corridor stretched ahead, and Brad hurried along it, left hand lightly touching the wall for balance. He felt naked, exposed, expecting any moment to hear someone from behind yell at him to stop. He could almost feel eyes piercing the back of his thin hospital gown.

Brad turned another corner and saw the double doors ahead. A sign on one of the doors proclaimed that this was an emergency exit and if it were opened, an alarm would sound. A thick chain loosely connected the two horizontal bar handles. The chain ends were joined by a huge Master lock. Why had he thought he would be able to leave the building? All he'd done was reveal that he was out of his stupor.

He padded on, more slowly now, defeated. Try it anyway, his inner voice told him. Maybe there would be enough play in the chain to squeeze his emaciated body through. Maybe he could get out and hide somewhere before night security responded to the alarm. Maybe he would sprout wings and fly away!

He pushed the handle on the right door, and the door opened with a sound that reverberated through the still building. It opened just enough for Brad to feel the heat outside, to smell the deliciously scented, natural air.

No alarm sounded.

What Brad didn't know was that smokers had routinely disabled the alarm sensor at the emergency exit so that they could grab a quick smoke without getting caught. They had religiously reset the alarm many times, but at some point it just seemed easier to leave it disconnected. After all, nobody was skinny enough to slip through the crack.

Nine inches. That was all the play in the chain. Was it enough? Brad knelt below the chain and slipped his head through the opening. He had read somewhere that if you could get your head through, the rest of the body would follow. But maybe that was only for mice.

Turned sideways, his shoulders and chest eased through. For a moment he thought his hips would stick, but, thin before, his weeks of illness-induced starvation had made him little more than skin and bones. Brad closed the door behind him.

He inhaled deeply, delighting in the asphalt smell. At least it didn't smell antiseptic. Crickets chirped loudly, and the shiny roundness of the full moon brought tears to his eyes.

No longer invisible, Brad looked frantically for somewhere to hide. There were no trees and no shrubbery. The building squatted like an ugly toad in the middle of a parking lot. A high wire fence topped by razor-wire surrounded the lot, which, at this time of night, contained only four cars.

Brad was amazed to find the asphalt still warm. The day must have really been hot. He trotted to the first car, a Chevrolet with a peeling vinyl roof. Locked.

The next car in the lot was a Mazda GLC. Three years before, when Brad was in junior high, he had ridden to school every other week in a car just like this one. He almost smiled when he spotted the car, seeing it as a link with his past and sanity. His incipient smile became real when the rear door on the passenger's side opened. Brad scrambled inside, fingers fumbling in the dark for the seat back release. He found it, lowered the seat, and slithered through the opening into the deep well of the trunk, molding himself around and over unseen objects. He pulled the seat closed, settled himself in the musty blackness, and exhausted, fell asleep.

CHAPTER 72

"Whatcha think, Jesse?" Stump whispered to his brother on the bunk below. He took a drag on his cigarette. Other than smoking a joint from time to time with his brother, Stump had not been a smoker until he landed in jail. He planned to quit when he got out, which he hoped would be very soon.

"Sounds okay to me, Stump." Jesse sounded excited, and Stump figured his eyes had their faraway expression. For a moment, Jesse's cigarette glowed brighter, and in the light from it Stump caught a hint of his brother's grin.

Somebody farted in one of the dark cells, a long sound ending wetly. Stump chuckled. "What you think of the food now?"

"I'm tired of beans," Jesse said. "Why'd they quit bringin' chicken, anyway?"

Stump's escape plan was simplicity itself. He would start a fire in his mattress and when Jerry Samuels came to put it out, he and Jesse would overpower him and run like hell. Samuels wasn't going to catch them. He would be lucky just to catch his breath. Stump figured any of the other cops in the station would be too surprised to stop them.

"How we gonna breathe with all the smoke, Stump?"

"Good question, Jesse," Stump said, and Jesse grinned at the words of approval from his brother. "Soak your t-shirt in the water in the toilet, wring it out, and use it to cover your nose." He hopped down and began to put his plan into action. When he finished, Jesse followed suit.

"Where we gonna go?" Jesse wanted to know.

"We're gonna split up when we get outside, Jesse. Make it harder for 'em to find us."

"I thought we was gonna stick together, Stump," Jesse complained, forgetting to whisper.

"Hold it down," Stump hissed. His goddam brother had shit for brains, and Stump already regretted telling Jesse he could leave with him. "Just listen. I'm gonna hide in Emmett's garage, maybe steal a car or something." Preferably one that wouldn't break down on an interstate. This time he planned to go south and west and try to disappear in Mexico. Maybe the 2 years of high school Spanish would be good for something, after all.

"Why don't you go home? Hide in that ditch back of the house. I'll come pick you up soon as I get a car." Like hell he would. He wanted to get as far away from Jesse as he could; Jesse was the reason they were in jail in the first place.

"Okay, Stump," Jesse said.

"You ready?" Stump felt his brother tense.

"Sure."

Stump blew on the glowing end of his cigarette, and then touched the hot tip to the side of his ticking mattress. A thin, acrid wisp of smoke curled away from the tip, and in the faint light Stump could see the mattress cover darken. This was going to take longer than he'd thought.

"Put your butt on it, too," he said. Jesse did, and they waited.

Time moved like cold molasses, but the dry ticking caught, and the thin wisp widened into a small cloud. The man in the cell next to theirs coughed and began to curse. "What the hell y'all smokin' in there," he yelled.

Stump felt his mattress getting warm on the smoldering end.

"How's it doin'?"

"Pretty good," Stump whispered, holding his t-shirt tighter against his nose. His eyes watered. "Gimme your mattress, an' I'll add it to mine."

A voice from a cell asked, "Is something burnin' in here?"

Laughter in the dark. "People are smokin', asshole." There was another fart, and someone said, "Shit fire and save the matches." More laughter.

Stump and Jesse knelt on either side of their cell door where the air was still breathable. Smoke billowed from the smoldering mattress. They waited for someone to sound the alarm.

"Fire," someone said, tentatively. Then another voice took up the cry.

"Let us outta here!" the prisoner in the cell closest to the door screamed at Samuels' fat face filling the screened window. The face disappeared.

The overhead lights flared on, and Samuels came charging through with a fire extinguisher. He saw immediately that the smoke was coming from the cell containing Stump and Jesse.

"Get back, you two," he yelled as he turned the key in the lock.

Instead of getting back, as told, the two came charging out, Stump putting a block on Samuels that his high school coach would've been proud of. They were out the door Samuels had left open before he could regain his feet.

CHAPTER 73

REM sleep. Grady's eyes moved back and forth, scanning the scene in his dream. It was a good dream, outlandish like most dreams, but good. In it, Grady was in the house where he grew up. Lots of his dreams were set in that place. Marge was also there, although he didn't meet her until after his parents had moved from the house on Sycamore. They were having a meal with his parents and Timothy, Grady's older brother who got killed in Vietnam. The dream felt so good he hated to let it go when the phone rang.

"For you." Marge handed him the phone. The clock hummed on her side of the bed, and Grady squinted at it, trying to see the time without completely opening his eyes. 12:25.

His father! What else could it be at this time of night?

"Hello," he said, sitting up, wide awake, expecting to hear his mother's voice.

"Chief?" the night dispatcher said.

Grady yawned. Relief. "Yeah?"

"All hell's broke loose down here," Cpl. Jones said. Grady's relief evaporated.

"What happened?"

The policeman's response was so garbled that Grady missed most of it, but the few words he caught raised the small hairs on the back of his neck. "Fire in the jail" and "escape" sounded ominous. "I'll be right down," he said, handing the receiver to Marge to replace. At 12:40, he backed into the street and rocketed away.

CHAPTER 74

Stump slipped through the deserted cemetery, stepping carefully over fallen headstones he could see by the moonlight, grateful for the excuse to stop running. Badly winded, his breath came in great whooping gasps. The smoke he had inhaled at the jail didn't help. He wasn't particularly superstitious, but he was still spooked at the idea of the cemetery at night. Still, cutting through would save him half a block.

Stump straddled the rusty wrought iron fence at the back of the lot. Looking back the way he had come, Stump nearly collided with a tree, throwing up his hands at the last instant to brush against the rough pine bark. A smoke smell clung to his nostrils; whether it was still with him from the jail or had drifted his way on the light summer breeze, he couldn't say. He heard a siren.

"It's about time," he muttered to himself. Stump started trotting again, putting more distance between himself and the jail. From time to time he paused to listen, ready to desert the road for the shadow of a house at the first hint of pursuit. None came, and the illuminated clock on the back wall in the office of his uncle's garage showed 12:15 when Stump slipped through the side door. He had found the key easily enough, secreted in the battery shell out back. He replaced the key after unlocking the door, and then relocked the door from the inside. Now all he had to do was to get the key to the

Toyota Camry parked outside, "borrow" the money in his uncle's cash drawer, and he would be on his way to Mexico.

It had all been so easy that Stump was unprepared for what he found, or rather, didn't find–the keys to the cars. The key rack was where it had always been, just to the left of the door from the office to the garage proper, but the rack was completely bare. Not a key in sight. It didn't take long for Stump to realize what had happened. His earlier theft had caused his uncle to change his habit of leaving the keys where they could be taken by someone inside the garage.

Stump thought briefly of calling the police and giving himself up, but that thought was quickly discarded along with the idea of taking a nap in the storage room. The sound of a big truck changing gears and accelerating into the highway beside his uncle's garage gave Stump the germ of a plan–he might be able to hitch his way out of trouble.

With a screwdriver from his own toolbox, Stump prised open the locked desk drawer where his uncle kept the petty cash. Taking what little money there was, Stump next rifled the cold drink machine. Here his luck finally changed, as there was a week's worth of small change in the coin box. His pockets bulging, Stump swiped a coke and left.

CHAPTER 75

Noland pulled in behind the car parked in front of First Presbyterian Church, which faced the police station. He hesitated before getting out, fighting the urge to turn around and head back home. "Did you throw away that letter I got about the job at Springhill, Marge? You been saying we need a change." Yeah, that was it. Run away from Harper in her time of need. He saw plenty of need in the smoke billowing out the front door of the police station. Could he use this as an excuse to get a new station?

Let it burn, boys, he thought, directing his silent prayer to the 25-year-old fire engine blocking half the street. It would have to burn to the ground before the town would get a new one.

"Make do, Grady," he could hear the mayor say. "Air it out and slap on a fresh coat of paint, that's what we'll do. Hell, you know we can't afford to start over."

An ambulance, siren fading, squeezed into the space between the fire truck and the sidewalk in front of the station. In moments, the ambulance was loaded and on its way back to the hospital. A line of men stood, sat, or lay against the station's front wall. Prisoners? Three men stood just close enough to be their guards.

The station door disgorged two men dressed in slickers, faces hidden behind gas masks. They walked unhurriedly toward the fire truck, and in their otherworldly garb they looked to Noland like extras from *Towering Inferno*.

Noland sighed and opened his door. Time to take charge.

"Chief," Jones said, and Noland caught the relief tinged with fear and something else. Guilt?

Noland nodded at his dispatcher and the two patrolmen standing with him, Buck Wilson and Todd Askew, and they nodded back. The prisoners appeared to be in shock.

"Well?" he said, arching an eyebrow. "How bad's the damage?"

"No damage, Chief," Jones said. "Jus' a lot of smoke." In the light from the streetlight on the corner, sweat glistened on his forehead. Normally natty in his starched uniform, the dispatcher looked wilted. "They put out the fire right away," he said, nodding at the fire truck and slickered firefighters. "Put a fan in there, and you'll never know there was a fire."

"Unh-huh," Noland said, disappointed, his dreams of a new jail vanishing. "Where's Samuels? Wasn't he on duty?" He remembered the ambulance scene when he drove up. "Anybody hurt?"

"Samuels is okay," Askew said. "Just got kicked around a little."

"Trapped!" one of the prisoners cried. "Trapped like fuckin' rats." A man on his right moaned, while the prisoner who spoke coughed productively and spat.

"What's he talking about, Jones?"

"The men in the cells, Chief," Wilson said, when Jones couldn't or wouldn't speak. Wilson was in his early 20s and looked younger. His sandy hair was clipped short, military style, and his blue eyes still had an innocence that revealed his inexperience at police work.

"I thought you said there wasn't much damage." Noland said.

"Smoke, Chief," Wilson said. Noland looked at the front door again, remembering the cloud he had seen when he parked.

"All of 'em?"

"Only three," Jones said, finding his voice at last. "They was all in the back cell. Samuels managed to get the others out."

"Who were they?"

"Bobby Murray, Joe Donaldson, and Rufus whatsisname, that guy from Mississippi."

"Carter," Noland said.

Jones nodded. The fire chief, who had been talking to his men near the truck, joined them.

"Hi, Grady," he said, ignoring the other three. "Hell of a time to have to get up, ain't it?" But in his unwrinkled white shirt with three ironed pleats front and back and black pants with a knife-edge crease, Freddy "Red" Benson might have been waving from a donated Ford convertible in the annual Christmas parade.

Noland rubbed his face and felt stubble. "Looks like it was harder on me than on you, Red," he said.

Benson laughed. The fire chief was short, pudgy, and red faced. He seemed endlessly good humored, even when there wasn't a fire to make him jolly.

"What's the situation inside?"

"Not much of a fire, Grady. Burning mattress is all it was." Benson produced a pack of gum and offered it around. Noland took a piece. "By the way, mattress fires are hard as hell to put out with water."

"Why's that?" Noland asked.

"The mattress fibers wick the water away from where it's smoldering, and the fire starts up again. Anyway, all that's left is to let the place air out. You'll be back in tomorrow. I called Major Curtis before you got here, and he said he's got a room over at the Armory where you can keep the prisoners tonight."

"Thanks," Noland said.

"Now, Grady, I hate to be an 'I told you so,' but ..."

"We put in a smoke detector a year ago, Red, if that was what you were going to say."

"Why didn't it go off?"

"Hell if I know," Noland said. "Any ideas, Jones?" Brian shuffled his feet, and his guilty look reappeared.

"Uh, Samuels took out the battery, Chief."

"Why did he do that?"

"He got tired of the damn thing bleepin' from all the cigarette smoke."

"Get it back in and put up a no smoking sign," Noland said. He turned back to the fire chief. "How'd it start, Red? Any ideas?"

"Yeah. Looks like one of the prisoners started it in his mattress. With a cigarette would be my guess. When he got it going, he piled on another mattress to get more smoke."

"You think it was deliberate then?"

"Sure."

"Uh, Chief," Jones said, and Noland figured from his tone of voice that there was more bad news.

"Yeah?"

"Couple of guys ran away when they got outside."

"Who?"

"The Watkins boys."

"Jesus H. Christ," Noland said. "That's all we need, to have those two running around loose." Jones avoided his glare.

"Anybody looking for 'em?" He waved at the departing fire chief. "Thanks again, Red."

"Johnson headed in the direction Stump took," Wilson said. "Him and Jesse split up when they hit the street."

"Why aren't you two looking for Jesse?" Noland said, addressing the two patrolmen.

"They're helpin' me watch the prisoners, Chief," Jones said. "Besides, Jesse oughta be easy to find. Where's he gonna go?"

"Anybody call the highway patrol to get 'em to set up road-blocks?" Jones shook his head. "Okay. Askew, you get the van and take these guys over to the Armory. When you bring the van back, get your car and start looking for Jesse. Check his house first. Wilson, you come with me, and we'll see if we can't find Stump." Noland started toward his car, stopped, and turned back to the two patrolmen. "Anybody notify the newspaper?"

They shook their heads.

"Give 'em a call from the Armory."

CHAPTER 76

Keeping to the alleys, Jesse escaped the downtown area only a few minutes after he and Stump left the station. As the business district thinned, Jesse was frightened by the sound of a car coming up the street behind him. He ran behind a building and hid in a loading dock. When the car had gone, Jesse trotted from behind the building to the next street over. Across the street from where he stood, an electronic message board behind a bank scrolled the time and temperature. Jesse didn't have to read the sign to know it was hot and late.

He also knew the police would come looking for him at his father and grandmother's house, and that's why he decided not to take his brother's advice and hide in the ditch behind the house. As for waiting for Stump to come pick him up, he didn't have any hope of that. He had figured from their time together in jail that Stump thought their situation was his fault.

Instead of turning right, Jesse turned left. If he couldn't get away, at least he could get even.

CHAPTER 77

Brad awoke to bumpy movement, the smell of rubber and rope and exhaust fumes, and to blackness, darkness so profound he couldn't tell whether his eyes were open or not. It reminded him of the time he and his family toured a cavern in Sweetwater, Tennessee. At one point, the guide turned out all the lights to give them the experience of total darkness. Brad, 11 at the time, had to chew the back of his hand to keep from screaming.

This time, relief soothed his terror. Movement, the hum of tires on pavement, meant he was leaving the asylum. But moving where? And what would he do when the movement stopped?

Wait. Brad waited until he heard the engine stop and the car door open and shut. He waited while he heard footsteps moving away. And then he waited some more. Finally, when he could wait no longer, he worked the trunk latch and cracked the lid.

Outside was darkness, but it wasn't as total as inside. He looked out onto a driveway and lawn illuminated by a distant streetlamp and a more distant moon. A dog barked, and he hoped it was inside a fence. Brad climbed out of the trunk.

He was in a neighborhood of small houses set close together. Most of the residents owned large American cars, Ford the most popular make. Many of the cars were parked either on the side of the street or in the owners' yards. Brad hesitated, feeling weak and dizzy, uncertain which direction to take. If he'd had a coin to flip, he would have flipped it, but penniless and barefooted, clad in a hospital gown, he walked away from the streetlight.

━━◀❍▶━━

Still barefooted and hallucination-free, Brad now wore blue jeans and a faded cotton work shirt as he tottered toward the big rig at the all-night truck stop. Each step sent a lance of pain into his calves. He was afraid to look at his feet, and with each step he cursed his stupidity for discarding the gown. Two blocks after he found the damp clothes hanging on the clothesline, he realized he could have altered the gown to make passable protection for his feet. But he hadn't gone back, and now he was about finished. He was ready to tell someone who he was and to beg them to take him back to the institution. Why had he ever thought he could escape?

As Brad approached the truck, the driver opened the door and eased himself out and down. He stood on the warm asphalt and stretched, took a last drag from his cigarette and flicked it away. Still stretching, the man looked incuriously at Brad staggering toward him.

"Whatcha say, good buddy?" the man said.

Call the asylum, Brad thought of saying. I'm an escaped loony. But instead, he croaked in a voice used for little except screaming for the past several months, "Not much."

The man looked at Brad's feet, blinked, and stopped stretching. Brad stopped. "Which way you headin'?" the man said. Like the rest of his body, his face was thin. It was also tanned a dark copper and was deeply creased. Fine wrinkles from squinting into the sun masked the man's eyes without hiding the twinkle of good humor Brad saw there.

Brad read concern in the man's expression and said, "North."

"Cal Drummond," the man said, extending a hand hard from gripping the steering wheel of an 18-wheeler, a hand whose top was covered with ropy veins. Brad lurched forward, grasped the hand with his, felt the pressure, and then his legs trembled and buckled. Drummond caught him easily and lowered him to the step next to the gas tank on his rig.

"Just lean forward. Put your head between your knees. That's right." Sitting on the truck, head down, close to fainting, Brad felt foolish, embarrassed at his weakness. Tears started in his eyes, and he kept his head down so the man wouldn't see.

"What's your name, Son?"

"Brad, Brad Childers."

"Listen, Brad," Drummond said, "I'm takin' a load of furniture to Nashville. You're welcome to come along if you want."

"That would be great," Brad said, looking up. He was sure Drummond could see his eyes glistening from the tears, but suddenly he didn't care. Hungry, exhausted, his feet macerated slabs of agony, he had finally reached the point where need overcame his teenage self-consciousness.

"You just sit there, and I'll take a leak and get us some burgers. Want some fries to go with 'em?"

"I don't have any money."

"Did I say anything about money? At this time of night, I'm just glad of some company to keep me awake."

CHAPTER 78

Noland rapped harder on the door, feeling rumpled and unshaven and slightly nauseated. God, how he hated getting up after a couple of hours sleep. He wondered how Randy Watkins would respond to being awakened in the middle of the night.

Randy Watkins had made no effort to hide his hostility. "What the hell you want, wakin' me up this time of night? I had just dozed off, and now I'll never be able to get back to sleep."

Watkins smelled like a distillery. "Sorry, Mr. Watkins," Noland had said. "Stump and Jesse broke out of jail, and we're looking for them."

"Ain't my fault if you can't keep them boys locked up, and if I never see Jesse again, it be too soon."

"Mind if we check their rooms?" he had asked.

Watkins grumbled but let them in anyway. They found nothing to indicate the brothers had been there.

"You might check the ditch back of the house," Watkins had said at the door. "That little shit Jesse used to hide back there when he knew I was lookin' to beat the tar out of him."

Listening to Randy Watkins talk about Jesse made Noland feel something akin to sympathy for the boy. Not that anything could ever excuse what he did to Peter Dewberry, but still, Noland could see how Jesse turned out the way he did. But maybe he had it wrong. Maybe Jesse was evil all along, and his father was just trying to beat the devil out of him. That would certainly be Randy Watkins' story, but it was not a story Grady Noland could buy. He had never seen a baby that looked evil.

At Emmett Watkins' house, the porch light flared, and the front door opened a crack. Emmett squinted over the chain. "Yeah?"

"Grady Noland, Mr. Watkins. Your nephews broke out of jail a little while ago, and we were wondering if you might know anything about where they are." The door closed and then reopened without the chain. Emmett slept in a ribbed undershirt and boxer shorts, and Noland studiously kept his eyes on the man's face. Watkins yawned.

"I ain't seen 'em, Chief. You try my brother's house?"

Noland nodded. "We were thinking they might have decided to hole up in your garage. Would you mind letting us check it out?"

"Naw. Lemme pull on some clothes, an' I'll come with you."

"Thanks," Noland said, and Watkins shut the door. He soon reappeared wearing overalls and slippers. Watkins followed Noland to the car, and in a few minutes Noland, Wilson, and Emmett Watkins disembarked in front of Watkins' garage. Noland left the motor running and the headlights on.

"Could they have gotten in?" Noland said.

Watkins nodded. "There's a key out back Stump knows about." He opened the door to his office, snapping on a light as they entered. The office was deserted, but the evidence of Stump's burglary was unmistakable. "Well, somebody's sure been here."

"Mind if we look around, Mr. Watkins?" Watkins shook his head, and the men took the door into the three-stall garage, Wilson leading the way. Two of the stalls held cars, and Noland nodded to Wilson to check them out. The sound of the doors opening and shutting sounded unnaturally loud.

Watkins had followed the men into the garage and stood by the cold drink machine, shaking his head. "Wouldn't a thought Stump would do anythin' like this," he said.

"What's behind that door?" Noland asked, indicating a door behind the last stall.

"Storage room," Watkins said. "Tires, batteries, car parts, that kind of thing."

"Check it out," Noland said, and Wilson walked over, opened the door, and looked inside. "Stump's not here, Chief," he called.

CHAPTER 79

When he saw the name on the streetside mailbox, Jesse grinned. He remembered something from the trial.

"Your name?" the DA had asked.

"Daniel Lyons Dewberry," the boy had said, looking pale and frightened.

"Address?"

"2837 Greenbriar."

Jesse rubbed his eyes, and a muscle twitched on the right side of his forehead. He couldn't remember shit at school, but he remembered Danny's address. Over the weeks and months he and Stump had spent in the Harper city jail, Jesse had questioned each new cellmate about Greenbriar's location until finally someone knew.

"Payback time for mister Danny fuckin' Dewberry," he muttered, sliding noiselessly behind a bush to the left of the carport. While he was at it, maybe he would have some fun with Danny's mother. She wasn't half bad looking when she wasn't looking at him like she wanted to fry his ass.

CHAPTER 80

When Peter was alive, Nancy loved their bedroom and their bed. "The bosom of buddy," she had called it, settling in, wriggling her toes, pulling the covers up under her neck on winter nights. She would snuggle up against Peter while he read, and she'd fall asleep without even trying.

But Peter was gone, and now Nancy watched and dozed through evenings and nights of television, avoiding the emptiness of *their* room. In the family room, Nancy awoke with a start. "Danny?" she said. On the TV, "Late Night" with David Letterman was just ending. Forgetting, she dropped her right hand to the spot where Skipper should have been, momentarily feeling for the dog's rough coat. Her hand met nothing, and she sadly remembered the squeal of tires, that awful thud. Her heart sank at the memory of Skipper's mad dash after a squirrel that darted across the street in front of them. She'd been holding the leash too loosely, she later realized, and Skipper was under the wheels of a neighbor's pickup before she could get to him. One squeal and he was gone.

At the time, she had wondered if she could handle the added grief. And the guilt. Peter had always told her she should have her hand through the loop on the leash when walking the dog, but she'd forgotten without him there to remind her. And one time was all it took.

"I was dreaming again," she said, talking to herself as she was wont to do these days. "Peter was in it."

Peter had been changing the oil in one of the cars, something he rarely did when he was alive. Why had she dreamed that, she wondered. And she wondered if she would ever fully recover from the trauma of his death and recover the ability to fall asleep in their bed.

Her physician had said, "Tincture of time, Nancy." Then Dr. Allen had repeated it, "Tincture of time." As though it was a prescription. Take a daily dose of "tincture of time." The only problem was that it looked like she would have to take it the rest of her life.

There were always the little reminders of Peter. When she shaved her legs, the smell of the shaving cream reminded her of the scent of his smooth cheek when he'd freshly shaved. Sometimes, taking a shower, she imagined she heard him whistling in the bedroom, getting dressed. How could he have been so happy in the morning?

If Danny cooked breakfast, something he had started doing on weekends, she pictured her husband turning the sausage.

When would she stop seeing men who reminded her of Peter, if only for an instant? How many times had she had to bite back a cry, a hail of greeting, to the back of some stranger in a mall or in the grocery store? And how many more times would she sit in front of the television set, crying, remembering her lost love?

Sometimes, when the memories of Peter were strongest, Nancy slipped into the study and turned on his computer, calling up files in which he had written journal articles. Although she didn't get much from them, she read the manuscripts compulsively, listening to Peter's voice reading the words in her mind. She cried then, too. She had spent a weekend skimming all his files, searching for some personal message, something Peter might have written just to her. But there was nothing, and she didn't blame him. How could he have known about Jesse and Stump Watkins?

When she thought of them, particularly Jesse, Nancy had dark thoughts. She saw herself as a gentle person, but the memory of his grins during the trial and of his description in his confession of how he had killed Peter made her think of doing horrible things. For once, she hoped what she had read about homosexual rape in prison was true. At least she could take comfort from the knowledge that the monster was not in Harper.

CHAPTER 81

Under a full moon, gleaming palely white, Jesse stole from tree to tree in the Dewberrys' backyard. A chorus of crickets hummed their mating tune. Pine straw crackled underfoot. Jesse peered in the lighted window and saw Danny's mother dozing in front of the TV. Colored light played over her pale features in the darkened room.

He grunted, and his grin consumed his face. As he watched, the woman's head lolled forward and then jerked upright. Although she looked in his direction, he didn't think she could see him. Behind him a wind chime tinkled, and Jesse jumped away from the window, heart racing. Shit, she mighta seen that, he thought, but when he eased back so that he could see in again, the woman had her eyes closed.

Jesse continued around the back of the house, looking through windows into unlighted rooms, trying to get a feel for the place. After the family room, there was a room that wasn't a bedroom and wasn't the living room. Without knowing its purpose, Jesse hated it, as bookshelves covered the walls. Next came a dark and empty bedroom. In the room beyond the empty bedroom, on the far end at the front of the house, a night light revealed Danny's sleeping form. Looking at Danny, Jesse felt a mixture of envy and hatred. He clenched his fists, aching to smash them against the boy's pale face. He turned and walked back the way he had come, back to the pet door he had seen when he started his inspection tour.

CHAPTER 82

T he truck roared steadily through the night, big wheels devouring the miles. Drummond had taken the interstate to
Birmingham, bypassing the city a little after 6:00 and picking
up I-65. On their right, the sky was just starting to lighten. From
time to time, Drummond made a terse comment into the microphone of his CB radio, speaking in a code that reminded Brad of his
foreign language class.

"Gonna be another scorcher, Brad." Drummond fumbled a cigarette out of a pack on the dash. Warm air whistled through the cab,
smelling of piney woods and diesel fumes.

"Feels good," Brad said, comparing the heat and road smells
with the chilled, medicinally scented asylum air.

"Where you from?" Drummond asked. He held the wheel with
his right hand, resting his left forearm on the window. Perhaps in
deference to his passenger, he held his cigarette so that most of the
smoke was sucked out of the cab.

"Little town just off the interstate. Harper, Alabama. Ever heard
of it?"

Drummond shook his head and took another drag. "By the way,
Brad," he said, "I'm just nosy, talkin' to pass the time. Anything you
don't wanna talk about is okay by me."

"Thanks," Brad said, wishing any of the psychiatrists at the asylum had been half as understanding as this truck driver.

"Anyway, I was wonderin' what you were doin' in Tuscaloosa."

"I was sick. In the hospital." He didn't want to say *which* hospital.

Drummond glanced his way. "You okay now?"

"Yeah."

With the sunrise, Drummond switched off his lights. He kept the big rig humming along at a steady 68.

After a while, he said, "How those feet feel?"

"Numb." Brad wiggled his toes in the athletic shoes and soft white socks Drummond had given him. Although they were too large for him, they certainly beat going barefooted. He had felt guilty about taking them, but Drummond said he never wore them anyway. "I bought 'em a couple of years back thinkin' I would jog a little in the mornings," he had said. "Back one time I was tryin' to quit smokin'. I thought if I ran, I wouldn't want to smoke. Didn't work, though. Damn near killed myself tryin' to run and smoke."

Brad thought that one good thing about his time in the asylum was that he had been able to kick his budding habit.

"Where you get off, Brad?"

"Decatur, I think."

"That ain't too far away," Drummond said. "Maybe 25 miles or so. How far is Harper from the interstate, anyway."

"'Bout 15 miles."

Drummond lit another cigarette, took a drag, and coughed. "Don't ever get started with these things," he said. "I started when I was about your age and have tried to quit a hundred times."

"My father smoked all through high school and college," Brad said. "And then quit cold turkey the day he married my mother. If he could do it, you could, too, Mr. Drummond."

"Cal."

"Cal."

"They got a truck stop in Harper, Brad?"

"I think so," Brad said, but he really wasn't sure. It wasn't something he'd ever thought about.

"Well, maybe I'll just drive on over. Get some breakfast and some diesel fuel."

"You don't have to for me, Mr. Dru ... Cal. I can make it from the interstate."

Drummond smiled, revealing a mouth with some spaces where teeth had once been. "I gotta eat sometime, Brad. Might as well be in Harper as anywhere else along here."

Brad opened his mouth to say that Decatur was closer, but he figured Drummond knew that already. "Thanks," he said, when Cal slowed and caught the exit west to Decatur and Harper.

CHAPTER 83

The house was on fire! "Get out," Grady yelled, and Marge just stared at him like he was crazy. "Where's Grady Jr.?"

"In his room, Dear," his wife said without opening her mouth. Grady felt his son's bedroom door, and his hand jerked reflexively away. White smoke curled lazily toward his legs. He kicked and the door swung inward. Behind it, wreathed in smoke and flames like a young Satan, stood Jesse Watkins.

"Guess your boy likes to smoke after all," Jesse said, grinning. Grady shoved him aside and clawed his way into the rapidly darkening, lengthening room. This can't be happening, he thought, and the thought brought him mercifully awake. His heart pounded alarmingly.

"Marge," he whispered. "You awake?"

"I am now," she answered. "What's wrong, Dear?"

"I just had a nightmare," he said, fumbling in his nightstand for a chapstick. He felt his wife's hand reaching for his under the sheet. Behind him the shade on the bedroom's rear window had a reddish-orange glow. "What time is it, anyway?"

"5:45," Marge said.

Grady groaned. "That's all?" He had only been asleep a couple of hours.

"Let's try to go back to sleep, Grady," she said, turning away.

"Okay," he said, but he felt wide awake. Grady slipped out of bed and stumbled into the bathroom to stand blinking over the commode. He didn't flush it. In the adjoining room, he squinted at himself in the mirror. He ran a glass of water and swished some around in his mouth. He spat the water, but not the foul taste, into the lavatory. The dark circles under his eyes convinced him to try for more sleep.

But sleep wouldn't come, kept at bay by a train of thoughts that centered on the fire and Jesse and Stump Watkins. Did they set the fire? It seemed mighty suspicious that the only two escapees were the brothers. And how could they have disappeared so completely? Grady had been sure that Stump would head for his uncle's garage again, and the stolen money convinced him that was what had happened. But where had Stump gone from there? Had he gotten away on the highway before the highway patrol put up roadblocks?

And what about Jesse? Grady worried more about the younger Watkins than he did Stump. If the truth were known, he halfway hoped Stump would get away, particularly if it was Jesse's idea to set the fire, if they had indeed set the fire. But Jesse was a loose cannon, and the idea of him running free in Harper made Grady's skin crawl.

Grady turned to his back and lay with his hands linked behind his head. He took a deep breath and let it out slowly. He willed his eyes to stay closed. Jesse's probably holed up somewhere, he told himself, and we'll find him in the morning.

But it was morning already, and they hadn't found him, and Jesse could be anywhere, up to Lord-only-knew-what mischief. Grady needed to urinate again. "One thing I'll do," he said to himself, finishing, "is call Nancy Dewberry and tell her Jesse's on the loose. No need for her to hear it on the radio."

CHAPTER 84

N ancy had been dozing in the family room, drifting like she often did, waking for the blare of commercials, then nodding off again, when she heard a familiar sound. "Skipper?" It was the sound she had heard so often when the dog slipped through his pet door into the utility room.

But she remembered Skipper was dead, so she drifted off again, forgetting the sound until she felt a body move by her chair. The body smelled of smoke and sweat, and Nancy knew before she opened her eyes that whoever had walked behind her didn't belong in her house.

"Oh, God," she had said, with that sinking feeling in her stomach that she had when they told her Peter had been found. She opened her eyes and screamed.

Jesse's right hand grabbed her throat, cutting off her wind so that her scream ended in a gargle. Nancy thought he was going to strangle her, but he thrust his face close to hers, and with breath that reeked of cigarettes and unbrushed teeth and a terrible diet, told her to shut the fuck up or he would cut her into little pieces. And then he showed her the knife. On his way through the kitchen, he had stopped and chosen her most wicked knife, the one she never used because it was too scary, the one that Peter had once wielded to mangle a Thanksgiving turkey. Now it gleamed in Jesse's hand.

The hand on her throat relaxed, and Nancy struggled to catch her breath. Jesse was stepping back, still brandishing the knife, when Danny staggered in from his bedroom, rubbing sleep from his eyes, lips mouthing, "What's wrong, Mom?"

In the eternity that followed, Nancy saw her son's pupils dilate, saw his lips retract in a grimace that somehow conveyed fear, anger, and hatred, and before she could scream no, he was charging Jesse. Surprised, Jesse fell back against the lamp and stereo. The lamp crashed, flickered, and went out, leaving the room in darkness except for the TV.

Shadows surged and heaved. Trying to escape from her chair and the feet kicking her shins, Nancy went backward in the chair, turning it over. She rolled free and scrambled to her feet, looking wildly for a weapon. She seized the broken lamp, hoisted it, as Jesse, on top, raised his knife hand and struck Danny on the side of the head. Danny lay still.

Jesse yelled, "Stop right there, Miz Dewberry."

She stopped.

"I'll cut out his heart with you watchin'," he said, grinning. Danny lay between Jesse's legs, face up, a spot of blood on the left side of his forehead.

"You've killed him," she said, dropping the lamp.

"Naw, he ain't dead. Just knocked out. But you do as I say, or he'll be dead."

Danny groaned, and Jesse raised the knife handle again.

"Don't," Nancy said. "Please don't hit him again."

Jesse ordered Nancy to bring him a rope, and she had searched frantically for something appropriate with Jesse hollering at her from the family room. Finally, she remembered the clothesline in the cabinet above the washer. When Jesse was satisfied that Danny was securely tied, he told her to take off her clothes, he wanted to see what she looked like "necked."

She shook her head, numbly, and Jesse slid the knife's blade under Danny's left ear and looked up at her, grinning. At the cold touch, Danny opened his eyes and Nancy could see his fear. She unbuttoned her shirt and slipped it off. Danny closed his eyes, and she was grateful for that.

Nancy undressed quickly, not giving Jesse the pleasure of a striptease. Nancy could see Jesse's eyes, magnified behind his thick glasses, glued to her body. He licked his lips, and she wanted to smash his face, knee him in the balls, take away the knife, and stab him again and again. But Danny lay beneath Jesse, his neck an easy target for the knife, now held casually while Jesse gaped at her.

"Lie down," he said, standing. She did, feeling the roughness of the area rug on her back and bottom. Jesse loomed over her, fumbling with his jeans, having trouble with the button because of the knife in his hand. He lay the knife on the arm of the couch, and Nancy wondered briefly if she might be able to overpower Jesse. As he struggled with his pants, she could see the hardness of his arms, the definition of the muscles there, and she discarded the idea.

Then his pants were down around his knees, and Nancy looked quickly away, hysterical laughter bubbling unbidden to her lips. She rolled into a fetal ball, hugging herself to try to stop the twitches and jerks of her shoulders.

"Goddam bitch," Jesse yelled. He knelt quickly beside her, his pants still down, and pummeled her back and arms with his fists.

A blow to the kidneys stopped Nancy's giggles, and she lay whimpering, expecting any moment to feel the coldness of the knife plunging into her back. Interspersed with the thud of Jesse's blows, she heard his hoarse breathing and his curses and Danny's cries for him to stop. As the blows slowed, she was aware that they no longer hurt very much, that they had a dull quality, and she sensed Jesse tiring. When the last one came, it was more of a tap. Jesse moved away from her, and she was sure he would retrieve the knife and skewer her with it. Her breathing shallowed and she felt faint. Thoughts of possible actions raced through her mind. Should she roll to her knees, spring up, run to the bedroom and lock the door and try to call the police before Jesse could get to her? That would mean abandoning Danny. Even though Jesse was stronger, should she try now to overpower him, maybe grab a book and smash him with it? Should she just tell her son that she loved him and wait for the stab? She heard Jesse's zipper, and then her clothes pelted her body.

"Put 'em back on," Jesse said. "You disgus' me."

When she was dressed, she asked, "What are you going to do with us, Jesse?"

Jesse looked away from the TV. "You're my ticket outta here," he said, "but first I'm gonna get some sleep." That's when he had tied her to the kitchen chair. As far as she knew, Danny still lay on the floor.

Inch by inch Nancy "walked" the chair toward the counter. Her goal was the utensil drawer filled with spatulas and spoons and long-handled forks and knives, all those lovely knives.

Nancy moved another half inch. Her problem was noise; she could have clattered to the counter in seconds, but she didn't want to wake Jesse.

How long had she been moving? It seemed like forever. Light filtered through the pine trees outside to color the curtains in the kitchen window. Her mouth tasted like she'd gargled with used toilet water, and the inside of her eyelids felt gritty. Her tightly bound hands ached dully, and her shoulders and back felt stiff and sore. She wondered if she could use her hands if she made it to the drawer.

Another inch. This time the noise she made sounded too loud. Holding her breath, she waited for Jesse to yell at her.

Silence. Birds sang outside, and a breeze tinkled her wind chime, but all she heard inside was the sound of her muffled breathing.

Another inch and another pause to see if Jesse had heard. What was Jesse planning to do with her and Danny? Was he planning to kill them after all? Force them to drive him out of Harper and then stab them both and dump their bodies beside the road? Did Jesse ever plan anything, or did he just react to the moment? Nancy didn't know, and the fact of not knowing strengthened her resolve to free herself. With a weapon of her own, she was sure she would have the strength to act.

Sometimes she caught herself thinking of Jesse as human, as just a kid not much older than Danny, who was desperate and hunted and probably more frightened than his captives. But then she remembered what he'd done to Peter, and her fingers twitched with the desire to grab anything she could use to hurt him.

The room was brighter now, but she only had a few more feet to go. She tried not to think of how badly she needed to urinate. If it came to it, she would just go ahead and wet herself.

Time seemed more of a problem now than noise. Surely Jesse would wake up soon. And when he did, he was bound to check on her. What would he say when he saw her across the room from where she'd started?

"Miz Dewberry, whatcha doin' headin' for the counter? Can I help?"

"No, I've made it on my own, Jesse," she said to herself, moving the last few inches in one burst, waiting one last time to see if Jesse had heard. Nancy slid open the drawer with fingers like clubs, then did a partial knee bend so that she could get her fingers inside. After that she groped, rooting for her paring knife, then found it, nearly dropping it twice before she got it turned the right way, blade against the rope, moving it a half inch up, then a half inch down, over and over, praying, sweating, feeling her bonds loosening, dear God she was going to make it.

The phone rang.

CHAPTER 85

Drummond hoped the boy would be all right. He had offered to take Brad home, or at least to the entrance to his subdivision, but the boy had insisted he could walk the rest of the way.

"No sweat, Cal," Brad had said. "It's just a few blocks from here." Here was a Gulf station next to a Dari Delite on the outskirts of Harper.

"Well, how about having breakfast with me and then calling your parents?" Drummond had asked, and Brad had said he wanted-ed to surprise his family and that he wasn't really hungry.

Brad held out his hand, and Drummond shook it while the boy mumbled something about how he would never forget Drummond's kindness. And then he was leaving, hobbling away in the heat, waving and smiling at the street to show he was okay.

Driving away from Harper, Drummond couldn't help thinking what a strange kid Brad was. He had an idea the boy was running away from a hospital in Tuscaloosa. Why else would he have been barefooted so early in the morning? Drummond didn't want to think about what kind of hospital Brad might have run away from, but the thoughts came anyway.

Drummond reached for a cigarette and lit it with a Bic. Surely Brad wasn't a mental patient; the boy seemed much too normal for that. Drummond's ideas of insanity were based on a few television programs and on things he'd heard from people who had little experience with it. He was thankful mental illness had never touched his family.

At 9:30 Drummond re-entered the interstate and headed north. He nudged the truck up to 72 and held it there. He had lost a few hours fooling with Brad, but he didn't regret it.

CHAPTER 86

Without a shade, sunlight poured unfiltered through the window, spearing Bone's eyes. He groaned and turned away from the light, drawing his bare knees up to his chest, trying to postpone reality with another couple hours of sleep. But sleep was only a memory, so Bone rolled out of bed and staggered into the bathroom.

He stood swaying over the toilet, his yellow stream striking a bubbling brownish-green soup that rose ominously when he pushed the handle. Bone watched helplessly, his bare feet seemingly glued to the floor. The noisome muck stopped just below the rim. Although he felt another urge, Bone ignored it.

"How in the hell can I take a crap in that?" he said, closing the door behind him.

In the bedroom again, Bone rooted through a pile of crumpled packs on the dresser for one that might have a cigarette. One by one, he threw the empty packs at the overflowing trash can next to one of Vicki's little tables. Instead of fighting over who got what, Vicki had left most of the furniture for Bone.

Finally, he straightened out the longest butt he could find and lit it. The lighter's flame seared hair in his right nostril, but Bone, undaunted, lay back on the rumpled, sweat-soaked bed, sucked his stale cigarette, and planned his day.

"Too hot to do anything this morning," he said. "Maybe I'll go by the employment office this afternoon." He rubbed his chin, felt stubble, and decided he had better shave before going. "Gotta make a good impression." Gotta quit talking to myself, he thought, inhaling a last lungful of the bitter smoke.

After a while, Bone tottered into the kitchen. More bad smells. If anything, the kitchen stank worse than the bathroom. "Rot smells worse than shit," Bone said, unaware that he had discovered an ancient truth and forgetting his resolve to stop talking to himself. "Maybe I'll clean the dishes," he muttered, already on his way out of the room. The sight of roaches crawling on the heaps of dirty dishes took away his appetite.

"One good thing," he said, smiling grimly. "Pretty soon all the roaches'll starve." Yeah, that was goddam funny, all right, except that he would starve first.

Running his fingers carefully along the top of the flue, Bone found in the chimney a bottle with two inches of bourbon. By nursing his find, he could kill the morning before he finished the bottle.

CHAPTER 87

Hannah found the half pint with an inch of amber liquid in the liftainer behind the church. She sniffed the whiskey, smiled, screwed the lid back on, and slipped the bottle into a pocket of her dress. She would save it for an after-lunch treat.

Just beyond the church, Hannah settled into her long-distance shuffle, feeling almost sprightly in the new (used) shoes Ida's oldest had given her for Christmas. Heat from the morning sun beat down on the old woman, warming her arthritic joints and diminishing their pain.

Every few minutes, Hannah held up her left arm to look at her watch, a birthday present from Ida. Its ivory case and band contrasted with her dark skin, and she delighted in the blinking digits. 7:53. 8:08. At 8:17, she saw the white boy.

"He's skinnier than I is," she muttered. And pale. Hannah had never seen anybody that white. He was so pale his skin seemed almost transparent, and his ankles, visible below the bottom of his jeans, were blue from the subsurface veins. The high-water jeans reminded her of the pants some of her nephews wore. The boy walked slowly by her, limping a little, eyes turned inward. Hannah didn't think he even saw her, but she was used to that from people.

She rattled on, remembering the boy's face. Something about it was familiar. Had she seen him before? Maybe in the newspaper but awhile back. "Shit," she said. "They all looks alike."

CHAPTER 88

"What the hell's that?" Jesse said, blinking, reaching for his glasses, scrabbling for his knife in the depression where the cushion abutted the back of the couch.

"Just the phone," Danny said from the floor where he had lain since his ill-fated charge. "How about letting me take a leak, Jesse?"

"How you gonna do that? I ain't gonna hold it for ya." Jesse sat up, feeling the pressure in his own bladder. The phone rang again, a long chime with a longer pause.

"Gimme a break, man," Danny said. "Either untie me or just un-snap my pajamas and let me sit on the toilet."

"Where's it at?" Jesse said. He had never thought of hostages needing to take a piss. That didn't happen in the movies and television shows he'd seen.

"Where's what?"

"The goddam toilet," he said, irritated and feeling slightly nau-seated from lack of sleep. He could still smell the smoke from last night. The phone rang again.

"Down the hall," Danny said. Jesse hooked a hand under Danny's armpit and pulled him up.

"You go firs'," Jesse said, prodding Danny in the back. He stood outside the door with his arms crossed, thinking how white Danny's legs were. Danny's stream sounded like it would never end. The phone's ringing had stopped.

Sometimes Jesse hated Danny for being white and having a father who didn't beat him. At those times, he wanted to do things to Danny to get even, to repay him for all the bullying he'd suffered at school and all the beatings he'd gotten from his old man.

He wasn't sure what he would do with the Dewberrys. He wished Stump was here to tell him what to do.

"I'm through," he heard Danny call. He helped the boy up and sat him in the hall.

"Don' go nowhere," Jesse said, grinning at his humor. He shut the door and laid his knife on the lavatory counter, holding himself and pissing while he stared at his reflection in the mirror. Jesse finished and zipped up. The tiny room smelled strongly of soap with just a hint of urine, and he felt another twinge of envy. The bathroom he and Stump shared was always nasty, with used rusty razor blades littering a brown-stained lavatory, a toilet that was rarely flushed, one permanently soggy towel stolen from a Motel 6, and a tub that took half an hour to drain. His granma had stopped cleaning the bathrooms, figuring their father ought to do it since he was home all the time. Jesse briefly thought of taking a bath in Danny's tub, filling it with hot water and soaking himself for awhile. After that, he thought about the breakfast he was going to get Danny's mother to fix. Yeah, that was a good idea. Maybe have eggs and grits and bacon.

Grinning from ear to ear at the thought of the great meal Miz Dewberry was going to fix, Jesse yanked open the bathroom door. Confronted with a double-barrel shotgun, both his hunger and his grin evaporated.

CHAPTER 89

Brad's pace had slowed dramatically since he waved goodbye to Cal at the Gulf station. When he had said he would walk the rest of the way home, he hadn't accounted for his months of inactivity. Now, he moved in a daze, each step feeling like it would be his last. Finally, three blocks away, he sat on the curb and cried. In the furnace of the noonday heat, Brad's hot tears dried before they hit the ground. When the voice came, he knew it was in his head.

"This is your second warning, Brad," the voice said, and Brad saw the soldiers raise their rifles. Their eyes were invisible behind polarizing sunglasses.

Brad laughed then, recognizing the scene from Stephen King's *The Long Walk*. If Garraty could walk for days, surely he could walk three more blocks. He stood shakily, eased his left foot forward–and nearly fell. Breathed through clenched teeth, "Unnhh." Then repeated.

On and on he walked, picking up a little speed as he got closer. At the top of the rise, Brad saw the familiar brick house through the fine mist of joyful tears. Before the hospital, he would never have thought homecoming could feel so good, so welcome. If only he could stay.

Brad let himself in with the key from the fake rock in the backyard. The house felt cool and smelled both familiar and different. He guessed correctly that the different odors came from the house's new occupant.

Brad opened the refrigerator and stood for a moment enjoying the frigid air. He took an apple and two slices of wheat bread, feeling like a thief. His moment of guilt was tempered by mild disapproval. His mother had never kept bread in the refrigerator. Well, he told himself, things are different now, and if I want to stay, I'll have to change. He ate at the kitchen table, carefully sweeping breadcrumbs into his hand to deposit in the sack under the sink.

Crying again, Brad stumbled through the silent house. He was glad the door was shut to his father's bedroom; the sense of the familiar was strong in the rest of the house, but he was sure Vicki's personal touch would be greatest there. There had been a few changes in the family room—a new picture over the mantle, some rearranged furniture, a ceiling fan—but overall the room felt achingly normal. What would he find in his room? Maybe it would be empty, stripped to the walls, his belongings in storage somewhere. Or, worse, maybe he would find artifacts from Vicki's former life. After all, they weren't expecting him to return. Ever.

The air conditioner came on as Brad reached for the doorknob, and he hesitated, startled. And then he was inside, and it was all right. Everything was the way he'd left it, only cleaner. Vicki or somebody had picked up, put away, made his bed. But it was still *his* bed, and he sat on it to ease off the shoes Cal had given him. The socks followed, and Brad winced when he tugged them off. His long walk had raised blisters on both of his heels.

Brad lay back on the rough spread and closed his eyes when his head hit the pillow. Gradually, he felt the tensions ease, the muscles in his legs unknot, the throbbing in his calves lessen. Still with eyes shut, he reached for the book he had seen on his nightstand, brought it to his nose, and sniffed. Still the same. He knew without looking what it was: *The Bachman Books: Four Early Novels* by Stephen King. He had been reading Rage before...before the hallucinations. Before the arsenic. Before the asylum.

Brad placed the heavy book on his chest and slept.

CHAPTER 90

Mayor Homer Wainwright was on the phone when Noland entered. The mayor waved the chief to a seat, flashed his politician's smile, and swiveled to face the window behind his desk, continuing his conversation as though Noland weren't in the room.

"You think they'll sue, Bill?" The mayor waited for a response while Noland pictured Bill Nabors. Nabors was the stereotype of the old-time lawyer, a heavy drinking, skirt chasing, slightly corrupt, good-old-boy with a Southern accent as thick as blackberry cobbler.

"Yeah, they were all black," the mayor said, and Noland knew he meant the prisoners who had died from smoke inhalation. He could hear the NAACP's accusation: "Discrimination in the Harper jail fire resulted in only black men being killed."

Wainwright turned back to face Noland, held his hand over the receiver, and asked: "How many of the prisoners were white?" Noland held up two fingers.

"Outta how many?"

"10. 2 outta 10," the mayor said into the phone. He listened a moment, then looked back at Noland. "How come there were so few whites?"

Noland shrugged. "Ask a psychologist out at the college," he said.

The mayor listened a few moments more and then hung up. "Want something to drink? Coffee? Coke?"

"No thanks," Noland said.

"Still on that health kick, Grady?" The mayor spoke disparagingly, as though exercising and trying to eat right were somehow socially unacceptable.

Noland nodded, thinking that his honor could stand to lose a few pounds, quite a few in fact, and that he really should quit smoking. The mayor lit a cigar while he waited for his secretary to bring a cup of coffee.

"What's the situation over at the station?"

"Madhouse, Mayor," Noland said. For once he hadn't minded coming to the mayor's office. Anything was preferable to the zoo he had left. "Next time I see some small-town policeman with a news camera stuck in his face, I'll be a heck of a lot more sympathetic."

The mayor's secretary entered with a steaming cup of coffee. "Sure I can't get you something, Chief?" she asked.

He smiled and shook his head. She closed the door softly.

Wainwright blew on his coffee, pursed his lips, and sipped. "Ahhh," he said, leaning back. "Who started it? The fire, I mean."

"Jesse and Stump Watkins."

The mayor snapped forward. "Why in the hell were they still in Harper anyway?"

"They were supposed to be in the state pen, but every time I called about taking them, the warden said there was no room."

"Thank God you got Jesse back, Grady. Sounds like he had you worried there for awhile."

"Yeah," Noland said, remembering his nightmare. "For some reason, Jesse went to the Dewberrys' house." That could've been very bad, and Noland shuddered to think what might have happened.

"I heard Jesse raped Miz Dewberry," Wainwright said. "Is that right?"

Noland shook his head, marveling once again at the spread of rumors in a small town. "No, thank goodness." Noland couldn't imagine what effect rape would've had on her already traumatized psyche.

"That's good. How'd she get loose?"

"Jesse tied her to a chair in the kitchen, and she managed to work the chair over to a drawer with some knives in it." That had taken a lot of guts; Noland wasn't sure he would've been able to do it. He really couldn't blame Nancy for urinating on herself when the phone rang. He hadn't told her he'd been the one calling. "Jesse was in the hall bathroom taking a leak when she finally got the ropes off. She got her husband's shotgun, and Jesse got a big surprise when he opened the door."

"I'll bet he did. Man, I would've liked to have seen his face. Why didn't she shoot the little bastard, Noland, after what he did to her husband?"

"The gun was empty. She couldn't find where her husband kept the shells."

The mayor sloshed coffee on his blotter. "Hot damn, Grady. That's fantastic. You mean she was bluffing?"

Noland nodded, smiling. What he didn't tell the mayor was that Nancy had told him she wouldn't have shot Jesse anyway. "He's just a boy, Chief," she'd said, and Noland saw the tears in her eyes.

"What about Stump?"

"Looks like he got away before we got the roadblocks set out. It shouldn't take long to find him, though." Again, Noland had the momentary thought that he hoped Stump wouldn't be caught. Still, Jesse said it was Stump's idea to set the fire.

"Thanks for coming down here to fill me in." Wainwright winked. "But you probably didn't mind getting away from all the activity, did you?"

"No." Noland stood, smiling. "Oh, by the way, to top it all off, I got a call a few minutes ago from the asylum Brad Childers was sent to. Guess who escaped last night?"

"Not Brad Childers."

"Yep."

"He on his way here?"

Noland shrugged. "Sure hope not. Who needs that?"

CHAPTER 91

Vicki sipped her Coke and stared out the picture window. Across the street, the words "ENJOY AN OLD-FASHIONED 4TH" scrolled across the bank's electronic message board. Before she could read the time and temperature, the door opened, admitting both her husband and a wave of heat.

"Boy, is it hot out there," Hal said, mopping his brow with a soggy handkerchief. He slumped into the chair in front of her desk and laid his sports coat across his legs. The front of his blue shirt was soaked.

"Want a Coke?"

"Naw," he said. "Just had one."

"How'd the meeting go?" Hal had been to his weekly Lions Club luncheon meeting.

Hal smiled. "We had a pretty good speaker, Vicki," he said. "Wish you could've heard him."

"Hmmm." Vicki took another sip of her Coke.

"Some guy from the college—Bud Wills or Mills, I'm not sure which—talked about angina and how you can recognize it. He was a young-looking fellow, but he'd had bypass surgery." Hal chuckled. "Sure glad he doesn't have life insurance with us."

Vicki, looking out the window again, nodded at her husband, not really listening.

"You're mighty quiet," Hal said. "Whatcha thinkin' about?"

Should she tell him? "The other night," she said, "when we heard the noise outside our bedroom window."

Hal looked blank. "What night?"

"I was getting undressed when we heard a noise."

"The car starting?"

"Before that. A clicking sound, like metal hitting metal." Vicki finished her drink and dropped the empty can into the wastebasket beside her desk.

Hal shrugged. "Probably the air conditioner coming on." The fan and compressor were right outside their window.

Vicki frowned, unconvinced. She thought she'd heard the sound before. Bone, on the day she left him, had sat in the chair in their bedroom while she filled boxes with her clothes and jewelry. Wordlessly, he had held the barrel of his favorite pistol against his temple, pulling the trigger time and again. The sound outside, muffled by brick, wood, and glass, reminded her of that.

"What do you think it was, Vicki?" Hal said, standing and stretching. He slipped his coat on.

The phone rang.

"Hal Childers' State Farm," Vicki said.

"Chief Grady Noland. Is Hal there?"

"Just a minute," Vicki said, nodding at her husband. He took the call in his office.

CHAPTER 92

Smoke drifted in the darkened room, creating a bluish haze that hung at eye level. Bone took a slow, pensive drag, holding the smoke for long seconds before letting it dribble from his nose. After a half-hour search, he had found the cigarette behind the dresser in his bedroom.

Images danced just behind his eyes, wanting to enter consciousness. Bone held them back, fearing that to free them would cost him all control.

"Vicki," he whispered, and the sound of his voice startled him. He sucked again on the Camel and felt the heat from the glowing tip on his thumb and forefinger. The sound of a car grew and then faded.

"It's all your fault, Vicki," he said, talking to the empty chair where she'd sat. "We coulda started over if you hadn't married that Childers. What's he got that I ain't got?"

Bone took a last drag from his cigarette before flicking it against the refrigerator. Sparks burst across the pile of dirty dishes on the counter, scattering roaches. The butt fell to the floor and started to cook the linoleum.

"A job," he said, answering his own question. And electricity that worked. Bone stood slowly, trying not to move his head laterally. Even so, the pounding started over, and he felt queasy. His pants hung on him, mute testimony to his sparse eating habits the last few weeks.

"Get movin', Bone," he said, leaning forward to get his legs going. He walked through the family room with his eyes half closed, down the hallway, and into the bedroom he had shared with Vicki. There, he laid out his cleanest dirty clothes on the bed.

In the bathroom, he shaved, brushed his teeth, and when he showered, the water jet felt good on his body. Bone was tempted to make an afternoon of it until the hot water changed to cold. Damn, he thought, don't tell me they've cut off the gas, too.

Bone was moving now, dressing, humming to himself. He had a purpose, although he wouldn't let himself think what it might be. The purpose, whatever it was, included his pistol, and this time he would take some bullets with him. Bone loaded the pistol carefully, and then emptied the box into his hand, impulsively raising the loose cartridges to his nose. He sniffed, loving the flat, hard, pungent scent of gunpowder, brass, and lead. The bullets filled his pocket, giving him ballast. He thrust the pistol under his shirt, between his belt and his belly, the cold feel of it reassuring.

CHAPTER 93

Hal and Vicki said little on the drive home. Hal drove absent-mindedly, while Vicki studied her husband's profile, trying to think of something that would take his mind off the call he had gotten about Brad.

"Wanna listen to the news?" she asked.

He shook his head. At a four-way stop, Hal slowed, then proceeded across the intersection even though he didn't have the right-of-way. The car on his right honked, and the driver gestured angrily. Hal was oblivious.

"Wake up, Hal," Vicki said, lightly. "Want me to drive the rest of the way?"

He smiled apologetically. "I'll be all right. We're nearly home, anyway."

"Whatcha thinkin' about, Dear?" As if she didn't know.

"Brad. Think I should call the psychiatrist we talked to on our last visit?" A red traffic light gave Hal the chance to show his new alertness. He left a full car length between himself and the driver ahead, something Vicki often asked him to do; he usually forgot, even on his good days. Overworked, the air conditioner spat condensation at them, then ice crystals. Hal cut it off, and they rolled down their windows. Instant sauna. The light stayed red.

"Couldn't hurt," Vicki said. She prayed he would discover that Brad had been found. Although she barely knew her stepson, she was aware of how much he meant to his father. She suspected Hal considered himself at least partially to blame for what had happened in the fall. Vicki had tried to draw him out about that awful night, to offer him the catharsis of repetition, but it was one area of his life closed to her—and probably to himself. Be patient, she told herself. Someday he would open up, and she would be there when he did. The light changed, and they crept forward.

Five minutes later, Hal turned into their driveway. A note taped to the carport door told them Sandy was studying with a friend.

"That kid's never home," Hal grumbled, unlocking the door. He held it for Vicki.

"At least she left a note, Hal," Vicki said, entering. She inhaled the cool air, then exhaled with a sigh. "Boy, does that feel good."

"Yeah." Hal locked the door but didn't replace the chain with Sandy still out. "I'm going to the bedroom to call, Hon."

"Okay," she said, disappointed he wasn't going to call from the kitchen. She pulled an apron over her dress as Hal, coat in one hand, tie in the other, left the room.

Vicki put a heavy black skillet on the large front burner, turned the knob to medium, opened the pound of meat she had moved from the freezer to the refrigerator that morning to thaw, and crumbled it into the pan. The night's main course would be meat sauce and spaghetti.

CHAPTER 94

B rad lay on his side, knees against his chest, hands between his knees. His eyes were open. He breathed softly, mouth agape, drool dampening the bedspread. Four inches from his nose, he could see a knotted thread that was part of the spread's design. He smelled his breath, and it was fetid. His bladder felt full, but he didn't want to move. Someone in the house might hear him.

He'd heard the carport door open and shut, the change in tone of the air conditioner as someone walked by the hall air intake, and the sound of a closet opening in his father's bedroom. He heard his father's muffled voice, and the even softer and more distant sound of a cabinet opening and closing in the kitchen. His father was in the bedroom, talking on the phone, while someone, probably Vicki, had stayed in the kitchen.

Brad listened to the small sounds, and their ordinariness soothed him. He strained to hear more, to understand what his father was saying, to catch the emotion in his father's voice. Was he happy or sad, angry or just tired? Brad held his breath, willing his heart to beat more softly. In the stillness, he caught another sound. A voice. No, voices. He had heard them before.

"Vicki's a whore," said a voice deeper than his father's. "You want to hurt her, do awful things to her."

"No," he breathed, knowing it was useless to argue. For a moment, Brad knew the voices were self-generated, but the knowledge was quickly gone. He wrapped his pillow around his head, but he couldn't block out the words. The main voice sounded like Dr. Provine.

"Bastard," Brad whispered. He hated Dr. Provine. All the man wanted to do was try a new kind of pill on Brad.

The first voice again. "How about Sandy, Bradley? Remember where you wanted to put some arsenic?"

"I didn't ..., he started, but the voice interrupted.

"No, you didn't do it, but you wanted to."

"Not true," he sighed, pleading.

But his pleas were, as usual, useless, and the chorus laughed, triumphantly.

CHAPTER 95

Bone's car died two blocks past Pizza Hut, drifting without power steering until he could wrestle it to the side of the highway. It had sputtered a few times earlier, but he'd ignored it since he didn't have any money for gas. Now, he stared in disbelief at the gas gauge needle lying well below the big red "E." Sweltering in the late afternoon's pulsating heat, he was tempted to empty his revolver into the dashboard, to shoot out all the gauges. But he didn't. Like the Blues Brothers, Bone was "on a mission from God," and he needed to save his ammunition.

He opened the door, eased out, and slammed it behind him. Too hard. Without catching, the door popped back and struck him in the right thigh, and Bone stumbled back, nearly tripping on the raised blacktop. A pickup swerved to miss him, and the driver honked while the passenger, unshaven and gap-toothed, shot him the bird.

"Sonofabitch," Bone yelled. He grabbed the offending door to keep from pulling his pistol and emptying it into the pickup. Then he kicked the side of his car—once, twice, three times—until a dent stayed in the panel. Satisfied, he walked around to the passenger's side and gave it a symmetrical dent. Only then did he walk away, moving fast, taking the first street off the highway. Traffic sounds receded, and the temperature, no longer fueled by the sun's reflection off acres of pavement, dropped slightly. A mockingbird sang behind a house, and the air was scented with the smell of barbecue. Bone continued into the subdivision. He crossed a small grassy island to walk on the sidewalk. At the corner, someone, probably a child, had carved initials in the damp cement when the sidewalk was laid. H.W., 1973. Bone grunted, sweat trickling down his back, wanting to take H.W. and smash his head on *his* block.

A young boy sped by on a skateboard, looking back over his shoulder to keep the stranger in view.

"Are you H.W.?" Bone called. He wrapped his hand around the handle of his gun. "Say yes," he breathed, smiling at the lad who stopped a few houses away. In one practiced move, the boy tilted the front of the board up with a foot on the back end, grabbed the front, and tucked the board under his arm. He sprinted across the lawn to his house. With his hand on the doorknob, the boy stuck out his tongue at Bone, then ducked inside, giggling. Bone read the name on the mailbox in front of the boy's house: Russell and Alice Lovett. The boy wasn't H.W., but Bone wished he'd popped him one, anyway. He walked on, aware that he was on the street where *she* lived. On a mission from God.

CHAPTER 96

Standing at the counter quartering tomatoes for the salads, Vicki heard Hal enter the room. The meat sauce simmered, and she had just turned on the burner under the water for the spaghetti.

"That smells good, Hon," Hal said. He pulled out a chair from the table and settled into it, unfolding the newspaper he had plucked from a nearby stool.

"What'd Dr. Provine have to say?" Carrot peelings flew into the side of the sink with the garbage disposal.

Hal folded over a corner of the paper so that he could see his wife. "They haven't found him yet," he said.

"Doesn't that seem odd to you, Hal, that Brad would have escaped when he was comatose?"

"Catatonic."

"Whatever. You know what I mean." Vicki broke spaghetti in half and dropped it into the rapidly boiling water. She set the oven timer for 10 minutes.

Hal closed the paper and put it back on the stool. "Apparently there was some commotion on the ward, some old guy died, and Brad must have slipped out when they came to get the body. Nobody saw him leave, but that's the only time the ward door was unlocked."

Vicki rinsed her hands and dried them on the tail of her apron. Facing her husband, she leaned back against the counter. "You mean he wasn't really catatonic?"

"I guess not." They both remembered the screams and the injections on their last visit.

"Is he still in the hospital?"

Hal shrugged. "Dr. Provine isn't sure. Since the emergency doors were chained and padlocked, they thought he must be at first. When they couldn't find him in the building, they took another look at the chains and decided one might have enough slack so that someone as thin as Brad could squeeze through."

"Jesus, Hal, sounds pretty careless to me. Why didn't an alarm go off?"

"It was disabled so employees could use the exit to grab a quick smoke outside. Any wine left? I could sure stand a glass."

Vicki had just taken the bottle from the wine rack when they heard the carport doorbell. Assuming it was Sandy, she unlocked the door without looking and set the bottle on the counter next to the dish rack.

"How 'bout givin' me some of that," Bone said.

CHAPTER 97

Brad heard the doorbell, and then, seconds later, a scream, bitten off. Shouts, then, either from the kitchen or from his head; he couldn't be sure. To test, he covered his ears, and the sounds diminished. Must be from the kitchen. But who, and why?

He slipped off the bed and nearly cried out when his feet touched the carpet. Blinking back tears of pain, Brad hobbled to the door and cracked it. In the kitchen, at the end of the hall and beyond the family room, his father sat in profile, facing the sink. Brad heard Vicki's voice followed by a man's voice. The voice was hoarse and irritating.

He would go into the hall, slip quietly out of his room on his sock feet, edge closer. See more. Hear more. He detected anger in the two voices. What were they arguing about? Was it about him? And why wasn't his father talking?

The door squeaked when he pulled it, surely loud enough for them to hear, but when he dared to look again, his father hadn't moved. He stole into the hall.

CHAPTER 98

"Shuddup," Bone said when Vicki screamed, and he shut the door behind him. He pulled the gun then and used it to motion Childers back into his seat.

"What do you want, Bone?" Vicki said, her voice too loud for the distance between them. Bone caught the quaver in her voice and smiled. He liked the effect he was having.

"You gonna introduce me, Vicki?" he said, looking from her to her new husband. Vicki took a deep breath, and he could see her draw into herself like she used to do after he hit her.

"Hal Childers," the man said, sticking out his hand like they were at a party.

"I wasn't talkin' to you, asshole," Bone said, narrowing his eyes to give the man his mean look. Put the fear of God into the sonofabitch. Childers started to say something, then closed his mouth.

"What's the purpose of the gun, Bone?" Vicki crossed her arms across her chest, and Bone could see her initial fear was gone. Only contempt remained.

"Why'd you leave, Vicki?" He heard himself yelling but couldn't stop. "Why'd you marry this sonofabitch? What's he got that I ain't?"

"He cares about me," Vicki said, "something you haven't done in years."

"That's bullshit," he shouted, waving the gun wildly. Vicki flinched, and Hal started to rise. "Sit back down, Childers." Bone

276

steadied the pistol on Hal's chest, then lowered it slowly. "Want me to shoot him in the family jewels, Vicki? Fix him so he won't be no good to you in bed, ever?"

"Put the gun away and go home, Bone. You've had your fun," Vicki said, and it might have ended there. If the timer hadn't gone off.

CHAPTER 99

Brad was halfway through the family room when he heard the stove timer. Vicki had just said something reasonable after the man (her first husband?) yelled, and then the timer shrilled and that's when it happened.

The shot.

Brad's head jerked, and he stubbed his toe on the ottoman, nearly screaming. It wouldn't have mattered. They were all deafened by the thunderclap in the house.

He was almost to the door and then through the door, moving fast. His father sat just inside the kitchen, his mouth a perfect "o" of surprise. Vicki stood just to the right of the sink from Brad's position, facing him, her hands curled around the edge of the countertop, knuckles white, her pupils dilated and her mouth round like his father's. Out of the corner of his right eye, Brad saw the effect of the shot, a neat hole in the clock timer, plastic starred around the hole.

Ludlow stood to the left of his ex-wife from Brad's perspective, slowly moving the pistol to aim at Brad. The smell of cordite was heavy in the room.

"Wha..., Bone said, and then Brad was on him, his momentum forcing the big man back against the refrigerator. Brad grabbed the thick wrist holding the pistol with both hands and tried to bend it over, but it was like twisting a flagpole. With a cry, Ludlow pushed him away, but Brad held onto the wrist. Bone again pulled the trigger.

Another thunderclap, and Brad felt pressure against his right side. He sank to the floor, still holding the wrist but not as tightly. For a moment, he stared into the black opening to death. His hands slipped off the wrist.

His father was up and swinging at Ludlow, flailing, and Brad remembered his only fight in junior high, when, tormented beyond all reason, he had finally struck back. Ludlow flattened his father with a blow from the pistol, and, as his father lay in the middle of the kitchen floor, groaning, blood starting to pool in a crease in the center of his forehead, Ludlow took aim.

Brad tried to move in front of his father, but he slipped in something wet on the floor and fell onto his right side. He screamed as boiling meat sauce pelted his upturned face.

The skillet caught Ludlow just above his left ear as he turned slightly toward it. He dropped like a pile of wet clothes, meat sauce burning the side of his face and neck.

Vicki had put everything into the swing, all the years of petty meanness, all the times Bone had struck her, all her anger at him for hitting Hal. With hands already starting to blister, she had felt the give in Bone's skull where the skillet hit. She dropped the pan and knelt beside her husband, brushing ineffectually at the blood on his forehead. His eyes were open. He was saying something she couldn't hear over the ringing in her ears.

"Brad," he mouthed, and she remembered the boy.

Brad tried to move and couldn't. Sensory messages bombarded his mind, vying with each other for attention, resulting in a strange paralysis. Pain was the foremost sensation, fiery where the sauce had scorched his skin and dull and throbbing where the bullet pierced his side. Next to the pain, he was aware of different odors. Each breath brought with it the cloying, coppery scent of blood, and beneath that he could smell Vicki's tomato sauce. His ears still rang from the sound of the shot in the confined area, but he thought he heard someone say his name. Another auditory hallucination?

"Brad," Hal said again, and the boy's gaze focused on his face. Brad's mouth curled in a half smile his father hadn't seen in years. "Hang on, Son. Vicki's calling 911."

"Dad," Brad said, struggling to speak. There was something in his mouth, some thick fluid that threatened to drown him. "You still love me, don't you?"

"You know I do, Son."

"Why are you crying, Dad?" Brad asked, and there was a quality in his voice that reminded Hal of Brad the child, his firstborn, the beautiful little boy he and Mary created. He squeezed Brad's limp hand tighter, trying to suffuse it with his vitality.

"Will you give me a hug?"

With the boy against his chest, Hal heard him whisper, "Mom really bashed that man with the skillet, didn't she?" Hal kissed his son's cheek. He would always wonder if Brad meant to call Vicki mother or if he had confused her with Mary.

CHAPTER 100

G rady hated everything about hospitals. He hated their smells, their sounds, their coldness. Most of all, he hated suffering the indignities of tests in hospitals. He could see why people often ignored dire symptoms. Sometimes it seemed better to die from a dread disease than to have to endure a test to detect it.

The upper GI hadn't been too bad. The barium milkshake tasted like chalk, and he thought he would gag on the last of the capsules he'd had to take the night before for his gallbladder X-rays, but, other than that, it was a piece of cake. Unfortunately, the test hadn't revealed the source of his problem.

"It's a process of elimination, Grady," Dr. Waters had said after Grady described the chest discomfort he'd been having lately. "We eliminate all the most likely problems."

"Which are?"

"Hiatal hernia, ulcers, diseased gallbladder, heart disease," the doctor had said, with no more emotion than if he had been reading a grocery list.

"Heart disease?" Grady had asked, sure the doctor could detect the anxiety in his voice.

"Unlikely in your case. You've quit smoking, you're exercising, you're not overweight, you're young. What about family history?"

When Grady told Waters about his father, the doctor just said, "Hmmm." That "Hmmm" had led to his present ordeal.

"Just step on whenever you're ready, Chief," Cindy Ames told him. He was in a hospital room converted to administer treadmill stress tests. Grady felt like a fool with his chest shaved, wearing a mesh shirt covering a gadget that reminded him of the movie *Alien*. Dr. Waters stood at a console to Grady's left, consulting a clipboard. He was short, had thinning hair, and an impressive mustache. The doctor looked at Grady and smiled encouragingly. Grady stepped onto the moving belt.

He took long strides, trying not to hold onto the bar at the front of the treadmill. "Don't grasp the bar," Cindy had instructed. "It'll make your blood pressure shoot up." Grady was breathing too shallowly; he felt faint.

"Hold out your arm." He did, and Cindy took his blood pressure, relaying the information to the doctor. The grade increased, and Grady had to take longer strides to keep up. In almost no time, his blood pressure was taken again, and again Waters increased the treadmill's pace. Grady was trotting now, mouth open, panting. The "alien" jiggled on his chest. In front of him, a narrow window provided a view of the gravel-aggregate hospital roof and a nearly empty parking lot. He could see the street nicknamed "doctor's row."

"Pulse 155, blood pressure 160 over 100," Cindy said. Waters increased the grade.

"How're you doin', Grady?"

"Not bad," Grady panted. He ran, sweated, and chanted in his mind, "I hate hospitals, I hate hospitals, I hate ..."

"You did fine, Grady," Dr. Waters told him when it was over. "No sign of any PVCs or any S-T depression."

"So, what's causing my pain?" Grady sat on the hospital bed near the treadmill. Cindy left after removing the monitoring equipment and the net shirt, and Grady felt almost normal again. Waters pulled up a chair.

The doctor favored Grady with that "Trust me, I'm omniscient" look peculiar to doctors and priests. "You've been under a lot of stress lately, haven't you?"

"I guess so," he said, thinking about the fire at the jail and the Bone Ludlow mess.

"When did you first feel the pain?"

Grady thought about it, and something clicked. "Come to think of it," he said, "it was around the time we caught Jesse Watkins." At least he didn't have to worry about Jesse anymore. He was in the state penitentiary, and with added sentences for manslaughter and escape, he would be there a long time. Stump had still not been caught; one rumor in Harper was that the police had killed him the night of the escape, and his body was buried beneath tons of concrete in the parking lot around the new bowling alley.

"What about all that with Mickey Ludlow and his ex-wife and that boy, Brad ..."

"Childers," Grady supplied. "Yeah, I think that brought on some pain, too. Did you read all the coverage in the paper?"

"Most of it," Waters said. "I have a question for you, Chief, but you don't have to answer if you don't want to. Did that woman really kill her ex-husband, or did her new husband do it?"

Grady had heard the rumors that Hal swung the blow that killed Ludlow. People thought it unlikely that someone Vicki's size could swing a pot hard enough to fracture a man's skull, but that's what had happened. Grady had seen the autopsy report. After the discussion of coup and contrecoup and depressed fracture of the left temporal bone, the bottom line was that Ludlow had died from the shearing of fibers in the medulla. He stopped breathing.

"The wife did it," he said. "She had the blisters to prove it."

"Blisters?"

"She hit Ludlow with a skillet full of meat sauce from the stove." What a mess in that kitchen. Ludlow's head dripped dark red hamburger and tomato sauce mixed with blood. Brad lay in a pool of blood, his face dotted with meat sauce. It was hard to tell where blood began and sauce ended.

"I think we've discovered the source of your chest pain, Grady," the doctor said. "Under unusual stress you unconsciously tighten your chest muscles, which then hurt. I'm going to give you a pre-scription for a muscle relaxant that you can take as needed."

Grady smiled, relieved.

"I do have one more question about Ludlow and the Childers family. Do you think the boy saved his father like the newspaper said?"

"Hard to say, Dr. Waters. Bone had already fired his gun once when Brad ran into the room. He might've been satisfied with that, scaring Vicki and her new husband, but I doubt it."

"Me, too," Waters said, stroking his mustache. "You read all the time about men killing estranged or ex-wives and then shooting themselves. Could easily have happened in this case."

A dark cloud had formed while Grady was in the hospital, and a cooling breeze swept over the hospital parking lot. Grady grinned and whistled tunelessly walking to his car. No heart disease! Relief lengthened his stride.

He swung the satchel containing his running gear onto the back seat of his car and slipped behind the wheel. He could hardly wait to tell Marge the good news. Well, he might tease her a bit, tell her he'd flunked and needed bypass surgery. Naw, better not; she had really been worried about his chest pain.

As he pulled out into "doctor's row," Grady thought of some-thing else Waters had said about Brad Childers, something the doctor remembered from the newspaper accounts when Brad had poisoned his family.

"Wasn't the boy's diagnosis catatonic schizophrenia?" Waters asked.

"That sounds right."

"Well, I don't want to sound callous, Grady. I mean, it was awful the boy got killed like that, but I don't think schizophrenics are ever really cured."

So maybe there was justice in what had happened to Brad. He had poisoned his mother and then died trying to save his father. With an incurable illness, maybe he was better off dead. At least that was the implication in what Dr. Waters had said. It would be hard to convince Hal Childers of that, and Grady wasn't about to try.

The first large drops splattered on the dusty windshield as Grady turned into his subdivision. He rolled down his window and turned off the air conditioner. He wanted to smell the sweet smell of dampness and feel the thunderstorm's breeze on his face. The drought's relief had been a long time coming.